Advance Praise for *The Tree Doctor*

"Marie Mutsuki Mockett's luminous new novel provides the hope and beauty we need after the isolation and disillusionment of the pandemic. If existential despair can kill, as the narrator thinks at one point, *The Tree Doctor* is about the opposite: how reconnecting with the world around you—and with your own soul—will help you survive. This coming-of-middle-age novel—a rarely dramatized but radically important stage in women's lives—will leave me thinking for a long time." **—Celeste Ng, author of *Our Missing Hearts***

"Marie Mutsuki Mockett's mesmerizing novel *The Tree Doctor* understands the drama inherent in having a garden. There is an unrecognized wonder to caring for plants: the genuine pleasure derived from planting new flowers, the amount of effort it takes to keep trees healthy and alive. Mockett's unnamed protagonist herself is much like a flower in bloom. *The Tree Doctor* explores one woman's sexuality at a time of life rarely written about, during a time in history that we are only now beginning to process. A beautiful and evocative, necessary book." **—Marcy Dermansky, author of *Hurricane Girl***

"This is a gorgeous and completely unique novel, bristling with life like the garden it describes. It is melancholy, erotic, hopeful, meditative, frightening, and even funny—a book about solitude that is never lonely, a book that is both timeless and utterly contemporary. I finished it grateful to Marie Mutsuki Mockett for this orgy of sensory pleasures, and this opportunity to pause and consider life in a time of collective fear and uncertainty. A balm to the spirit and a lovely work of art." **—Lydia Kiesling, author of *Mobility***

"Sex, death, rebirth, and literature—it's all here, in one astonishing book. *The Tree Doctor* made me want to go have an affair!" **—Gish Jen, author of *Thank You, Mr. Nixon***

"This finely calibrated, groundbreaking chronicle of one woman's midlife awakening captivated me from the very first sentence. With deadpan humor and deep compassion, Marie Mutsuki Mockett perfectly captures the vast social, political, and cultural changes wrought by the pandemic, spinning them into a gorgeous, utterly original novel. I loved it." —**Joanna Rakoff, author of *My Salinger Year***

"What I love about Marie Mutsuki Mockett's work is every book has its own unique concern, landscape, texture, mood. *The Tree Doctor* is unlike anything I have read. In it Mockett tells many stories at once: how the most luscious flora coexists among the mundane and often impossible concerns of suburbia and cities; how reckonings operate when you are mother and daughter and wife and lover; how illness makes its way from the personal to the universal and back again— and more! A California book, a pandemic novel, a cautionary tale, a romance in which descriptions of plants brush up against scenes of global catastrophe and build into thrilling sequences of forbidden love. This is a novel to highlight and underline, to get lost in, to dream of, to share, to study, to surrender to." —**Porochista Khakpour, author of *Tehrangeles***

"*The Tree Doctor* is a remarkable novel: sexy and profound, cerebral and corporeal. Never before have I been so turned on by trees and flowers, or laughed so much about the mysteries of sex and sexual desire. Marie Mutsuki Mockett depicts grief and self-discovery with such beauty and restrained vulnerability. I loved being in the singular world of this book." —**Edan Lepucki, author of *Time's Mouth***

"Like the best of literature, *The Tree Doctor* allows us to see ourselves, but reading this beautifully honed story is also an act of healing. Every page brought new color, feeling, and wisdom into my life, changing me, not unlike the narrator's mended cherry tree with its surprising spring blooms. Marie Mutsuki Mockett is an exquisite writer." —**Alan Heathcock, author of *40***

The Tree Doctor

THE Tree Doctor

A NOVEL

Marie Mutsuki Mockett

Graywolf Press

This publication is made possible, in part, by the voters of Minnesota through a Minnesota State Arts Board Operating Support grant, thanks to a legislative appropriation from the arts and cultural heritage fund. Significant support has also been provided by other generous contributions from foundations, corporations, and individuals. To these organizations and individuals we offer our heartfelt thanks.

Published by Graywolf Press
212 Third Avenue North, Suite 485
Minneapolis, Minnesota 55401

www.graywolfpress.org

Published in the United States of America

ISBN 978-1-64445-277-6 (paperback)
ISBN 978-1-64445-278-3 (ebook)

2 4 6 8 9 7 5 3 1
First Graywolf Printing, 2024

Library of Congress Control Number: 2023940228

Cover design: Kimberly Glyder

Cover art: Cory Feder

The Tree Doctor

One

She would always say she called the Tree Doctor because of the fuchsias, not the sickness. It was early March and the fuchsias should have been sprouting. There were eight plants and they would usually grow to reach four feet each summer if they had been trimmed properly during the winter. A few fresh shoots were growing out of the trunks, but the leaves were mostly gnarled. The leaves looked arthritic. If an elderly hand were to emerge from the trunk of a fuchsia, it would look like these leaves.

Many plants in the garden seemed to be faltering, but the fuchsias, which she had loved as a child and which supplied food for the hummingbirds, who would now have less to eat, were one wrong thing too many.

She recalled a plant nursery in the valley, near her grade school. It was seven miles away. She could not tell from the internet if the shop was open. The website showed rows and rows of plants in bloom—azaleas, snapdragons, newly sprouted tomatoes. She imagined the plants sitting there, waiting to be purchased, but unclaimed because of the sickness. She picked up the phone and dialed and a man's voice answered after the first ring.

"Hello! G . . . Nursery!" There was noise in the background. She heard a woman yelling, though she could not make out the words. She heard a brief beeping, like a front-end loader, or perhaps a car reversing.

"Hello! I was just wondering if you have any fuchsias."

"I got lots. Depends on what you want . . ." His voice was cavernous, but not so booming as to frighten her. It was an inviting voice, and even over the old-fashioned landline she could feel it pulsing through her ear and into her skull.

"Bush fuchsias," she said, holding the phone away from her ear, but then his voice was garbled and she couldn't make out the individual words. "What was that?"

"Not right now." Her ear pulsed again.

"Wrong season?"

"People plant them in winter. Why?"

Briefly, she described the problem, idly massaging her lower back with her free hand while she spoke. She was sore and stiff after pulling weeds, a chore to which she was unaccustomed.

"How old are the plants?"

"Over fifty years, I imagine."

There was a pause, as though he needed to finish sucking on a piece of candy. "Did you just buy the house? Doing some remodeling?" Now there was an edge to his voice.

The question surprised her. "No. It's my childhood home. I'm back here to shelter." She left out the fact that she was only visiting California and that the sickness had made returning to Hong Kong temporarily impossible.

"Oh." Her answer had surprised him. She imagined him turning the phone around as if to examine it. "If you have plants that are over fifty years old, it would be a shame to throw them out." He sounded a bit stern now.

"Yes! I agree!" Briefly she explained the condition of the fuchsias, making sure she stressed her concern for their well-being. "I thought maybe they are dying due to the drought. My mother stopped watering—"

"There's enough water," he growled. "Just the governor lies and tells you there isn't." He drew in a breath as though to calm himself. "The leaves are curled because you have mites. It's an insect that bores. Attacks everything. You can treat it. You'll just have to do it every year. Cut it back so it's at fifty percent.

Medicate the roots. Give it fertilizer. It'll take time but it should come back."

"I've cut it back . . ." She had, in fact, nicked her left index finger when she mindlessly picked up the clippers while trying to balance a box half full of clippings on her hip. Her finger still stung when she washed the dishes. It had been years since she had cut, nicked, or pricked herself, and her carelessness had momentarily filled her with fury.

"Fifty percent. And you'll need anti-boring medication."

"Anti-boring." She laughed.

"It's a kind of mite that's microscopic. Starts at the roots and travels up the stalks and into the leaves. Twists everything. The leaves come out curled?"

"In some places." She liked how much he wanted her to understand the feelings of the flowers, even if he didn't understand her humor. "What's the medication?"

"We have it."

"Can I order it online?"

"You can. But—" He left the admonition unfinished. He had just helped her on the phone, and she ought to buy the medication from him. "You can order it from us over the phone. Drop by and we'll put it in the car. You don't even have to get out."

"Is it busy there?"

"Pretty quiet early in the morning," he said. "Otherwise. Lots of people are home gardening now."

"I see." And here she imagined a world of frightened people and unadopted flowers.

"Well, you give me a call . . ." He was going to hang up.

"I'll take some," she said, pulling the credit card out of her wallet. "However you sell it. I can come by tomorrow morning."

"Good. Your name?"

. . .

Just south of Carmel-by-the-Sea, Highway 1 narrowed to a two-lane road and would remain that way as it hugged the coastline and winnowed its way south to Big Sur. Often this road was slow because it was the only throughway for lone, grizzled VW bus–driving sentimentalists and stalwart semi-haulers with loads of lettuce destined for the Michelin-starred restaurants and the bare-bones, backpacker-friendly log cabin grocery stores along the coast. Today it was empty. She had a feeling of exhilaration, as though she were getting away with something. She was nervous, too, as this was her first time venturing out into the world since the mandatory lockdown, and she had already put on a pair of the latex gloves from one of the two boxes she had found by her mother's bedside. She had on a face mask, a stiff blue one that the care workers had worn during flu season last December.

Carmel Valley was now increasingly home to the superrich. She knew this only because it was what visiting golfers would tell her whenever she spoke to them in the airport lounge, waiting for the small puddle jumpers that flew from San Francisco to the tiny World War II–era airport in Monterey. She also knew because she occasionally read references to the valley in glossy magazines. But she didn't personally know this part of the valley. For her, the valley was a place where people kept horses and where homes were simple, low, and long, in the manner of the rancheros who had settled there when California belonged to Mexico. At the first light, she made a left onto Carmel Valley Road, passing an endless line of construction equipment. The small valley cottages were, one by one, being remodeled into villas that, like women with augmented bustlines and newly symmetrical faces, would in their altered state now be worth much more than they had been previously.

She had never longed for a dream home as a goal of adulthood. But in so many of the classic books she loved to read there was some kind of magical house—Pemberley, Howards End, Tara. Even in her favorite novel, *The Tale of Genji*, the eponymous hero, a prince, is said to have finally surpassed the Emperor only after he has built a grand estate comprising four residences, each featuring a garden focused on one distinct season.

Carmel Valley was narrow and the hills that bordered it felt close and accessible; most peaks were only two to three thousand feet high. It was winter and the hillsides pulsed with translucent greenery—nature's answer to the neon canyons of the city. In the summer all the grasses would turn brown and she would feel the irritating dry heat on her skin and sense the prickliness of the spiny oak tree leaves as she passed under their branches, which were awaiting a fresh season of rain. She would say she loved summer, since that was what a good Californian said, but she would be longing for this winter greenery. The nursery was located to the right, after a turn on the road to accommodate the riverbed. Farther ahead was the Carmel Valley Village, and beyond that, the reservoir.

The driveway to the nursery went up a short, steep hill and led through a wooden gate. Ahead of her there were hundreds of flowers, bushes, and trees grouped by type. There were the container fuchsias, begonias, and petunias. There were geraniums under a greenhouse roof, the profusion of scarlet petals ruffled like a row of flamenco dancers.

The man on the phone had told her she would not need to get out of the car. But there was no clearly marked location for a shopper such as herself, no sign that read "Park Here." She sat in the SUV, gripping the steering wheel and wearing a mask. What was she supposed to do? Was there now a conventional way in which people went shopping in the world? She had seen nothing on the news or online. It was too soon, she supposed, for new conventions to be established, and the sickness was just a visitor. In the nursery proper she could see customers—mostly middle-aged women—unhurriedly pulling specially made carts with long, flat beds, on which were arranged various flowers. These were not the furtive shoppers she had expected. In fact, she was the only one sitting in her car and refusing to get out. A couple wandered by holding hands. Married, no doubt. They had on wide-brimmed canvas hats and their leathery skin suggested years of tennis and long-abandoned sunscreen routines. The couple were wearing masks. They walked over to a very tall third figure she noticed only just now, a man wearing a bandanna over his mouth. She guessed he was Latin American— maybe Central American—from the part of his face she could see. She could make out his name spelled out in large block letters on a name tag, like something from the Large Print Book Club: "JUAN." She wondered if his name really was Juan. Her mother's name was Kazuko, and the one other Kazuko they had known in their small town had told people to call her Costco, like the store, because Kazuko had been so difficult for Californians to say and to remember. Juan and the married couple had a brief conversation, which ended with Juan pointing at a corner at the far end of the lot. At a tree, perhaps. What would they buy? Apple? Crab apple? Maybe a lime tree? No, it would need to be something romantic, she thought, as she watched the couple walk away, still holding hands. A flowering tree, perhaps.

She should park the car and get out. And yet if she got out now, wouldn't she simply be succumbing to some kind of peer pressure, and wasn't she too old for that? Still, she felt like an ambassador from the land of uptightness. She had never quite felt like a good, laid-back Californian and had been happy to go to the East Coast, where people seemed to keep an invisible tabulation of things like who was where in line, and whether or not dogs were supposed to be on a leash, and certainly whether or not someone should wear a mask—all things that, if violated, would make the average laid-back Californian say "neurotic" and maybe even "high-maintenance" and even, quietly, "kind of a pain in the ass, if you want to know the truth."

Juan was heading her way. When he got close enough to hear her, she yelled out the window: "Hello! Hi!" As soon as she did this, she felt ridiculous clinging to her car and flagging a gardener. She was not this person! On the other hand, she had paid for the boring poison and wanted to get it.

The man seemed surprised to see her sitting in the car. She could tell from his brow that he was confused. Perhaps he was supposed to know who she was? Then the plane of his forehead went smooth and slack and she understood that he now understood she was one of those people who did not want to get out of the car.

"Yes, miss. Can I help you?" He bent over to look at her through the window, folding his tall frame into a crisp angle.

"I'm here to pick something up. I was told I could just park."

"You paid already?"

"Over the phone."

"What is your name? No. What is the thing? A plant?"

"Poison."

"Herbicide?"

"No. I mean, it is a poison for bugs. A boring medication." It didn't sound the least bit funny in this context.

"You got a boring problem."

"Very boring."

"Who helped you?"

"With my boring problem?"

He rolled his eyes. "Over the phone."

"A man. He said his name was . . . he didn't give me a name."

"Oh." Juan nodded as though suddenly everything, even the boring problem, had become clear. "The Tree Doctor. Stay here." Juan walked away.

As she sat in the car, a middle-aged blond woman trundled by pushing her flatbed shopping cart, whose top layer was completely covered with petunias. Something about the way the woman shuffled made her look unsteady, like the grown-up version of a toddler pulling a toy cart. Had her mother come here looking like that? Wasn't it just like an elderly person to love visiting this neonatal intensive care unit for plants crossed with a grocery store? The older a woman became, the more likely she was to love plants and pets, seemingly unaware that she loved these fragile things only because she, too, was growing more frail. Occasionally, some writer or thinker, who was usually male, came along and made it cool to love bugs or birds, but mostly, to love the natural world suggested a kind of weakness.

Another man was coming out to her car. He walked ahead of Juan and wore no name tag. The two men had very different gaits. Juan was taller and walked more slowly. Juan strolled. There was a note of hesitation in his step, and though he was very tall, his caution suggested gentleness. He must be beloved in the nursery. He could pick up trees and move them around without breaking any branches. The other man was perhaps five inches shorter. He wore cargo shorts that were faded and had a fraying hem but that must have been expensive, she guessed, because the fabric was matte, the seams crisp and tight, and the individual pieces of the pants were asymmetrical. The pants were like the Sydney Opera House of REI hiking pants. They were probably all-weather pants—light and thin and stretchy and practical, and now very worn. He had on boots and white socks and his legs were tan. He had a bit of a belly, but his legs looked perfect. Men so rarely had good legs in shorts, but everything that she could see—the thighs, the glossy knees, the chiseled calves—looked kneaded and baked like a chewy pretzel. He had on a wide-brimmed canvas hat with mesh along the sides. He wore a red bandanna over his mouth and all she could see were his eyes, which were the color of saffron, or perhaps the pistils on a tiger lily. Maybe they were the color of a Japanese maple turning dark. Whatever the color, they were not merely brown but some shade of gold and suggested to her something molten whirling around at his core. Inside him.

He was carrying a blue plastic jug. She rolled down the window of the front passenger seat. "Hello!" she yelled. She tried to sound friendly and casual and not at all like a high-maintenance woman who would buy anti-boring medication over the phone and then refuse to get out of the car to pick it up.

He passed the container through the window and set it on the seat. "Something else," he said. Then he tossed a brown paper bag into her car. "For fun." As he said this, the corners of the bandanna flexed and his eyes narrowed. She couldn't see the smile but she could feel it pouring through the fabric of the bandanna. The world would worry whether or not the virus would penetrate the fabric on this man's face, and in that moment she was merely interested in the smile she could not see. The one under the mask.

"What is it?"

"Surprise." He put one hand on the halfway-rolled-up window and leaned his head partway into the car. She smelled earth and sweat.

"I thought . . . I mean, you said I didn't have to get out . . ." She was too old to apologize.

He withdrew his head. "You'll need to do the application on your fuchsias for the rest of their lives. You won't ever permanently kill the bugs."

"No," she agreed.

"Sure you don't want some flowers?"

"I've never gardened that way." Actually, it was her *parents* who had never gardened this way. Her father had handled the big jobs, transplanting and landscaping, and her mother had kept things organized, weeding and clipping, though they had been as one when it came to the genesis laws of gardening, which included raising all flowers from seed. But she couldn't stop herself from sounding like some kind of plant snob, in an effort to impress him.

"Come back if you run out." He turned and walked away. She rolled up the window and began to work her way through the parking lot and back out to the road to drive home. She had never left the vehicle.

. . .

That afternoon, she put on a pair of spare sweatpants and, ignoring her sore muscles, weeded the entire iris bed. She weeded the round island of dirt where the begonias had bloomed when she was a child. She mixed the anti-boring medication with water and poured it on the roots of the fuchsias, as the Tree Doctor had instructed, and she followed this with fertilizer she found in the toolshed. She put fertilizer on the sixty-year-old lemon tree, which was standing on the patio like a rebuke, stripped of leaves, but still gripping fistfuls of lemons. Every last ounce of the lemon tree's energy had gone into producing and saving its fruit. She would save the lemon tree. She would save all of it.

She was surprised by how easily her body adapted to the chores she had not done since childhood, when her mother had told her to pick snails off the bird-of-paradise, or to collect the fallen camellias. It was like riding a bike. It was like having sex. It was an intimacy with plants that she had forgotten she possessed, a way of knowing how to help the plants feel better. When she was done, she took out her iPhone and, on impulse, took a photo of the tidied iris bed and of the lemon tree; when it was healthy again, she would have her patient's before and after photos. She sent the photos to her mother's caretaker at the facility with an explanation.

It was five p.m. when she was done and she sat on a rock by the pond. She remembered the package that the Tree Doctor had tossed into her car, and went back to see what it was. Inside the bag she found what at first she thought was garlic. She pulled the shiny cloves out and realized they were bulbs. Some were gold and some were brown and others were nearly orange. "A bulb has magic," her father had once said. She could hear her mother's voice too: "If you find a bulb while weeding, just re-plant it."

These knobs of vegetable matter contained all the encoded information necessary for a plant to unfurl—flowers, leaves, roots, and all. If there were any plant that could survive a holocaust, or something as traumatic as an interstellar jour-ney, it would be a bulb. She had only twenty bulbs, and so she spaced them out around the garden with the idea that when they bloomed, there would be color everywhere. Then, as dusk began to fall, she stood on the patio and wished the garden good night.

. . .

Before the airlines suspended all nonessential travel, before in-person classes everywhere in the world had been canceled or gone remote, she had had a job teaching in Hong Kong in the Global Literature program at the Hong Kong Open University, a private college focused on helping its Chinese and foreign national students receive an American-style university educa-tion. The university, like the apartment where she lived, was located in Discovery Bay, a resort town inhabited by expats and wealthy Chinese to whom China's stricter laws were not ap-plied. At the university she had been a tutor, then a compo-sition instructor, and then the previous fall had finally been granted her first class. She had intended to fly back to Hong Kong from California in time to resume the yearlong course, but then she became stranded in the United States, and anyway her class, she found out, had been moved out of the physical classroom and into her computer. The few people in her social circle with whom she still communicated about teaching and writing bemoaned this shift to the online world, but she found it convenient, at least initially. Teaching online allowed for the maintenance of appearances. She didn't have to commute and she didn't even have to put on proper pants.

She taught a class on Japanese aesthetics, running the gamut from anime to food to film, with *The Tale of Genji*, the world's first novel, at the center of the curriculum. Written by an anonymous female courtier whom history called Lady Murasaki, the novel is set in the Heian era, which fell between 794 and 1185 CE and is considered Japan's golden age, akin to Queen Elizabeth I's reign, or Enlightenment France.

The text generated countless works of art, from paintings to plays to poems; there wasn't a Japanese art history or literature class in the world that didn't reference *The Tale of Genji*. Though it was generally believed to have been written by a woman for women, Japan's warring shoguns and warriors also cherished the story. Throughout Japanese history, male warriors would attack and loot castles, gleefully making off with precious hand-copied and illustrated volumes belonging to their rivals. "Imagine a book other than the Bible," she had told her students, "inspiring such devotion among men."

The afternoon after she planted the bulbs, her computer screen reflected her face back to her in a rectangle of moderate size before bisecting, then exponentially fragmenting into increasingly tiny, glowing frames, each holding hostage a blinking and yawning miniature face of one of her students. She smiled hard and effected what she hoped was confidence. She needed to be their teacher and their mother. "Thank you so much for coming to class," she said. The school had given her no guidance at all on how to handle virtual instruction. "I am so glad to see that you are safe. I want to assure you that we will still have a good class this semester. Everything is going to be fine." She went on to tell them that the Heian period was book-ended by plagues. Their reading assignment was timely! Fear of illness and death was partly why there were so many Heian poems about cherry blossoms and beautiful, transient things; between these curtains of death, there could be moments of light and life, stars in a dark, moonless sky.

She could see that her students were bewildered, and a few were resentful. She could feel their near panic, and she pushed hard against it, as though she could be like that Dutch boy with his finger in the dyke. If she smiled hard enough, the way she had tried to do around her daughters when they were little, the class would go well. There was Ravenna, whose red hair filled the entire box in which she sat. Astrid was her bright-est student, and supposedly her three parents—accessories designers—lived in some kind of secret polyamorous arrange-ment she didn't understand but had pretended to comprehend when Astrid had confided in her about it.

There were slim white girls with dirty-blond hair—children of expats—whom she struggled to tell apart. Henry was gay and Black and the son of a computer security expert for a bank. Momoko was the most vocal of the students from Tokyo, and had opted to take the class because her grandmother had, for twenty years, been leading a neighborhood discussion of the text with other women; Momoko wanted to read the book for herself and, after a lifetime in International Schools, was going to attempt to do so in English and in modern Japanese. There were the Chinese students of wealthy local parents who wanted their children to learn English and to mingle with Westerners.

The translation she favored was over a thousand pages long in English, fifty-four chapters interspersed with 795 poems. She

tried to split the semester into three parts, reflecting the tradi-
tionally acknowledged three parts of the book. To complement
part one, she added lessons concerning hair, clothing, poetry,
architecture, marriage, and ghosts. In part two they would
examine gardens, Buddhism, and Japanese painting. And tricky
part three—chapters 43 to 54—well, she had never really gotten
this far. Just as well, since Genji doesn't even appear in those
later chapters, having died in part two, and scholars still de-
bated whether or not Lady Murasaki had even written them
herself, because the tone was such a departure from that of the
earlier chapters.

But she loved the beginning, which had for her the magic
of a fairy tale. They were all supposed to have read the first six
chapters by now, but she wasn't sure if anyone had.

"So *The Tale of Genji* begins with an aging emperor who
has two sons by two women of different ranks. The older boy,
Suzaku, is the son of the powerful concubine Kokiden, while
the younger child, Genji, is the son of the Emperor's most beloved but lower-born Intimate, Kiritsubo. In the world of Genji,
concubines and Intimates are not the same thing. Genji is so
stunning that at birth he is called the Shining Prince, which
makes Kokiden furious. She wants her son to be the most important man in the court—not Genji, whose mother isn't even
all that important."

When she saw her students fidgeting, she said: "Think about
William and Harry, or JR and Bobby Ewing. History is full of
brothers at war and in partnership—and at odds over women.
Which is what happens in *Genji*." Her students perked up.

"Okay. Moving on. Genji's mother dies before he is three,
and the Emperor is heartbroken. And he replaces Genji's dead
mother with Fujitsubo, who looks nearly the same as Genji's
mother! And then when Genji meets this Fujitsubo for the first
time, at twelve, he also falls in love with her. It might sound

crazy. But people do have types. Marla Maples looked a lot like Ivana Trump. Johnny Depp replaced Kate Moss with Vanessa Paradis. It happens." They murmured, which she took as a sign of assent.

"Then Genji marries Aoi, but despite having his own wife, he pursues other lovers, and eventually gets both Fujitsubo *and* his wife, Aoi, pregnant. And then, when he is caught in bed with Oborozukiya, whom Suzaku had hoped to marry, Genji's shame is so great—and Kokiden's rage is so pyrotechnic—that he is sent into exile."

"I have to be honest," one of the blond girls said, leaning toward the computer, as though doing so would bring them closer. "I am finding Genji . . . *triggering.*"

"He's a rapist," Ravenna said bluntly.

"Maybe it isn't rape?" someone else asked. "Is it rape?"

"You only think that because you spent your last semester in San Francisco," Momoko said.

"Well . . ." Her kindness and smiling were not holding back the unsettled emotions of the class. "That's the subject of a lot of debate. By our standards, maybe? But it's also argued that women had to seem vulnerable as part of courtship. Remember, potential lovers can't even see each other. They are hidden behind curtains and layers of clothing and they have to create tension through . . . seduction."

"Oh, like Rhett Butler *seducing* Scarlett O'Hara." Ravenna rolled her eyes.

It was true that *Genji* features rape as a matter of course. People who read *Genji* in its first hundred years hadn't seemed to mind too much, but by 1100 CE, Genji's sexual escapades started to become a problem, and the commentaries began to rebuke him for his womanizing. The teachers she had had in college had dealt with the book's troublesome morals mostly by focusing on its aesthetics, which was also what she did. They had done what in the world of parenting was called "redirection." "Ha-ha, Genji is so *bad*, but let's look at all the poems! Look not at how Genji is acting like a creepy Peeping Tom in this hand scroll, but at the composition and how Genji stands on the right-most side of the scroll as he peers over a fence to look at the scenery to the left, which only reveals itself as you unroll the paper, making you, the viewer, complicit in what and how Genji sees. Wasn't that a genius move of visual storytelling!"

"I've made a tally of all the women he sleeps with from chapters one to fourteen. It's fifteen. And one guy," Ravenna said.

"Genji only sleeps with the brother because the sister won't. It's revenge sex."

"The brother doesn't give consent."

"It never says 'rape,' though," someone pointed out.

"None of the women have any agency," Ravenna complained. "Of course it's rape."

"There *are* women who want to have sex with him, like the Lady of Evening Faces," Momoko countered. "She answers his morning-after poem with her own morning-after poem and it's clear she wants more sex."

"I still think the book needs a trigger warning," the first blond girl said.

"I think so too. I just . . ." Ravenna sighed. "I can't . . . relate to this book."

She didn't know how it had happened that people now confused what transpired in a book—a work of fiction—with something that was happening to them. Was that really the point of fiction now, that one read in order to see oneself in the world of the protagonist? Then again, she'd usually experienced the characters in the classics—most of whom were white—as living lives different from her own. Maybe that was not normal. She did not read and imagine that anything that happened to someone in a book might happen to her. It had not occurred to her that she had the right to ask for such a thing.

But this was not completely honest. Maybe she loved *The Tale of Genji* because she saw herself in it, or at least wanted to. The truth was that something about the book had always evaded her. She said she loved it because it was the world's first novel and was written by a woman of color and had generated so much beautiful artwork, not to mention all those paintings of women with long black hair like her own. But what was the book *really* about? She knew what she was supposed to say, but she didn't necessarily know what she was supposed to say for *herself*. It would be impossible to overlook the instances of rape in *Genji*, but it was also not possible to read *Genji* if all one focused on was the rape.

Astrid came to her rescue. "We can't read this book like it's a nineteenth-century exploration of the psyche," she said. "I mean, this book is from a time before anyone was worried about being a girl boss."

"Those poor women." Ravenna shook her head.

"Maybe we are the ones who should be pitied, thinking that love is real," Momoko replied.

Astrid continued, "I'm thinking about what you said the other day about the main point of the book. About *mono no aware*. You know?"

"That's right," she said. "An awareness of things. Life is always passing us by, so the Heian Japanese would try to capture these little moments that are beautiful and painful at the same time." She began to display reproductions of paintings of kimono-clad nobles riding in boats on a waterway beneath cherry blossoms, and photos of modern-day Japanese tourists riding in similar boats while videotaping the blossoms showering petals on the water. With each love story, Lady Murasaki had tried to capture both the beauty and the futility of earthly love with a parade of details often drawn from nature.

"Audre Lorde kind of said the same thing about the power of the erotic," Henry said. "Real erotic power is about feeling things deeply. And then she said if we cut ourselves off from authentic feeling, we engage in what she called pornography."

"The point, I think, is that you can't just divorce sex from aesthetics or the act of living," said Astrid, of the polyamorous family. "Sooner or later you deal with your body, right?"

"And yet," Momoko countered, "the body barely exists in this book."

And this was also true. Even in the images she loved to share, the faces were interchangeable—small eyes and little curved noses. Most attention was paid to the sweep of the hair on the women, and the many layers of clothing.

"I don't know." Momoko yawned. "Reading this book and listening to all of you . . . I realize just how asexual I am."

"*No one* is asexual," Ravenna said.

"Sexuality is a spectrum," Henry told her bluntly.

When she had been in college, which was longer ago than she liked to admit, she had thought that the only people who needed to figure out something about sex were gay people. She had naively assumed sex was a fairly simple flow chart with two routes: Were you gay or were you straight?

"You can't think of this book as being the story of individual people, all trying to live their best lives," she said. "They are all in a very rarefied world—the Heian court—and they express their feelings in poetry, and the poems all utilize nature. They often express what they feel through watching the plants, or the mist, or the seasons."

"Humans aren't plants," Ravenna said.

"Humans are a part of nature," Momoko replied tartly. "Maybe you need to change what it is you think a human being is."

The class came alive and began debating, using words like "Anthropocene" and "anthropocentric," and she was relieved that they had, at least for now, stopped arguing about rape.

When class ended, she shut down her computer and rubbed her eyes. She knew that the sickness would keep everyone home and inside except the reckless and those who mistook caution for weakness. The sickness was searching for her body. She would likely not see her students all semester, and no one would touch her for weeks. She was, it must be said, accustomed to a lack of touch and had for years now gone to the local mall to receive anywhere from a fifteen-minute to a one-hour massage from a rotating cast of mainland Chinese immigrants. Now she could not pay even for the most chaste contact.

Her phone chirped. She had a new text message. "Kids in class. Talk to you later?"

"I'll be asleep," she wrote back. No matter how many times she explained the time difference or the fact that the iPhone made the calculation of time differences easy, Thomas seemed incapable of keeping track. He could set his timer for business meetings around the world but could not arrange his schedule to suit hers, fourteen time zones away. She waited for a reply, and when none came, she stood up and went to turn up the heat in the house. The sun had gone down, and the rooms had all gotten colder.

The thermostat was in the dining room. She hit the little digital up arrows, raising the temperature to seventy. As she waited to see if the old boiler would begin to spew out hot air, she cast her eyes to the side, sorting through the clutter on the dining room table. The house had once been spotless and organized, and now she could see a layer of dust on the vinyl tablecloth, unopened bills, a pile of checkbooks and stamps. Her mother had stopped cleaning and had ceased to put things away in the weeks before she was persuaded to move to the care facility. There was a supply of rubber gloves; these had been worn by the nurses who had tried to look after her mother to keep her in this house.

There was also a package of masks, still unopened, and labeled with Japanese characters. She picked it up. It was the last of her mother's stash of masks from a trip she'd made to Japan the year before. It had bothered her how her fastidious mother had always come back to America with a surplus of masks, like some stereotypical anal-retentive Asian and not a confident, body-positive Californian. Now there was a shortage of masks in the world, but she would have enough.

And then she saw ten packets of seeds and a note in her mother's handwriting. Carrots, peas, three kinds of beans, beets, lettuce, radishes, two packets of California wildflowers. The corners of some of the packets had been torn open—they were from previous years. But otherwise the seeds were laid out as though they had been arranged the night before by someone who knew that around the country, grocery store shelves were being stripped bare of produce and basic supplies.

She read the label on the back of the bag of carrot seeds: "Plant after the first frost has passed," it said. Well, she was in Northern California, where the frost often never arrived.

She picked up the note. Her mother's cursive letters were shaky but still elegant. The note read: "Vision Board." How could her mother—who never watched Oprah, Gwyneth, or even CNN, and who never, ever read *Elle* or *Vogue*, who never looked at any media aside from Japanese cable TV—know what a vision board was, and why had she placed this strange missive in among the vegetable seeds?

The whole house was whispering *sssh*, the sound of the boiler pumping warmth through the vents. She would be warm enough now, unaware of the temperature, and she could take her body for granted again. She turned off the dining room light and waded through the darkness to the bedroom, where the blinds had been left open. Standing by the bed, she could see deep into the night. Outside the window, the patio furniture slouched on the glittering salmon-pink tile. Moonlight rained down into the back garden and onto the daffodils and narcissuses, which were clustered like lanterns receiving the light, their white nature becoming known in the dark. How she had loved playing among these flowers as a child! The garden sloped gently down to a man-made pond, beyond which the grounds ended in a row of trees and scrub belonging to the neighbors, who were not gardeners. At the left edge of the garden, she saw one mammoth figure rising out of the ground, a leafless tree she called Einstein because of the way its branches stood atop the silver trunk, like the stray wisps of the brilliant physicist's hair. It had been her mother's favorite tree, and now it, too, looked half-dead. The tall trees—the still-skeletal frames of the maple and wisteria—cast calligraphic shadows on the lawn. Behind them, the cypresses and redwoods rose into the dark, reminders of how grave and mysterious trees could be.

She woke up only once in the middle of the night, raging with heat. Who had turned the heat so high? But she had only herself to blame. Her skin was lightly coated with sweat and she lay on top of the covers. Try as she might, she could not give herself over to sleep. This was happening often now—some middle-aged wiring would jolt her awake and she would be unable to sleep again and would spend the following day in a stupor. She had to sleep.

She had put on seven pounds earlier in the year, eating bread at two a.m. because it knocked her out enough to sleep, but there was no bread in this house. She had no sleeping pills and she had stopped drinking. She would have to masturbate, but it seemed like such a chore. For a few minutes, she searched the internet for something pornographic for a woman of her age and situation, but the only porn she found was for younger people. Far in the distance, she could hear the sounds of the ocean, and then she remembered something. Those kinky Japanese in the Edo period had evaded the censors by representing sex and nudity in unpredictable ways. There was Hokusai's print *The Dream of the Fisherman's Wife*, in which an octopus uses all eight legs to bring pleasure to a woman. In the nineteenth century, Westerners had interpreted the octopus as raping the woman; today, art historians were confident the octopus was not.

She pictured this and reached beneath her underpants and pictured one mouth and eight hands.

She came quickly and felt her body sinking so deeply it was like falling. Had she really been that stiff a moment ago? As she surrendered, she was relieved not to be out there, awake and in the world, where the virus raged, but here, inside and in her imagination.

Two

One morning a week later, she made the mistake of reading the news and looking at social media. Everywhere, people were dying, and the world she had known only ten days ago had come to an end.

Her students would have access to some of the same news that she did; at the very least, they would know they were on lockdown because of a deadly virus. Clear on the other side of the world, they were in their apartments or, if they were lucky, home with their parents. Seven of her students emailed her to say they could not, for various reasons, make it to class at all. Astrid sent her an email thanking her for the last class, along with a link to a transcript of an interview with Audre Lorde. She was supposed to be grading their reading responses, but she did not want to grade their papers. Who cared about grades? She was exhausted.

She considered baking a tray of brownies, but this would require her to assemble eight ingredients and retain the presence of mind to distinguish cups from tablespoons and teaspoons. She was not able to focus on the very first instruction—"about a cup of sugar"—and so left on the counter the few items she had found in the house, and went to lie down. By noon, she was still lying in bed in her childhood room, overcome by depression. This would not do. What would the vision board advise?

She decided to go to the garden center. The nursery would cheer her up.

. . .

This time she parked her car and got out. Since her last visit, the ground had been painted with arrows to direct foot traffic, as if the nursery were now a maze. It was early in the morning, but already the nursery was busy. As before, mostly older women pulled the carts and stacked them with flower pots and wended their way along the prescribed route. Dutifully, she began to follow the arrows, too, looking at the flats of flowers for sale and sold in packs of six.

Because she was wearing her face mask, she was swimming in a sea of half anonymity like everyone else, which felt both freeing and oppressive. A paper burka. On the one hand, no one would remember her. On the other, she worried a little. Did she look more Asian to people who could see only her eyes and not her Anglo nose? She wasn't sure.

She had taken a few photos of the most troublesome plants in the garden and of the beleaguered cherry trees, thinking she would ask the Tree Doctor if there were an ointment she could apply to kill off whatever fungus was bothering them.

"How are the borers?"

She hadn't seen him coming. Her skin prickled and she wondered how he had recognized her so easily. She couldn't see the lower half of his face, but there was no mistaking the way he walked and the way his hands seemed to vibrate, even while dutifully holding a potted petunia.

"I think maybe it's too soon to tell."

"It'll take a while. Petunia?" He held the flower out to her.

"I don't know." She hugged her body. "Do you have any more bulbs?"

"All out. You could probably find some online. But you'll be dealing with gophers at this time of year. California menace. You need to poison them."

"I have a few questions. I brought some photos."

"Show me."

She pulled out her phone. She wanted to show him pictures, but of course they could not stand next to each other, as they might have before the sickness. She held the phone out in front of her, thinking that perhaps they could scroll together, an arm's length apart. But middle age meant she couldn't see as well as she used to, and neither, apparently, could he. He took the phone from her, intending, she assumed, to look at the photos himself, but just then the screen went dark. Exasperated, she took the phone back and unlocked it, and he closed in beside her, a little dramatically, as though to emphasize that he was next to her only because of the phone.

They began to go through the pictures she had taken of the trees, and as they looked, she again became conscious of the fact that he smelled. It was not an unpleasant smell—it was earthy and natural. They were in a nursery, with their face masks on, diagnosing the problems of her trees. The thought occurred to her that if they were naked, she would be smelling this same smell from him, and the fact that she had imagined them naked together embarrassed her. Still, she liked the smell. You were supposed to dislike body odor, and men in particular were supposed to stink, but he did not smell bad. He smelled very good. Did she smell to him too?

"This tree is grafted." He was talking about an expired apricot tree.

"What does that mean?"

"The nursery or the breeder took a hardy root stalk and split it around here"—he pointed to a knob on the tree—"and stuck in a clipping from the flowering cherry. And now the root stalk has sent out branches from its own root."

"Why would it do that?"

"It's under stress. The roots know it's in danger of dying and it doesn't want to, so it's sent out its own branches. The top part is fragile, which is why it was attached to this stronger part here. But the whole thing was under threat, so it sent out—"

"An ambassador."

"You could call it that."

"There's another whole tree, maybe twenty feet away from this one. And there was a third one but the gophers killed it."

"Must be an old tree, then, with extensive roots, for the babies to be so far away. It's still trying to survive."

Over the course of their conversation, the distance between them had narrowed and now they were nearly shoulder to shoulder. "Like Jor-El sending Kal-El out into space."

"I've never heard it put like that, but I suppose that fits. Some people say that life on Earth began with some kind of bacteria coming down from outer space."

"The bacteria ambassador."

"What else do you have for me?" His voice was serious, but she could see from the way his eyes sparkled that he was amused.

She showed him the constipated cherry trees and the spot on the trunk of one tree where she had found an open sore. He whistled through the face mask when he saw the gash. "Something's been eating them."

"Eating?"

"A rat? A gopher? I don't know. But that looks like a pile of chips."

"Isn't this a fungus?"

"Any sap? Oozing?"

"No."

"That's an animal, then," he said. He was quiet for a moment. "You understand, they will not come back."

"Can't I patch the hole and cut off the dead branches—"

"That looks like a twenty-year-old tree."

"I think that's right. My parents planted it after I left home." He looked at her and she thought for a moment that he was going to ask her a question. Instead, he continued to talk about the cherry trees.

"They don't last too long. They're weak here too. And see? That's another graft. Cherry trees actually want cold and humidity—all the things we don't have in Northern California. Anyway, it's going to die." He said this with finality. Weren't doctors supposed to display tact?

"So I should take them out—"

"And replace them, if that is what you want to do. Or you can wait. They are partly alive."

She showed him one final photo: of the Einstein tree. "I'm just wondering," she said. "Do you know what's wrong with this?" This time he took the phone from her before it had a chance to lock and go dark.

She had taken several photos of Einstein, and the Tree Doctor swiped through them all, then reversed, went through them again. He took off a glove and used his bare fingers to blow up the photo, and then let it diminish. He was quiet for a long time and she watched his hands. They were hands that had worked a great deal—not like her husband's smooth and pale fingers, which were so slippery she often feared the platinum wedding ring would slide right off. The Tree Doctor's hands were like the branches of an oak, each knuckle a whorl where a branch had once been. His hands weren't clumsy. His fingers were accustomed to precision, like a bonesetter's, and he magnified the picture to a specific size only in certain spots, then moved the photo around to examine something else about the tree. These were hands accustomed to pruning dead flowers, and testing soil for moisture so little plants could grow. People who touched plants every day, as the Tree Doctor must, had particular hands that mimicked the tough, gentle, and persistent nature of trees.

When he was done he looked at her over the top of his face mask and she had the feeling he was seeing her for the first time. And what did he see? "I can't tell what this is," he said at last. "It's not dead. I see growth. From your photos, there is no fungus. It looks like it just hasn't come out of hibernation yet, though it's awfully late. It looks like some kind of cherry, but it's not a tree I know."

"What do I do?"

"Wait?"

"For?"

"To see if it produces leaves or flowers. It has so few branches. It's like some kind of living bristlecone cherry tree."

"Does that exist?"

He didn't answer her question. Instead, he said: "This doesn't even look like a graft. It looks like a whole flowering tree. But it would be very unusual for something like that to grow to be this old in California. Not impossible. But unusual. Cherry trees didn't come over from Japan until the early twentieth century, and they've mostly been grafts."

"It bloomed when I was a child. My mother was very attentive to it. She's Japanese."

"That explains it."

"What?"

"Have you asked her for help?"

"She's not very . . . well. I can't ask her for much."

He shifted the conversation. "Cherries aren't my specialty. Not one like this. I'm a conifer man. Simpler and older reproductive mechanism than flowers." Then he seemed to consider carefully what he would say next. "I could come take a look."

There was a slightly self-conscious casualness to how he tossed out this offer. He couldn't possibly be flirting. That would be silly. But was it silly? It had been years since she had navigated casual attraction. He must just be nervous, she decided. Or very polite.

"I would appreciate that," she said. She gave him her address, and they agreed on a date and a time. He would stop by late in the morning, he said, when he would be doing a tree delivery in her neighborhood anyway. A rhododendron. As if a person couldn't drive a rhododendron home in their car and plant it themselves. They rolled their eyes together and laughed out loud at the helpless person who had been unable to plant a rhododendron. She refrained from asking him if the offender was a doctor or a lawyer, but as if reading her thoughts, he said: "Software designer."

"Like my husband!" she said.

"Oh, I didn't mean—"

"No, no, it's okay. It's just that I completely get it!"

Then they laughed some more until the CB radio called him over to the succulents, and she was by herself again in the middle of the petunias. Just as quickly as she had felt the lightness of making an unexpected friend, she was gripped by panic. The Tree Doctor was coming to her house, and though he knew the trees were sick, he did not know that there were no flowers. He would know that she was a hack gardener if she now bought fifty petunias and planted them in a flurry, like one of her students cramming for an exam.

As she was browsing plants, she received her daily photo of her mother from the caretaker in the facility. It had been a month since she was last able to visit her in the care home. She could see that her mother was smiling. Today the photo came with a video, and her mother, with the help of an aid, told her how proud she was that she had managed to string up the berry vines, and that she was trying to save the lemon tree. Her mother was glad she was weeding. Her mother was adamantly proud.

She crammed her cart with petunias and South African

daisies and snapdragons and fragile begonias. She stuffed the car full of blossoms and drove home. Once she arrived, she found she was exhausted and left the plants on the lawn, vowing to plant them in the morning. She washed her hands thoroughly and took a nap, and when she awoke, she began to scour the internet for deals on dahlia bulbs and plants whose roots could be delivered to her home. It turned out there were plenty, and what she saw was on sale. She filled her online basket and ordered. She would replenish the garden with flowers and she would take a photo when they bloomed and she would send the photo to her mother.

. . .

She was ten the first time her mother had been sick. "Truly sick," as the family called it. There had been a mystery illness undiagnosed for months, until someone at some point determined her mother had been in the ICU with viral meningitis and not an intense migraine, as the doctor on duty had insisted at the time. Nothing, as the saying goes, was ever the same for them again. By the time they finally got the meningitis diagnosis, her mother's body had moved on to embrace other ailments, chiefly advanced rheumatoid arthritis, an autoimmune disorder, which in the 1980s was, again, blamed on her mother's hypersensitivity and diagnosed as likely "another bad headache," until a physician at Stanford confirmed that in fact the body did rebel and attack itself on occasion, which he insisted was likely what was happening to her.

The family entered a world of cataloging and avoiding foods that might cause inflammation. They learned not to hike, because her mother could not hike. She pushed her way without shame onto every train and bus to reserve a seat for her mother, who always boarded slowly behind her, and then she stood stoically if two seats were not available. She learned not to complain about ordinary feelings like pain, tiredness, or boredom. To be truly sick was worse. She adapted to her mother's physical needs, and learned to read her mother's little cues, which might signal scheming, exhaustion, or needing an ingredient to be brought down from a high shelf. She walked quietly when she came home from school, so as not to wake her mother from a nap. She asked waitresses for a list of ingredients in the dishes on the menu, and eventually they stopped eating out altogether. After she got married, after family life took her away from the constant vigilance and obligation that accompany life with someone who, through no fault of her own, was becoming an invalid, she often felt she occupied a liminal zone, unable ever to truly be free of feeling in her body what her mother needed, and also unable to give herself over to what she heard people refer to as "the pleasures of adulthood."

There followed more years of mystery ailments, which a parade of generally sensitive and enlightened doctors had been able to combat. There were hospitalizations and surgeries, miracle drugs that provided relief before their side effects were discovered and the pills jettisoned. There were new diagnoses, and after her father died, a decade ago, she began coming home on occasion to accompany her mother to the new doctors and hospitalizations and surgeries, before returning to her husband and children.

The first time she had left her own family in Hong Kong to sit through a surgery for her mother, she marveled at how supportive Thomas had been. He never complained about her lengthy absence. He also never called to check in on her, and only recently had she begun to wonder if what had looked like stoicism in the face of family stress had actually been a kind of emotional blankness. Maybe he didn't seem bothered by her absence because he didn't feel bothered. He had certainly minded when she had, tentatively, brought up a three-week residency to revive her dream of being a writer, because that trip would have meant leaving the children in his care while she attempted to work on a long-abandoned manuscript. As it happened, her mother was often sick, and getting worse, and then her mother's illnesses became the sole reason she ever left the family to go anywhere. Illness got her out of the house. She traveled for illness. Her mother's illness had made her crafty. For instance, she knew how to buy a dress at Anthropologie in twenty minutes when she went out "to pick up your prescriptions" and how to charge the dress to her mother's credit card and blame the "slight delay" in getting home on "beach traffic." But this didn't mean she was friends with illness. She didn't *like* sickness.

People wanted to know how her mother was doing. Most people her age had healthy parents—only a few had lost someone, and those losses were generally sudden. The changes to her mother had been slow, if you considered that they had occurred over a lifetime. Her mother had never been good at the difference between "a," "an," and "the." There were so few pronouns in Japanese, and so her mother often confused "he" and "she." In the last few years, when her mother had said things like "But it is frozen" with no context at all, she had, uncharitably, assumed this kind of speech was a continuation of a tendency to rely on her to help render her words in English. And then she assumed that her mother's firing of one caregiver after another had been due to her poor impulse control. Childishness, really. But now her mother could barely speak at all, and when she did, it was in a whisper.

A few weeks ago there had been a diagnosis of dementia. And she now questioned everything about any of her mother's behaviors that she had once dismissed as crazy. Her mother had not been crazy; she had been sick. Her mother was not rude. Her mother had been coping as best she could, due to an additional illness they had not known about. Her mother was still in there somewhere. Her mother loved her and this was why her mother had wanted her to fly over from Hong Kong: so they could be together. Her mother had been angry when they had not come two Christmases ago, not because she was overly possessive and unable to respect boundaries, but because she had known in some way that death would separate them soon.

Now in the dining room, she looked again at the piece of paper on which was written "Vision Board." It was so peculiar. Was the paper there to remind her to make a vision board, or to suggest that the house itself was a kind of vision board? There was nothing special up on the wall, for example, aside from the family photos that had always been there.

She wondered if behind the little pieces of paper floating around the house and the objects that had been moved, there was in fact a conscious order that spelled out a message impossible to express in full sentences, and that message was for her. A vision board. She should assemble the clues—the seeds, all the notes, her mother's will—and then the vision board would tell her what she was supposed to do. Maybe her mother knew. Maybe, in that space between wellness and sickness, between sickness and death, her mother had perceived something about the world of the global sickness. She would begin by planting her mother's vegetable seeds. This seemed to be what the "Vision Board" note implied she should do. She put everything in a wire basket, then took the long way around from the front of the house to the back and began to work in the garden. First, as always, she must remove the weeds, the dense accumulation of narcisuses and dandelions, and, toughest of all, the grasses.

. . .

That evening just before midnight, her iPhone clattered and her body lurched into wakefulness. Blue light winked up at her from the floor and she pawed at its source. She couldn't see very well—her newly found middle-aged self required low-level reading glasses, which she had begun purchasing from Walgreens just after the first of the year—and she felt around the headboard for the blue plastic frames. Then she picked up her iPhone and assembled herself to see who might be calling.

It was Thomas. She had expressly asked not to be woken up in the middle of the night, but here he was, calling her anyway.

She slid the green button on the screen to answer the call and was surprised for just a moment to see the sleepy but intent face of a fourteen-year-old girl whose long brown hair was pulled back into a sloppy bun. "Sophie?" she said.

"Mommy."

"Honey, it's after midnight here."

"But I need to talk to you."

It was almost four p.m. there. Saturday. Thomas was probably napping. She sat up and took a sip of water. Her stomach, unaccustomed to food or drink at this hour, began to gurgle and then moan rather like a whale. Hopefully Sophie could not hear.

"All right, honey. What is it?"

Sophie started chattering. There were anecdotes about school conducted in Hong Kong over the internet, about the housekeeper and the nanny no longer coming to the apartment, per lockdown orders, and about too many meals involving Japanese curry. "Pia watches too much YouTube," Sophie said, reporting on her little sister. "Daddy doesn't monitor her viewing. She's into Barbie torture."

"I'll talk to him," she soothed.

Then there was silence. "How's Grandma?"

"I haven't seen her since lockdown. I get texts and photos." Was this really why Sophie had woken her up in the middle of the night? "I need to sleep, Soph. I don't—"

"I want to know something," Sophie interrupted.

"Okay." She sat up straighter.

"Did you know—"

"What?"

"—about the virus? I mean, did you know this would happen?"

Interesting. Her daughter had waited and planned not only to retrieve Thomas's phone while he was napping, but to ask this question to her directly with no one else around. "No one knew! I mean, sure, SARS and H1N1 happened, and I guess I knew that hypothetically it was possible that something might one day affect all of us even worse."

"But they say that the virus started in December. Before you left."

"It was in the news, yes."

"I heard that there were warnings that the virus might spread."

"The Chinese government always says that."

"They say that they warned us and that they warned—"

"I had no idea that it was going to spread like this! Anyway, I had to come here to move Grandma from her house into the nursing home."

"But if you knew that the sickness was coming . . ." Sophie's voice was trembling.

"It won't be forever. Just for a bit."

"Mommy, please come home."

"Hong Kong has restrictions. I would have to live in a hotel for two weeks before I could see you. And that would only be after I took a test showing that I'm negative, and I can't even find one in America right now. And not only that, a one-way ticket back to Hong Kong is, well, thousands. This will all be over in a few weeks and then I can come see you." Everything she had said was true, except for the last line of reassurance. She did not know that it would all be over.

Sophie was wholly unconvinced. She could see it in the way

her daughter was watching her through the glass, listening to the way her voice came out in an unconvincing whinny. The talking heads in America were predicting that the virus would be cleared in a matter of weeks, though she had also heard some officials saying that the virus was likely to be with them for many months. But her message to her daughter was in complete congruence with the story most everyone in the West was being fed now.

"That's not what they say here." Well, yes, of course Hong Kong would have a slightly different take.

"That's what they say here."

"But you knew before you left—"

"There are things even Mommy cannot control. I was only supposed to be gone for a short time—"

"Mommy, we are a *family*." Sophie sounded exactly like Thomas when she said this. Her daughter must have overheard one of their fights, perhaps the one last Christmas when she had cried and cried in the hotel bathroom the night before the flight back to Hong Kong. It was true. She hadn't wanted to go back. She had wanted to stay in America.

"Of course we are, Sophie. The virus was a fluke! I will come home soon! When I can!" But it was also true what Sophie had said. Back then, in December, she *had* known the virus was coming, that it was marching across China and toward Hong Kong, or rather that it was flying toward them, and she had chosen to go to the United States in what turned out to be a narrow window before travel became restricted. She had looked at the news and listened to the Chinese, American, and Japanese newscasters and told herself, vaguely, "Well, it'll all work out," and ignored the voice in her head that had asked: "How?" She had ignored the voice in her head that told her that if Hong Kong was starting to panic, then something was seriously wrong, even if, in December, neither Europe nor America was paying much attention.

She sat back in the bed, and while the autopilot Mommy part of her began to speak reassuringly, the other part of her questioned everything. Had she known that if she left Hong Kong there was a good chance she would be separated from her family for a while? Had she *wanted* this?

She felt terrible. "I did not leave knowing that I was going to be separated from you. Really. Sophie. It was only supposed to be for a short time." She had been ten when her mother had become so sick and she had learned to fend for herself. The girls would too. Sophie was fourteen, and old enough to take care of herself and to get to school. Pia was younger, at nine, but old enough to understand that Mommy would leave but still come back. And Sophie would help out with Pia. She had even sold this as some kind of *feminist* thing—"Grandma matters too!" It was all supposed to be okay.

"If it gets really bad. Like really bad. Can you just come home?" Sophie asked.

"Yes," she said. "I can. If it's really, really bad, I'll find a way. But for now they say we should just lock down, like you are."

She knew Sophie was not comforted, and yet, everything she had relayed to her daughter—the lack of tests, the price of a ticket, the few airlines flying *to* Hong Kong—was true.

"Why can't we come to you?" Sophie asked.

There was an answer, of course, but she thought that telling her daughter the truth might violate one of the laws of a Good Marriage, which was to present a united front to the children. The truth was, Thomas and the girls could come to the United States much more easily than she could return home to them, as many more carriers could enter America, no matter what the president said. They had American passports, after all, and the airlines would let them in to California.

But she already knew how this conversation would proceed. Thomas would say: "I'm the breadwinner." And then, maybe realizing how 1950s this sounded, he would add: "My job is in this time zone and we can't afford for me to risk my job. Especially with the cost of International School. Which was something *you wanted*." Being the breadwinner had been the punch line to most of their fights. As Sophie had now apparently divined from their many fights, "breadwinner" was why it had been okay to leave New York, where she had been happy and had had a job she loved, for Hong Kong, where he would make more money. Not that he was happy with more money. He was forever tortured between being "management" and "on the product side." Currently he was on the product side, designing an algorithm to identify eye movement and eye engagement, with the ultimate aim of providing retailers, software users, and, he joked, dating sites, detailed reports of exactly which inch-by-inch section of any visual field received the most attention from any human being. It was a kind of eye-tracking software initially developed for high-end weapons, and now translated to the marketplace. This reduction of physical space to tiny, trackable quadrants was why they could live on the forty-sixth floor of their high-rise apartment with a sparkling view of neon and distant airplanes landing at Hong Kong International Airport. She knew he considered her time in California a kind of indulgence— a favor he was doing for her due to her sick mother.

Suddenly the image on the screen refracted and Sophie's movements froze, then became fluid, and then froze again. And when the picture finally recovered, she was looking at the faces of three people: Sophie; her husband, Thomas; and little Pia, who appeared to have drawn a triangle on her nose, from which lines radiated out across her cheeks. "Mommy!" Pia screamed. "I'm a cat!" She put her hands over her head in the manner of ears.

"Hello!"

"We are okay," Thomas told her before she had a chance to ask him directly how they were.

"Me too," she said. Then "Sorry this happened. If I had . . ."
His eyes drifted to some point off camera. "Priority is that
you stay healthy. Anyway, I think this will be over soon."

Again she knew it would *not* be over soon. She did not know
why she knew. But she knew. "Thomas, I think this could be the
real thing."

"And I think you worry too much. Because—"

"My mother."

He nodded. Her mother—her sick mother—had made her a
little bit nuts.

"I could . . . I mean, I would have to quarantine if I flew back,
but . . . ," she began somewhat timidly.

"I looked at tickets. Way too expensive. We wait long enough,
the price will go down. When this blows over. Shouldn't take
too long."

"Right." She paused before surprising herself by making a
suggestion. "Why don't you come here? Everything is virtual.
The kids could go to school and . . ."

"Honey! You know!" He jerked his head toward Pia, a bit of
pantomime, which she understood she was supposed to translate as "not in front of the children." "The company needs me
here. I can't be in some totally different time zone."

The girls turned to look at Thomas at the same time, all four
eyes fixed on his face as though willing him to look back at the
camera in the phone, the little device that was, for now, keeping
them all together. The children knew, she realized, that something was wrong beyond what was being stated.

"Meow! *Meow!*" Pia purred and they all laughed on cue.

She laughed extra hard. "Ha-ha-ha! Pia! You look so cute!"
She did not want Pia to feel the need to try even harder to be cute
for the sake of the family. There was quite a bit she understood
about acting, as a mother. She understood that they were all in a
crisis and that she must appear calm. She knew that her children

trusted her to be far more aware than Thomas of what was actually dangerous and what was not; Thomas didn't know. She also knew that she had to outwardly appear to support him—"This will be over soon"—until such time as she could present the opposite and realistic position. She repeated that she was happy to see them, but sleepy, and for the next twenty minutes she listened to more updates about lax internet-watching times, and the preponderance of Japanese House Curry for dinner, and after she had fallen asleep twice while clutching the phone, they hung up and the sixteen-hour time difference, where air was fattened with tiny spiraling particles of the virus, reasserted itself.

Three

The frogs began singing the night before the Tree Doctor was scheduled for his first visit, after a few delays. She was teaching her online class when the first frog belted out: "Ribbit." It was April now and the days were lighter and the world outside the window had a faintly dark blue glow by the time class ended. She left her curtains open, so she could make out the outline of the roses and trees, but her students could see none of this. She could, however, see them shuffling around in their boxes on the screen as though they were all suddenly caffeinated, and then Henry asked finally: "Are those frogs?"

She said they were frogs and they were mating.

"How can you sleep?" Astrid asked.

"I'm used to it," she told the class.

"But it's so loud." The class was genuinely perplexed.

For the most part, her students were agreeably keeping up with the reading and engaging in her carefully orchestrated conversations. But then today she had brought up the dramatic moment in chapter 5 when the Shining Prince struggles to recover from the illness he has experienced as a result of being in proximity to his dying lover, Yugao, and things took a bit of a turn. She then showed them photos she once took of the mountain monastery to which Genji travels to see a hermit who is said to cure the sick. Her mother—her mother!—had stayed behind with her two daughters at the hotel as she had gone up into the mountains for an overnight visit. Had her mother not been there to help her when the girls were young, there was so much she would not have been able to do.

"Wait, does Yugao really die because of some jealous spirit?" someone asked.

"Yes, Rokujo, one of Genji's former lovers. It also kills Genji's wife the same way. She projects her spirit into Aoi's body and makes her sick and kills her too," she said.

"Astral projection assassin," one of the boys said. "Cool."

"Some people say that Rokujo is the most interesting woman in the book. She's never really presented as anyone's enemy before she dies, and Genji is devastated when she does."

"Maybe Lady Murasaki was rooting for Rokujo?" Astrid asked.

"That would be a very feminist reading," she said. "But none of this is what I want to talk about. I want you to focus on the cherry blossoms." The key thing she hoped to share was that while the cherry blossoms in the city of Kyoto were past their prime, the wild mountain cherries were still blooming where the hermit lived. She had experienced this phenomenon herself. Just as the cherry trees help Genji emerge from his lingering illness, she, too, had experienced the piercing joy of spring re-emerging. "This ability to feel rejuvenated in nature is a treasured Japanese attitude," she said.

"Like forest bathing," Henry offered.

"I heard some journalist made that up," Ravenna said.

"No, it's a real thing," Momoko countered. "Especially in springtime."

She was running through a series of photos of Japanese screen paintings of cherry blossoms and her own pictures of cherry blossoms, when Ravenna asked: "And this is also when Genji decides to become a kidnapper, right?"

It was, in fact, the case that in this chapter, the teenage Genji, who is assumed here to be around seventeen, first spots the character Murasaki, who at this point in the story is ten years old. She looks rather conveniently like Genji's stepmother, Fujitsubo. The child Murasaki has no mother, and her father is absent, leaving her in the care of a nurse. And the moment Genji sees Murasaki, he knows he must have her and asks to make her his ward. He is rebuffed initially, but when the nurse dies, Genji kidnaps Murasaki from her house in the mountains and moves her into his home in the capital city.

"It's not much different from Elvis grooming Priscilla," Momoko said.

"Except Elvis didn't rape Priscilla," Ravenna said.

"Do we know that Genji rapes Murasaki?"

"She doesn't write him a morning-after poem the way she is supposed to," someone answered.

Some translations portrayed Genji's actions with Murasaki as a "seduction" and not as "rape," and yet it is quite clear that for the four years during which the child Murasaki grows up with Genji, she is tutored by him to become exceptional in all the arts, including the writing of customary morning-after-sex poems. During this time, they sleep together as parent and child on the same futon, before he finally decides, the night after his actual wife dies, to make Murasaki his new wife.

"Why is he the hero of the book again?" someone asked.

"Because the gods admire him," Henry said. "They make sure he outranks his brother in the end."

"How?" Ravenna asked.

"Through his children," Momoko said. "His daughter becomes an empress and his son becomes an emperor."

"No," Astrid said. "It's not the children. It's the actual sex. With his mother-in-law. The gods reward him for it."

She attempted to redirect the conversation, pointing out a few lines in the text just after Genji goes into exile. He survives a disastrous storm on the coast, after which he has a prophetic dream.

"He woke up and understood that the Dragon King of the sea, a great lover of beauty, must have his eye on him. The gods are attracted to his capacity for beauty," she read.

Critics often wrote that Genji expresses himself best through the rituals of the Heian court; he is an excellent dancer, speaker, artist, and writer of poems. Lady Murasaki spends countless pages describing Genji's meticulous attire: Heian garments were sheer and great attention was paid to the color and order of their layering; Genji is a master at communicating aesthetics and mood through his robes.

"You might say he had style," she continued, "and made everything beautiful, and the gods loved this. To be a person in Genji's time was to participate in an ongoing performance."

"All influencer, all the time," Henry said.

"But real.life isn't a performance," Ravenna argued. "That's fake."

"Or real life is a performance," Momoko countered. "You only think you aren't performing."

Her younger self had once pitied people in the past, stuck in their prescribed roles as serf or minister of this or that and unable to express their true and essential selves by hopping on a plane and flying down to Tulum or wearing ratty jeans for a run to the grocery store for an impromptu microwavable pie. That was being *free*. She had been certain she was *free*. Now she was less certain. How much of what she wanted, including microwavable pie and ratty jeans, was because it was what other people wanted?

There followed, then, a conversation she had never had in conjunction with *Genji* before. The class did not admire the paintings she showed them of Genji and Tō-no-Chūjō dancing, or the tea ceremony bowl with the morning glory flower that was Yugao's namesake, or even the cherry blossoms north of Kyoto. They argued instead about whether or not Genji could in any way be a real person.

There were her students, constrained in their little boxes on the screen, and no, they couldn't socialize in person, as it was healthy for young people to do—and yet they were free too. She could be anywhere and no one would know the difference, and so could they.

. . .

In the morning she reminded herself that the Tree Doctor was coming. In the kitchen, she looked at the abandoned bowl of sugar and considered finishing the brownies. But in the newspaper, which she read online, she had seen a recipe for something called "comfort pound cake," which involved a cup of sugar and grated zest from a lemon. She went out and looked at the tree. The tips of the branches had lost their hard and brittle quality and seemed out of focus. It was trying to grow new leaves. She considered this to be a sign and plucked a lemon from the tree.

She found that she could now concentrate on baking, and she set to work assembling the ingredients and grating the lemon, which was so ripe it fell apart in her hands, so she had to dump the juice and pulp into the batter all at once. She put in half a cup of cornmeal, as directed by the recipe to give the cake more texture—a genius idea—then put the batter in the oven.

The act of putting together the cake took her back to her childhood and the first cakes she had made for her parents. Her mother had learned to cook from a *Better Homes & Gardens* ring binder found at a garage sale. It had been part of the training her mother had put herself through to become American. Like her mother before her, she had adopted the cookbook as her own, too, working through the recipes and cooking dinners for her parents, though nothing had made her happier than baking a cake.

As she was musing on this, she heard a faint *rat-a-tat*. It sounded like the stand mixer. The sound stopped and she stood still in the kitchen as the smell of burning sugar began to swell in the air, and the oven began its magic of congealing the ingredients in the batter so it would transform into cake, a metamorphosis that was perhaps not quite as spectacular or mysterious as caterpillar to butterfly, but which nonetheless filled her with a sense of awe and suspense. The tapping continued. It was consistent enough that she decided it could not be some valve or pipe or mechanism in the heating system that had broken and required attention. It wasn't dripping water and, anyway, it wasn't raining. She looked around the kitchen. The sound repeated and she came to the window over the sink.

She was face to face with an Allen's hummingbird. A male. He was hovering like some kind of miniature helicopter from the world of the bird police, and as he made eye contact with her, he scooted forward and tapped the glass with his beak. *Tap-tap-tap-tap-tap.* It was ludicrous to think that a hummingbird might know Morse code, but in that moment she felt there was an urgent message that only she was able to decode. He repeated the action and then, as if in disgust at her inability to speak the language of window tapping, he backed away until he was clear of the eaves of the roof, then scaled the air and disappeared.

Why would a hummingbird be speaking to her? A romantic voice suggested that the bird was the spirit of someone deceased, but this was silly. What would a hummingbird want her to know?

Birds were chattering over by the bird feeder—titmice were angry at a jay. Always the same birds. How she wished for something unusual, like a goldfinch. She moved over to the other window to look at the hummingbird feeder and saw that it was depleted of juice. She had let the feeder run dry. Fortunately, there was still enough sugar in the house after baking to fill the feeder.

. . .

The Tree Doctor parked his van on the street. This was interesting, because most people parked in the driveway, right in front of the garage, and she always had to ask them to move their car so the garage door could open if necessary. Perhaps the Tree Doctor had already made this assessment. Or perhaps, because he delivered trees, he was accustomed to thinking like a delivery person and thus parked on the street like the gardeners in the neighborhood.

She put on her mask, then opened the door and went out to greet him.

He was wearing his mask, too, and she realized she had never seen his uncovered face, and since she didn't have his name, she had not been able to google him to look for a public profile. He was walking up the driveway casually, with his feet springing in the way of athletes. He raised his hand when he saw her and his eyes narrowed as he smiled beneath the mask.

The cake had been out of the oven for an hour, and the kitchen still harbored perfume from the sugar and the lemons. "I made a cake." She gestured toward the house. "Would you like a piece?"

"I really shouldn't." He patted his stomach. It looked flat to her. Inside she cringed; she had mentioned the cake too soon. He was still walking up the driveway, looking at the six trees in the center island. Two Japanese maples, a dogwood, a cherry, a redbud, and two plums. At the front of the garden, she had transplanted the flowers from the nursery, and they blended nicely into the rest of the greenery.

But the Tree Doctor took little notice of the flowers. His focus was on the trees. "A little bit uneven. The redbud is shorter than the others."

"It's the newest," she said. "There was a golden chain tree in the corner—"

"What happened?"

"It died."

"Maybe the heat wave."

The red maple had remained in its skeletal form for so long, she had been sure it was dying. But now its leaves were un-peeling in a way that reminded her of a snack her children's classmates had eaten—the fruit roll. The leaves were not the firm, dry leaves of an apple tree, but felt like latex. The leaves emerged red and became maroon but never turned green. The Tree Doctor touched the tree and felt the leaves, as though to take its pulse. He turned to the dogwood and the cherry. As they stood in the garden, two juncos leapt onto a branch of the cherry and began to chirp with great intensity.

"Hello," he said to the birds.

Both birds lunged in a way that was comical, but that she also could not help but respect. They were defending their ter-ritory. One of the juncos edged out to the tip of the branch closest to the Tree Doctor's face. In little darting moves that made her think of a fencer, the junco jabbed at the air between them with his short beak. *Chirp chirp chirp.* Alert alert alert. The meaning of the high-pitched sound was without question.

"Let's go to the back," she said. "That's where Einstein is."

On their way, they passed the two constipated cherries and he knelt down on one knee, like a cavalier, and gingerly touched the most affected tree with his hand. Then he very gently touched the bark. He pulled a pocketknife from his pocket and began to chip away at the wound. Filings poured out. It was as though the tree had been holding back the full extent of its rot and injuries, and now that he was here, it revealed just how much of its interior had deteriorated. Then he stood and shook his head. "I'm sorry."

"Is it a fungus?"

"No. Like I said, flowering trees like this don't last much lon-ger than twenty years. There is a new one you might try called a

Pink Cloud. It does well in Southern California and doesn't need the cold winters you have in Japan to wake up. We just started to carry it. If you get a couple, you'll probably want to wrap something around the base so rodents won't chew it up too. I can take care of these for you."

"I would appreciate that."

They passed through the orchard on the side of the house. He noted her handiwork with the berries, then suggested she trim the suckers off the fruit cherry, which he told her would never produce a crop: "It doesn't get hot enough here." Yet she showed him where she had planted tomatoes and cucumbers and the tiny grapes that had begun to form on the vines along the western side of the house. As they walked, little kinglets, chickadees, and juncos continued to chide them on their progress. She was about to point out the Einstein tree when he paused. "Wow." The garden spread out before him. "You grew up *here*?"

She could not make out his full reaction or expression. She could only see his eyes over his mask scanning the property, gaze gripping the scenery like a hawk's gaze piercing through shrubbery to look for signs of prey. What did he see, exactly?

Maybe he saw the potential of the place—what her parents had intended. Maybe he was taking in that it was a wide piece of property, perched on a hill, where it would have been susceptible to flooding. Maybe he was reading the property as her father had; there was enough sun for plants, and once there had been a view of the ocean. Maybe he was deciphering the landscaping and how the edge of the property was lined with camellias, because they loved shade and their flowers would be among the first to emerge in February and March. In front of the camellias there were rhododendrons; these would bloom later. There were various other plants mixed in—a bed of azaleas and, beyond that, an iris bed on a raised mound of dirt. As they walked on the lawn, she had to remind him to be careful because the ground was pockmarked like a moon heavily bombarded by comets over millennia—actually, the ground was punctured only by gophers, but they were insistent and thorough. Somewhere she had read about a lawn restoration system that involved digging up the dirt and laying down gopher-proof mesh and planting grass on top of it, a treatment that sounded, frankly, as labor-intensive as the gold-wire face-lift Catherine Deneuve was said to have received. In other words, only a movie star, and a French one at that, deserved a lawn with a deceptive underlayer of firmness. The Tree Doctor lurched as he walked and stuck out his arm for balance. She felt embarrassed. If she had converted to wood chips, this balancing act wouldn't be necessary. She would just have a simple garden and not an obstacle course. He didn't seem to care.

They paused in front of the pond, by the overgrown bonsai pine. She tried to make a joke. "Is it still a miniature pine if it looks like a Chia Pet?"

"How many years since it was trimmed?"

She shrugged. "Maybe three? I was watching instructional videos—"

"I could do it." His eyes feasted on the little pine.

Then they stood there for a long time. The goldfish were mating. It was embarrassing, actually, the way they were in an orgy on top of one of the planks usually used by the birds for bathing. Instead, the fish lurched up onto the plank—three or five at a time—and shuddered in ecstasy against each other, disturbing the water so it lapped and splashed chaotically. Then the fish swam over to the low-hanging branch of the wisteria and rubbed their bodies against each other again. "Goldfish are pagans at heart," she said.

"As are we all. Why goldfish? Why not koi?" he asked, his voice flat.

It was a reasonable question, and she began to narrate an abbreviated history of the pond, and how the water had attracted mosquitoes, which had first prompted her father to put in mosquito fish, tiny minnows that ate mosquito larvae. But then the frogs had appeared and sung so loudly at night that they had all had to learn to sleep to the sound of amphibians, and soon there were little tadpoles, whose metamorphosis into froghood and emergence from the water to land had been a childhood delight.

There had been a transition from mosquito fish to goldfish and then to koi, but this had brought a host of new problems: raccoons, kingfishers, and herons. Her parents, birders, had been delighted by the waterfowl, but eventually had to take recourse in creative measures to fend off the predators. They had strung a net across the top of the water to keep out birds who dove or fished, and wired the perimeter of the pond with a shock wire attached to a power source and timer; sometimes at night they had heard the raccoons scream.

But the koi had died in the unpurified water, an incident so traumatic that she glossed over the details of their deaths, only to say that her mother had insisted on small graves in the rose garden. There came a period when they installed a water purifier and once a year fished out all the koi into a bucket, then moved them indoors to the guest room bathtub, while her father drained the pond and scoured it of scum. And yet this intention of kindness, too, had been met with tragedy when the koi, unaware that they had only temporarily been dislodged, jumped out of the bathtub and onto the floor of the bathroom, where they died in the middle of the night. It was the first incident that demonstrated to her how existential despair could kill. Her family had responded with increasingly detailed measures to keep the koi in the tub—wooden planks and tape to secure the shower curtain—but then at night had woken up to the sound of urgent splashing, as the koi, not understanding their situation, had hurled their bodies against the curtain and attempted suicide.

"Koi are really high-maintenance," she finished. She felt giddy. In high school, each time she made a new friend and introduced them to her parents and thus her home, she would give this spiel about the fish in the pond. But it had been years since she had had an opportunity to do so; everyone in her life already knew the story. It made her feel strange and young again to have to tell someone something so personal about herself for the first time.

"So, goldfish." He nodded. There were six now on the wooden plank. One was white and gold and had a particularly long tail battering the water like the long lashes of a doe-eyed woman. Or was that a boy fish? There was no way to be sure. "I didn't know goldfish got so big," he said.

"I was always told that goldfish usually die because the tanks are so small they run out of space to keep growing. They die before their time."

The Tree Doctor sighed. She was expecting him to either remark on the futility of trying to have a backyard pond, or perhaps suggest she hire a gardener to upgrade the garden, or maybe even comment on the sheer eccentricity of worrying so much about the care and maintenance of backyard fish, but he said none of these things. Instead, he told her: "There is this guy in Silicon Valley whose trees I sometimes trim. He has a couple ponds, too, and has to hire someone to care for the koi. You know—fifty-year-old fish. I never realized it was so complicated."

He understood. "That's right!" She was overjoyed. "Who has a koi pond—?"

"Oh, this rich software guy with an obsession with Japan. People who love gardens all automatically love Japan." He paused. "So. The Einstein tree?"

She walked him over to the cherry tree by the iris bed.

He spent a few minutes with the tree, touching its bark and examining the ends of its branches with the kind of tenderness she had seen her mother's physicians employ to inspect her swollen fingers and toes. It was like he was communing with the tree. Then he walked around the base of the tree and over to the iris bed, kicking at the dirt with his toe. "It's dry," he observed.

"I water it."

He walked the other way and looked at the azaleas. They were covered with lichen and had bloomed unevenly. She was embarrassed for their leafless appearance. "What happened here?"

"I don't really know."

"Maybe the same lack of water. And some bugs. You can spray them with neem."

"Won't that kill the bees?"

He looked at her. "How much fruit do you have?"

"Berries. And the apples and plums we walked through earlier."

"It'll take time for the azaleas to come back. You could rip them out and plant new ones. Enrich the soil first and spray to get rid of fungus."

"Or keep them—"

"—and let them heal. It will take time. But they'll revive if you are patient."

Her father had been the kind of person to try to heal every plant. If a storm knocked a branch off the apple tree, he would carefully graft the branch back, fixing it with tape and tar, and very often the tree received the branch it had lost. Her mother, on the other hand, had tended to move plants around and throw out what was not thriving. During the drought, she had let things die. In the last few years she had spoken often of plants that were "volunteers."

She mentioned this now to the Tree Doctor. The wisteria

by the pond, she said, was a volunteer. No one had planted it there. Her mother had begun to favor plants that could grow in California's drought conditions and to abandon anything requiring extra effort. Her mother had such clear feelings about plants and gardens!

How had she failed to pass on any of these values? Her children had come to visit and had gone to the beach, played catch in the backyard with Thomas, and eaten barbecue. In short, they had treated this house as a kind of VRBO experience, and hadn't really learned any of the lessons that the garden had to teach them. She supposed that was her fault. Then again, the pace at which her parents had lived and expected her to live— the slow observing-koi-in-the-pond pace—was out of step with New York and Hong Kong, where vacations were doled out a few days at a time and meaningful interactions had to be packed into the space of an hour here and there.

"And what will you do?" he asked. His voice rippled with amusement.

"I don't know," she said and then gestured toward the Einstein tree. "What do you think?"

"It isn't dead," he said. "And what's really weird is it definitely isn't a graft. That's the same tree from root to tip. Where did it come from?"

"I don't know," she said. "It was my mom's tree. Every year she made some kind of special fertilizer for it."

"Can't you ask?" Here he was, asking about her mother again. People always wanted to know.

"She's in a nursing home and I can't see her."

"I'm sorry. How long—"

"It's only been about six weeks. She was diagnosed a year ago with this . . . brain condition. I forget the name." She could feel herself starting to panic. She did not want to think about any of this.

"Doesn't matter."

"She wanted to stay here. But she had several falls. After the last hospitalization I was told . . ." She should not cry while talking with this man. Somewhere behind her, she could hear two hummingbirds fighting over the feeder. She focused on the sound.

"Sure. Look at this place. I wouldn't want to leave either." He held out his arms as if to sweep up all the rhododendrons, the birds, and the trees.

"But—"

"You had to," he assured her.

Had she, though? It had all made sense before the virus. She couldn't leave her own family or her life in Hong Kong to care for her mother the way her mother needed, and yet now here she was, stranded, apart from her family, and her mother was still a two-hour drive away. She could bring her mother back here to the trees and flowers and birds while they waited out the virus together. She could do this, and her mother could watch as she—with the Tree Doctor—restored the garden.

And yet. There had been that terrible Thanksgiving just a few months ago, when she had come from Hong Kong after her mother returned from her most recent hospitalization, which had been prompted by the latest fall-rehab combo. They had both adapted to the condition of her mother's body again. They had adapted to the two ramps, the bars in the shower, the bath transfer stool, the bedpan, the diapers, the medical alert button, and a baby monitor—the kind with a camera. They had also added a rotating staff of nurses, the cost of which, in a year, would equal the full tuition of a private four-year college. The nurse had gone home for Thanksgiving to give them "time as a family." And that night, before going to sleep after eating a small plate of Whole Foods takeout turkey, she had extracted a promise from her mother not to go to the bathroom alone. Her mother might fall. Her mother must call to her over the baby monitor if she needed to go to the bathroom. And what had happened? Some as-yet-unvanquished maternal instinct had prodded her awake at 1:34 a.m. and she had glanced, bleary-eyed, at the black-and-white baby monitor to see the wraith-like figure of her emaciated mother crawling across the screen, on her way to the toilet. It was like watching the grainy play-back from one of those security cameras positioned on a front porch and discovering that your home was routinely visited by mountain lions or pilferers of Amazon packages. This had been the moment—heart thumping and pulse screaming as though fueled by the jet stream as she ran from her bedroom to her mother's—when she knew without any doubt that a nursing home was now needed. Her mother needed care that she could not give, even when they were together. The plants in the garden would lose their champion.

"I can fix the bonsai on the steps and by the pond for you and maybe save the juniper on the corner of the pond. But a tree like this . . . I would have to ask a specialist. I could ask around. Do you mind?" He pulled out his phone and gestured that he wished to take a photo.

"Please," she said.

While he took pictures, she told him about the quick recovery of the lemon tree and how this had given her confidence that other things in the garden might revive too. It made her happy to share this information. Even now there were rhododendrons pushing forward new growth. The other day, behind the pond, she had found a giant oval-shaped pink-and-white blossom that was on the verge of blooming. It looked like a Fabergé egg, the kind of thing that would emit a click once the blossoms unfurled. "I wonder," she said, "at what point a plant decides it will have blossoms. Like, does it know by spring? Does it make a late decision?"

"Do plants have free will?" He seemed at once amused to be considering this and delighted by the trajectory of the conversation.

"Or do they just respond to stimuli? Like if you feed and water them, they just . . . react?"

"That would be how Westerners see nature. Plants are a bunch of nerve endings."

"In Japan, there are these things called Noh plays—"

"I know what Noh plays are—"

"—where trees are characters. There's one with a talking cherry tree and another with the spirit of a pine tree. Six hundred years ago, the samurai were watching talking trees, and Shakespeare wasn't even born yet."

Without speaking, they went over to the redwood steps in the center of the garden, and sat down on the topmost step. There was another unruly bonsai here. "Needs a haircut," the Tree Doctor said.

"I could pay you," she said softly.

"Or you could watch YouTube videos and do it yourself."

"I don't want to kill it."

"Plants are harder to kill than people think."

While they were sitting a socially distant and respectable six feet apart, a leaf coasted diagonally down from right to left. It spiraled like the single blade of a helicopter. "It must be a maple tree seed," she thought, remembering how her mother had shown her in Japan that such seeds could whirl in the air as they fell. They had collected the seeds and tossed them loosely as they whirled down. The Tree Doctor, seeing that her attention had drifted, scanned the air for what had caught her interest and also saw the falling seed. It was small and light and had not fallen as quickly as most maple seeds did, and then she realized it could not be a maple tree seed at all. It was falling from too great a height and, anyway, the maples had not even fully emerged from winter to produce leaves, let alone seeds. This "seed" was actually a feather. Behind it, another feather was falling, and as she turned her attention farther to the right, she saw a cloud of soft down wafting in the air. The sun caught all the feathers and shone through them, and she was reminded of the soft down of willow trees—of the time, as a college student on exchange, when she had gone punting through the soft down of willows in Oxford, but of course this down could not be from an English willow tree.

High up on a branch of the pine tree she called the Penthouse, a Cooper's hawk was plucking the carcass of a songbird. His feet gripped the body, and with his beak he was methodically stripping the little bird, who was already decapitated. He had ripped out the wings and the tail; the dead bird's pink feet stuck straight out.

There was a gray titmouse sitting on a branch not too far away, and it was screaming. It was neither the fretful sound a titmouse made while eating, nor a sound of warning. It was something else entirely. The titmouse was screaming in agony, and she realized that the dead bird, now being flayed by the hawk, was most likely the titmouse's mate.

Another hawk landed beside the first hawk. They squawked to each other, and then the first hawk—slightly smaller—who had been preparing the titmouse for eating, held out the captured prey with his foot, and the other hawk received it and began to strip bits of flesh off the carcass, while the titmouse continued his or her lamentation. Every now and then the hawk who was eating paused to rip out some of the feathers, so the air continued to whirl with feathers, which the breeze picked up and scattered far across the garden, all the way from the weeds beneath the Penthouse, to the iris bed, and over to the orchard. And as the titmouse cried, the smaller of the two hawks, whom she would soon understand was the male, leapt neatly with his hawk legs and, with his wings batting at the air a few times, landed on top of his mate and they had sex as she continued eating. With an instinct no engineer could hope to replicate, they balanced there on her feet, which were gripping both the pine tree and the dead bird, and he sat on her and flapped his tail up and down, and she hers to receive him, and as she ate the headless bird, the titmouse cried for what was lost.

It was only a backyard garden, and he had come only to look at her cherry tree. Gardens were just places where flowers bloomed.

She cleared her throat. "Are you sure," she began, "you wouldn't like a piece of cake?"

"I could take a very small slice," he said. "In a napkin."

"In a napkin," she repeated, and stood up to go into the kitchen to get the cake and look for a knife. She came back outside with the cake and held it out to him. She felt like Eve with her apple. Like a temptress. But it was just a cake.

He took the cake from her slowly, and transferred the small packet from his right hand to his left. Then he held it and used his right hand to remove the mask. As he did this, his eyes never left her face, and she, understanding that a question was being asked in the act of their interlocking eyes, did not look away. He disrobed his mouth.

She was thrilled to see his face.

She wasn't thrilled to see his face.

He looked about as she had expected. She was disappointed. She wasn't disappointed. Her feelings about his face were like one of those balls in a small wooden maze, rolling around, and coming to rest, and falling down the little hole, and she examined them all over again, from the start. She had wanted to see what he looked like for days now, and here he was, apparently unconcerned and unaware of how his face was affecting her. He had a long and strong jaw. She liked this. His mouth was wider than she had expected. She loved the way his lower lip was wide and full and muscular. The top lip was arched and tense, and when he spoke, it was mostly the lower lip that flexed. When he concentrated, he drew his lip in and ran his tongue over it, and then his full mouth pursed. She could not stop staring at his bottom lip.

She no longer looked at men the same way as she had as a young woman. Then, even though she knew she was not supposed to worship men, she did anyway, for the magic she had imagined they could confer on her life. To be chosen by one of those men and deemed beautiful had seemed to complete a transformation of her body at a cellular level: A man had chosen her. A man had found her smart—smarter than other women, whom he had not chosen.

All this was nearly past her now. She was no one's potential mate or potential partner and was not going to contribute her eggs for the creation of a child. This fact seemed to change everything, just as it did for the older female characters in *The Tale of Genji*. What was more, when she looked at men now, she did so as someone who had her own children. People would appear in front of her as their present selves, but sometimes their voices or their stories seemed to fracture them into their former incarnations, and she would see the events in their lives that had brought them to her now. This was one of the gifts of parenting: the knowledge that all humans passed through stages when they were small and helpless.

The Tree Doctor moved the cake to his mouth and took a bite, and a moment later he moaned. He jerked his body, too, overtaken, it seemed, by the flavor. "Oh my God."

"It's the lemons," she explained.

And here he laughed. "Do you always do that?"

She shook her head.

"Do you always give credit to something other than yourself?" He took two more bites and she continued to stand in front of him, watching. "This is making me nervous," he said.

"Oh. I—"

And then he reached out and drew her to him. It was so simple to close the distance. He pulled her into him and kissed her and she smelled and tasted the earth and the sugar and the fruit all at the same time. He was holding her so she did not sink into the ground. He tested the additional boundary of her lips with his tongue and she opened her mouth. And the kiss went beyond a thank-you for the cake and into the realm of exploration. She was now a territory to be explored. Or maybe he was planting something in her—the seeds of possibility. She was still holding the potential future of his spit in her mouth when he let go and took another bite of cake and grinned at her, and his eyes gleamed with mischievous light. "I love lemon," he said.

She laughed. The blood in her ears was churning in spite of herself. She was like one of those lava floes on Hawaii that perks up after a period of dormancy. "Thank you," she said. "I mean, you're welcome . . ." She felt like she must sound stupid.

He nodded at her, and turned away to return to his work.

. . .

That evening she spoke to all the members of her family in Hong Kong. Her children floated around the screen, while her husband's conversation ran like a Twitter feed, recounting a list of articles he had read about the world, and which he had dutifully sent her earlier in the day. She had not read any of the articles, but it hardly mattered, as he continued to elaborate on his thoughts about most of them, so all she really needed to do was punctuate the conversation with an "Aha" every now and then while her mind drifted back to her conversation with the Tree Doctor. How unexpected it was to have met someone in her little hometown who could talk to her about trees and art! Meanwhile, her husband explained how the majority of his opinions had been covered in the comments that appeared at the end of each article he had read and forwarded to her, how his feelings allied with "JohnnyinAtlanta" and "AGuyRick," and fretted over whether or not to type out his own opinions, given that Johnny and Rick had already offered theirs. As she had not truly paid attention to any of the articles or to her husband's opinions, she merely defaulted to her standard position in their relationship, which was to encourage him to express himself and to affirm that once he started typing out his comments, he was sure to bring a dimension to the conversation that both Johnny and Rick had failed to do.

She heard his voice swell with color immediately, and she let her mind wander again while he dissected Johnny's comments in particular. How much she had longed to get out of her hometown as a young woman. Who knew where and how that longing had arisen in her; she knew only that she had wanted, like a house cat with an eye on a bird feeder, to get *out*. She had been so relieved to end up in New York City and to meet other young people like her who understood that in the place where they congregated, things were *happening*. She had found people like this all over the world, in every major city, and they had all shared the language of traveling, and good coffee, and little-known but about-to-be-discovered bands. The desire to be part of the center of things had never left her. She wondered if the Tree Doctor had been similarly surprised to find a like-minded person here in this small town.

She struggled to keep herself composed on-screen. She wondered if Thomas's algorithm would have detected that something was amiss with the quadrant of screen space she occupied. Would it tag her eyes and know that kissing the Tree Doctor had provided an intravenous shot of some mysterious elixir that had caused her organs to liquefy, sort of the way one of those caterpillars is said to turn into soup before its molecules are rearranged into a butterfly? Her skin was barely holding her together, everything right under the epidermis was churning, and there was no difference between her heart, her blood vessels, her bones, and her brain. She wanted to go back outside. Back out there, to the garden with the trees and the fish and the hawks.

And on and on Thomas prattled.

Eventually, however, he grew impatient with her and asked her to comment on the state of the world. "So what do *you* think?" he asked. He did this when he suspected she wasn't listening to him.

"I mean, that all sounds very smart."

"What does?"

"What you said."

"Which was?"

"Honey, I'm not going to repeat everything. I mean, this is not school."

"Well, what do you think? You can at least tell me that?"

Flustered, she composed herself sufficiently to rattle off recent events, beginning with the latest report from the nurse on her mother's condition—stable—and then the goldfish mating in the pond and the nearby hawks, and then the class momentarily rejecting *The Tale of Genji* on the grounds that the Shining Prince is a rapist. She left out the Tree Doctor's work in the garden. As she spoke, she understood how trivial all these matters sounded in contrast to the sickness and the upheaval in the greater world, as covered by the news links. In truth she didn't want to memorize the headlines or shape her thinking based on what all the reporters were saying. She preferred this new and distracted state she was in, where she thought about the Tree Doctor and his mouth. *That* was an obsession that would keep her alive.

Thomas seemed dissatisfied with her account, but before he could say so, Pia found her father and climbed into his lap and asked: "Mommy? When are you coming home?" And they were able to join together in reassuring Pia that Mommy would be home as soon as the sickness had passed and she was able to travel again. And Pia, a far less watchful and suspicious person than Sophie, accepted this explanation readily. Or perhaps it was because she was aware of the need to dispel family tension that Pia began to meow and paw at the air, relishing the attention of everyone laughing over her resumed cat antics and applauding her for her comedic nature, and perhaps this was why the conversation took an unreservedly mirthful turn. And if the family recognized the undue pressure on Pia to be a cat in that moment, there was very little they could do beyond comforting her; they were helpless before the sickness.

Then, acknowledging the now-fifteen-hour time difference between them, daylight savings time having come, and that Mommy would soon need to sleep, she thanked her husband for caring for their two daughters and acknowledged the gross inconvenience of her remaining so far away.

"I'm so sorry this happened," she said meekly, as though she had caused the pandemic and thus saddled her husband with primary care of the children. He nodded at her in return. Graciously, she thought.

It would change, they promised each other. And then she hung up on her computer screen, leaving her family to stay quarantined in their home while daylight streamed over the Hong Kong penthouse. She wondered what the hawks were doing outside. She wondered about the goldfish. She went outside.

In the little bit of light left, she could see that the maples were now starting to leaf. And there beneath the maples were some purple flowers and little pale blue ones—forget-me-nots. She realized they were wildflowers, and that when the narcissuses were completely gone, the wildflowers would remain and perhaps even take over the empty space.

She remembered the package of vegetable seeds she had found on the day she arrived. The vegetables were now sprouting, but there had also been two packs of flower seeds—morning glories and wildflowers. She understood then that her mother had stood there the winter before and thrown out handfuls of wildflower seeds and this was what she saw now. Before she had placed her mother in the facility, her mother had somehow managed to make it out of the house, perhaps with the aid of a walker or perhaps with a nurse, and throw those seeds onto the ground. Enough had burrowed under the dirt to germinate. Her mother had done this in order to try to pull her through from winter to spring, so that when the days lengthened, she would at least have these flowers to color the garden, hopeful that both she and they would be here in the spring. She took a few photos with her phone, then sent the ones that seemed brightest and best to her mother's nurse.

Four

It became clear that the world had been engaged in a relay race. In conversations with her family, she and her husband had told each other to "just get to this week" and then "just get to that week" and then "the week after," promising each other that once they reached these goals, there would be the possibility of life returning to some condition loosely defined as "normal." In fact, she and they were simply wading into the darkness along with everyone else, not knowing when the planet would no longer be blanketed by the virus. There would never again be a "normal" for a sustained period of time.

Thomas, she realized, lacked the imagination to grasp this. He needed the relay race, while she did not. There were likely many people who needed the relay race to ease them into understanding what the world looked like now, which was not how it looked even a week ago. But it was impossible to have a civilized and meaningful conversation if she didn't pretend to believe in the version of the world that included a relay race. Sometimes she even half believed it was true that "by the end of May this thing will have burned itself out." Why would a virus burn itself out? It wanted to survive as much as she did, and it would adapt the same way she and her mother had adapted to the ailments that piled up in their lives.

So on the phone or on FaceTime, she would agree that "next week things will all look different," and then she would hang up and go to sleep or go out into the garden and cry, before looking to see what the plants might need. Sometimes she could feel her mother reaching out to her through the garden to comfort her. "Feed me. Prune me. Admire me." Late spring was a time of lush color, dominated by violet and blue. The color purple in Japanese was *murasaki*, she recalled with delight. In the iris bed, there were now five flowers blooming, and the wisteria had, like Rapunzel, sent down its lilac curls. The word for wisteria in Japanese was *fuji*; Genji's stepmother, Fujitsubo, with whom he is so obsessed, was named for wisteria. Both Murasaki and Fujitsubo are named for purple flowers. She found the irises to be curious. Before blooming, they sent up swordlike leaves, which fanned out one by one, until seemingly out of nowhere they emitted a stalk with a bud at the top. Given how fat and round the stalk was, she thought she ought to be able to tell when an iris was going to birth a new flower. But she couldn't. They just seemed to appear.

She remembered a trip to Kyoto with her mother one May, when the restaurants on the Kamo River had just opened. They had lined up with perhaps fifty other elderly women hoping to buy tickets to see the beautiful young geishas dance in their elaborate kimonos as part of the welcoming of spring. Because she was so much taller than most Japanese women of her mother's generation, she was always asked to try to push to the front of the line to get a ticket, she did not like standing out so rudely as a Westerner. But her mother, already frail, insisted. "You get ticket. We may never get a chance again."

They sat in the auditorium with two booklets—one in Japanese for her mother and the other in English for herself—and watched as the geishas moved in the controlled and hinged yet smooth manner of Japanese dancing that sometimes seemed to fore-tell popping and locking. The geishas could dip down on their knees and tilt their chins and pivot while holding out a fan. They could bob their heads like little solar-powered dolls while twirling a parasol. And the kimonos! Such a celebration of spring colors. The younger geisha in the group, properly called *maiko*, wore pale blue and fresh green with splashes of red and pink—the colors of her mother's early spring garden. She knew the geishas would change their clothes as the year went on, and that by June, some would wear the dark indigo of the iris and wisteria, the saturated colors the garden was now sporting.

This love of flowers, the geisha dances, the exquisite taste of green tea—these beautiful things about Japan—had all been aspects of the culture she had adored from childhood. These trips were the highlights of time shared with her mother—moments when her mother's handicaps and illness could not reach them. It was this experience of transcendence through beauty that she wanted to share with her students, but they seemed to be insisting on going beyond what they saw as "mere aesthetics."

Other aspects of Japan had been harder. There was often a somberness that had irritated her in childhood. All these ancestor shrines and offering incense at altars to people who had died and whom she would never know. And all these temples with Buddhas! They were forever visiting temples and praying to Buddha to cure her mother. It hadn't worked. Now here they were—in fact, here was the entire world—swaddled in sickness, and her mother was sicker than ever. But as it happened, the ancient festivals they had attended together had their origins in plagues. The Gion Festival, with its eighty-foot-tall hand-drawn carts; the Nebuta Festival, with its twenty-two-foot-long lanterns, not to mention the many enormous wooden temples with statues of the Buddha holding a pot of medicine. "Built to commemorate a plague." "Built to ward off a plague." This must be why she had known the sickness was real. It had happened before and it was happening again.

Had people then been paralyzed by the fear of getting sick, and had they not left their houses, and moved with precision and caution? It must have been like that, and so they had clung to springtime flowers to remind themselves that the world would go on and provide beauty. She, too, should put her faith in flowers.

There would come a day soon when the irises would fade, and if she was to keep color in the garden, she would need new flowers to replace them. Late one night, after chatting with her family, she sat and binge-shopped for lily, peony, and gladiolus bulbs. She had tried in that conversation to ask Pia and Sophie about school, but Pia was absorbed in a cartoon and Sophie was resorting to one-word answers. At one point, Pia left the cartoon and crawled into Sophie's lap, and Sophie put her arms around her sister to hold her securely in place with such automated motions, she realized they must sit together like this often. They were quiet, though, and only Thomas had managed to talk, but his conversation bored her. He complained about his boss, who had left him out of a management meeting. "They wouldn't even have a product without me," he told her, and her head bobbed like one of those solar-powered nodding dolls. "Do you think it's racism? Everyone in there is probably Chinese or Japanese except for Renny, and he's from Australia. I mean, it was a meeting with this department store. They want to put in a prototype of the eye tracker at a makeup counter once the stores can open again, but I should have been there. Don't you think?"

She had become adept, while using the video chat, at running the internet in a separate window, and she was just then, yet again, browsing bulbs.

"Babe?"

She focused on the chat again. "Thomas, it may be a while till stores open."

"We are planning for Q3. It's why I can't leave Hong Kong."

She considered the bulk order of irises and lilies, which were on sale and sitting in her virtual basket. What if Thomas was right? And even if he wasn't, surely by the end of the summer she would be rejoining her family?

She told him not to worry about missing the meeting. She told him to at least shave so he looked tidy for his next camera appearance. Then she ordered the bulbs.

. . .

The Tree Doctor came to the house three days in a row, arriving at six thirty a.m. and sitting in his truck for an hour until it was light. Nothing had transpired between them since the kiss, and she began to wonder if perhaps she had dreamed it. He did not behave as a man who had kissed her, and she did not ask him for reassurance that she had been kissed. Was the kiss a promise?

Because he parked under the cypress trees, his body was always in shadow and she could not see his face, even if she set the alarm to wake up early to take a peek at him. By the time he emerged from the pickup, his face was covered with a mask and she could make out only his eyes. Gradually, the feeling of elation that had come from that kiss began to wear off. She wanted it to come back.

The first day, he removed the two half-dead cherry trees at the side of her house, then coordinated with Juan from the nursery to deliver two new Pink Cloud cherry trees, which he planted for her. The following day, he returned to start pruning.

He was remarkably self-sufficient. He had a little celadon-colored flask of water, which he kept half-wrapped in a customized canvas skin tucked in the pocket of an apron made from the same material. As he moved around the garden, he carried a little bag, the kind of fastidious thing only German and Japanese men would appreciate. He had a pair of black scissors, which had a customized holster attached to his hip. He was trimming the pine trees. He had warned her that they were so far past the ideal point of pruning—two years—that he would not be able to bring them back to their original shape, but would need to improvise. She had said she did not mind.

In his hands, the first bonsai, by the steps, went from being an oversize Chia Pet to a segmented bonsai, the needles clustered like the individual atoms making up a model of that most profound compound of nature. He found the branches that needed to be removed, he sharpened angles, and he nudged the needles into pompadours and tidy beehives and coiffed updos.

She wanted him to remove his mask again. She wanted to know what he looked like and she wanted to know what he thought when he saw her unruly garden and imagined the network of roots, plant viruses, gophers, and bugs all living just beneath the skin of dirt that kept everything somewhat cohesive.

It was not as though he ignored her altogether. "What do you do all day?" he asked her at one point when she went out to offer him a glass of water, and he demurred, explaining that he had his thermos for when he was thirsty.

"Oh, I . . . I'm teaching a class. An English class for a college in Hong Kong."

"You're a professor?"

"No! I'm a writer." It came out of her so easily. She rarely confided this to anyone anymore. She explained, then, about the novel she had published twelve years ago and how that had gotten her a series of teaching gigs.

He seemed impressed. His eyebrows flew up over the face mask. "You writing another book?"

"I don't know. Hard with a family."

"I don't see any family." He said this as though she had tried to get away with a lie. They were standing in the center of the garden, on the lawn, and with so much empty space around her, she felt exposed. There was no tree in her immediate vicinity to which she could instantly turn the conversation. "Do you miss your kids?" he asked.

"Of course," she said.

"Isn't there some way—"

"It's a little harder than it sounds." She explained all the travel restrictions, and the difficulty of timing a ticket with a test. Not to mention the cost.

"Your husband—"

"His job is in Hong Kong."

"But no one is working in an office right now," he said.

"This is true."

"So why—"

"He keeps saying the virus will be gone in a week."

"Oh, one of *those*."

"Yes."

"Hard for a man," he said. "We want to give you all the answers."

"Still."

"Still."

She appreciated that he did not push the matter. Instead, he said: "You could work on another book now."

This was true and it also made her uncomfortable. She *could* work on another book.

"Do you have, like, an editor? Or, like—"

"An agent. She died."

"I'm sorry."

"I have friends who write."

"Do they encourage you?"

"Actually, they do. Did. Most don't have kids. They've stopped asking me about my writing."

"But they do ask—"

"Sometimes. People used to ask me all the time how my new novel was going. They also used to ask if babies are like books."

He snorted. "And how does *that* make you feel?" She recognized the tone he was using. Her father had used it. He was talking to her the way men did when they were genuinely interested in a woman. Her father had been such a man, which was not to say he had been a womanizer. As far as she knew, he had not been. But his errands around town—to banks, shops, law offices, the post office—invariably took three times longer than they would have for her mother, because he always stopped along the way to talk to the women behind the desk, behind the counter.

She felt moved by his interest. She told him that babies and books were not at all alike, since a book, as far as she knew from her one experience, had nothing at all to do with the colossal suppression of self that for her accompanied motherhood. She had not known she was capable of so much fierce love; this part about being a mother was true. She had learned and continued to learn lessons about love that nothing else had ever taught her. Certainly not movies. Movies made it clear that it was the *falling* in love that was love. And this was true, but there was a reason most movies ended with the falling part. Falling had a shape and a destination. Would she get her man? Would they end up together? Loving a child was an endless activity.

She had known since she was a child herself that people lie. But one of the biggest lies she had been unprepared for was the oft-told homily that a woman could be anything she chose to be. This point had been repeated to her—women were liberated and could do anything, and she had absorbed the lesson with such thoroughness that even if she had had any doubts about herself, she made sure to hide them, because women were supposed to be only badass now.

What the world did not tell you was that it needed mothers to take care of the children offscreen, and it needed the mothers not to work, so as to make certain that play dates and activities and coding classes and athletics and confidence-building karate classes for girls were all attended. To be a mother meant to care for something small and weak all the time. It meant that her daily emotional state bordered on a sentimentality that had nothing to do with "complexity" or "irony" or being at "the height of her powers." To care for a child meant reducing herself nearly always from the capacity for large thoughts, for which her mentors—generally men and sometimes childless women—had always praised her. For this, she was paid nothing.

All this poured out of her as she stood, still holding the rejected glass of water. And the Tree Doctor listened. She thought she should stop divulging quite so much about herself, but then he was a stranger. It didn't matter if he found all this to be too much or not. However, she also wanted him to kiss her again, so maybe it did matter. Maybe the fact that he had kissed her once meant that he was not truly a stranger, and this was the reason why she was now unable to stop talking. She decided she had enough dignity that if he found her to be a lunatic, standing in the garden in her face mask, she did not care. "Someone once said that for every baby a woman has, that's two books she doesn't write."

"You're down four now, then?"

"If we accept the accuracy of that calculation, yes."

"You know," he said as he stood up and brushed his apron free of bits of pine, "I am familiar with most of the gardens in this town, and yours is . . . different. You definitely did not have parents who taught you to value regular life." He walked over to the second bonsai, the one by the pond, and turned his back to her as he began to assess its shape.

What was this supposed to mean? She felt nervous and excited and afraid. It had been a long time since she had experienced this combination of emotions and the cocktail that in aggregate could be described only as youth—that searing feeling that had driven her to flee this house in the first place. How had her body produced this feeling now, of all times? Her periods had been spotty the last four years, and now she had not had one at all for months. She was on the brink. She had been blazing hot the night before and turned off the heat, even though the thermostat was set to sixty-seven.

Today the palpitations had stopped, and her body temperature was manageable with a sweatshirt and a hat, and her body was excited and she felt young again. Did the irises feel a sudden rush of heat when they sent up a blossom? Was the suffering Einstein cherry tree, which seemed on track to miss spring altogether, undergoing something akin to menopause? Or did it have a sickness like her mother did, where the parts of its body would not cooperate with one another and death was around the corner?

There were only so many springs left in her life. She had grown up in this house with this garden, taking for granted this passage from white to blue to the saturated reds of summer and then fall and on to the brittleness of winter and then spring again. Her mother had fed the birds and reported discovering nests, and then the birds had disappeared and then reappeared in the winter. It had all come and gone and come and gone, and one day it would not arrive at all. This must have been what her mother had understood when she had stood in the garden, either alone or with a caretaker, and thrown about those handfuls of wildflower seeds. One day there would be no more spring. All people must pass into this knowledge. Was this the point of the vision board? Was he ever going to kiss her again?

She asked the Tree Doctor: "Why are you interested in trees?" She sat down on the steps, a respectable six feet away from him, while he continued to clip the bonsai. She was waiting for him to remove his mask and take a sip of whatever was in the thermos, but he wasn't budging. For someone who had such fluid fingers, he could at times be very stiff. He reminded her of a hawk when it was sitting on the tree branch with its shoulders hunched up around its head. Only his eyes were alert, scanning the garden. His dexterous fingers were at rest and gently folded over a pair of shears, like talons wrapped around the branch of a tree. She hated him for being so stubborn. Surely he knew what she wanted.

"Flowers are a gateway drug. You start out wanting flowers in a garden and then eventually, you realize that trees give the garden a structure. Seasons come and go and the trees are still there."

"Why conifers?"

"I like their personalities," he said. "They don't ask for too much, as long as they are growing at the right altitude. They make homes for animals. They can survive extreme weather. And fire."

A pine tree was self-reproducing, but the fruit it bore was open—a pine cone—and it rained seeds out of the cracked shell. Fruit trees had arisen later in evolutionary history, and their seeds were encased in the flesh of fruit, which needed to be eaten, or to rot away before the seed could be produced. It was not appropriate, he said, but he thought of conifers as being like men, and fruit trees as being like women.

She could see him smiling under the mask. He seemed to want to add something further and she nodded to let him know it was fine for him to say whatever he wished. But then he closed himself off from her again, and a slight coolness descended between them. She didn't like this. She had liked it when he had warmed to her and told her about the trees and asked her to talk too. She imagined those gentle yet strong fingers pruning the bonsai with his Japanese cutting tools. He seemed like an unusual man—someone so sharp and so particular about how the candles of the tree were cut and about the shape the tree would take, yet tender, too, that he would devote all this energy to the trees.

Then he did speak. His eyes drifted out over the garden toward Einstein, and he said: "A tree is like a human being on its head. The roots are the nerve system. The brain. A tree sticks its head in the ground and holds up its sexual organs. They are more like us than we like to think. And they communicate down there, underground, to each other."

"Is this something you think about or visualize when you are working?" Was that why he had kissed her?

"Sometimes. Sometimes I feel like I'm just standing there with them. One of the trees." The whole thing about the trees with their heads in the ground and the sexual organs on display was just this side of creepy, but she liked it. He said it so matter-of-factly, the way a botany professor might speak of such things. Trees had sexual organs. It was a thing that had to be said if someone was going to talk about trees beyond surface politeness. And she had asked about trees, and he had told her about them, politely and dryly. He was not the sort of person to pretend that plants were a mystery. He would not pretend that flowers were a decorative item that just emerged in nature; they had a purpose.

"Would you like some cake with your tea?"

He angled his head.

"I assume you are drinking tea? I was thinking of having some tea. I thought you might like some cake. We could have tea and cake."

"I won't be able to stop at one piece." He patted his stomach. "Also, I'm not twenty anymore."

She felt irritation. She thought he ought to just give in to the cake again. But he was firm and he would not take off his mask. "I don't want to minimize what you are feeling. You know. With your family. I believe it's very real to you. But, you know, it happens to lots of people. To men too. In my opinion, your feelings are totally normal and, frankly, the only healthy way to feel."

"What . . ."

"Wanting to be alive, if you are going to go to the trouble of staying alive." Then he turned, and keeping his back to her, he continued to trim the tree and he did not see her face when she removed her mask to drink the water, and still he did not turn around, though she tried to talk to him. He liked to work in silence. Finally she went inside and tried to grade her students' papers until she heard the rumble of his pickup, and she knew he had left for the day.

· · ·

While she was looking for toilet paper, she found her mother's backup supply of tea. She had not noticed it before, because it was kept in two cardboard boxes, opened but with the flaps shut, in the garage on a table that had formerly been used to repot orchids. Also on the table were two stacks of plastic plant trays, a jar filled with bamboo chopsticks accumulated from many years of buying takeout sushi, another stack of empty flowerpots nestled one on top of the other, a vacuum-sealed rectangular package of canned sardines, and at least thirty packages of instant ramen.

The sight of the ramen tore at her heart. Her proud mother must have been eating instant ramen. This was a food she had begged her parents to buy for her as a child. "This is not food," her parents had explained. They were forever willing her to eat the chewy, woody asparagus and chard from the garden, when all she wanted as a ten-year-old was the salty, briny, slimy concoction of instant ramen.

The ramen told her how desperate her mother's last year had been in this house, where she could no longer care for the garden. Beside the packets of ramen was a box—the backup tea from Nagoya, Japan.

Sometimes she read her students a passage from *The Book of Tea* by Okakura Kakuzō: "The Philosophy of Tea is not mere aestheticism in the ordinary acceptance of the term, for it expresses conjointly with ethics and religion our whole point of view about man and nature. It is hygiene, for it enforces cleanliness; it is economics, for it shows comfort in simplicity rather than in the complex and costly; it is oral geometry, inasmuch as it defines our sense of proportion to the universe. It represents the true spirit of Eastern democracy by making all its votaries aristocrats in taste." If *The Tale of Genji* was concerned with aristocrats, *The Book of Tea* made it clear that the pursuit of beauty belonged to everyone.

She and her mother had different teas. Her own tea came from a 350-year-old shop in Kyoto and was available online.

Her mother, however, drank a different kind of tea. Her mother's illness meant that her body was somehow sensitive to teas that were grown in Shizuoka, which was not far from Tokyo, and which had a more acidic flavor than teas grown in Uji, which was closer to Kyoto. Her mother's Uji tea was not available online. It came from a small store in Nagoya that would not ship internationally.

When they went to Japan together, even if their main itinerary did not include a side trip to Nagoya, they always had to stop there anyway, checking their luggage into a locker if possible, before taking the subway to the tea shop, which was located on a side street near the center of town. Their different teas also meant that in the house for the past twenty years, there had been two canisters: one for her mother's tea and one for hers. And as her mother spent progressively more time in bed, like a good daughter, she had made two pots of tea and brought the cups and pots to the bedroom, where they had sat and talked and watched the garden and the birds outside. In recent years, there had been less time for tea. "You sit and drink tea," her mother had said, bossing her around. "You will regret when you cannot." It had struck her as so overdramatic, all this pre-grieving. Her mother had been telling her the truth, though. There had been only so many more days to drink tea together by the window with a view of the garden. For now, here was the tea, without the tea drinker. She took a bag of tea out of the box and decided to drink it.

That morning she had received a text from her mother's caretaker. It was a photo of her mother, listing to the right and trying to smile with the muscles still controllable by the puppetry of her brain. It was a half smile and her eyes were half-bright. Her mother as object, posed before the camera, dutifully greeting her daughter. She had sent back another picture of the lemon tree, noting its increasing return to health. It was like an answer to a question, or like a sick challenge. "Can you, too, get well?" Now her breathing was sharp, and her heart, despite the slow-release beta-blocker recently prescribed for the stress she was enduring as a caretaker, and still circulating in her system, was flopping wildly, a fish without oxygen. She tried to steady herself. She sucked the emotion back inside her body—her mother was the one who was sick, not her. It was selfish to panic over the exchange of photos.

She found more toilet paper and went back into the house.

It had started to rain. The rain did not abate, and perhaps an hour later she began to fear the wind. The lights flickered and the power snapped off. The refrigerator simply gave up with a soft whine. The lights all clicked. The heater gurgled and was silent. She looked for matches to light a candle if the power outage lasted the night, and to light the stove for hot water in the morning. She found candles easily. Her mother was prepared.

She opened the damper above the fireplace, then pulled two logs out of the metal bin on the hearth. Her father had chopped this firewood from a downed tree branch years ago. Outside there was more wood, but it would likely already be damp. She would need to make do with what was in the house. When the logs did not immediately light, she cast about the house for something to use as kindling. Paper bags? Old tax forms? She settled on a combination of junk paper and old rags, watching the threads of what had once been her mother's flannel shirt catch hold of the flames from the match. Then she blew so the fire could ignite the logs, which it finally did. The fireplace exhaled heat.

She pulled an old wool blanket off the bed and wrapped herself in it and sat in the living room by the window and watched the water strike the pond and fill it so the fish would have more space to play.

The garden was drinking rain, but it was a hard rain and the leaves bent under the barrage. It was like a Korean massage, the kind that left a human body pink and stripped of old skin, newly born. All around the garden the heads of plants nodded. They were like adherents to some strange religious sect where they needed to show repeated deference. The wind picked up and she could hear it passing through the trees. From far away she heard a crack. Somewhere a tree had fallen. Then the wind would enter a lull and then it would rise again. She sat there for two hours on the sofa, rising only to boil water on the gas stove to make more tea to warm herself. The birds were hiding out, perhaps clutching branches of the camellia trees that lined the property. They did not come to the feeders. And so for the next few hours she and the birds tried to ride out the storm.

Occasionally there was a hush and then a few birds arrived frantically at the feeders. When the birds landed in the rain and ate the seeds, she felt a swelling of warmth, a tenderness she had not felt since her first child had been born, when the nerves inside her body had seemed to extend in sensitivity beyond a point she had previously thought possible. Having a child, especially the first one, had been a lesson in extremities of care, alertness, and often worry. Because babies cannot talk, she liked to joke to her husband, she had felt like a veterinarian, reading the moods and tiny changes in behavior of her child as a vet examines a cat that appears to have a malady. But the veterinarian analogy was only half-right; she had really felt like a medium. She had crawled inside her children's bodies to feel how they felt, and to respond accordingly.

The phone rang once. Of course her mother had an old-fashioned landline, which still worked when the power was out. She went to answer and listened to an automated voice from Pacific Gas and Electric inform her that the power was out in her neighborhood. The voice told her that crews were even now repairing whatever had caused the outage and that another call would follow with an estimated time for the power to be restored. She hung up the phone.

If her mother were still here, they would have slept in the same bed, but her mother was not here. She made more tea and drank the tea. She replenished the logs, finally falling asleep before the fire with a pillow under her head.

It rained all evening and all night. The house heaved and creaked as though to let her know how hard it was straining to keep out the storm and the rain. Occasionally there were peals of thunder and a great crashing. She drifted in and out of a light sleep and felt very alone. She tried to hug her body for warmth, or touch herself to see if she could relax into comfort and thus into an easy sleep. That comfort, though, seemed too mechanical this time. She couldn't even be bothered to help herself.

She woke up once and her mind wandered. How had she come to this point where she felt she existed on a far shore, away from people to whom she had until recently felt quite close? Her hands were starting to wrinkle. Her face and neck too. She found herself thinking of her mother's tea and how she could not have known that it would be the last tea purchase they would make together. She felt distressed to have ever thought of her mother's tea as an inconvenience. The facility had recently told her that her mother did not drink tea, but took Ensure in coffee. Her mother had left her and had left all the tea, and yet her mother was still alive.

Again she considered bringing her mother back home. If the reality she perceived were true—that the virus would not disappear anytime soon—then she would not be leaving for Hong Kong. She could bring her mother home. They could have a little more time together.

There would come a day when she, too, would no longer drink tea or travel anywhere. She was turning into one of those older people who had memories and who would tell stories of what she had done and not of what she hoped still to do. She knew that the next phase of her life would depend on her ability to navigate this change from a person who hoped to a person who looked back on the past.

She wanted to walk through the rooms to check for leaks from the roof, but in the dark, her childhood imagination began to inflate the house so the rooms grew and she feared becoming lost in her own home. It got so thickly dark here when the electricity was out; it was never this obscure in the city. She put another log on the fire. One more log and she would run out of things to burn. As a child, when there was a storm, she had been afraid of the howling, of the trees slapping the roof, and of the proximity of lightning. Her parents had always consoled her. There was no one now. She *was* the parent. "It is only sound. It is only a storm. It will pass." Her body rigid with cold and fear, she got up only once more to put on a wool sweater, then climbed back into her nest by the fire.

. . .

She woke early in the morning after a fretful night of sleep. The sky was still gray and the afterburn of the storm still kicked up the trees with weak gusts of wind. The house was cold; the heat had not come on. The lights were still out, but the birds were gossiping frantically while they ate. They must know, she decided, that the storm had all but passed and the skies would soon be blue, and warm air would dry everything that was wet.

She took a match from the Buddhist altar and lit the gas stove to boil water for coffee. The refrigerator and freezer had had no power overnight, so she was quick when she opened and shut the door to remove the half-and-half. The caller ID announced an unfamiliar number.

"Hello," she said, already bored by what would most likely be another robocall.

"Hey, it's Dean. I'm sorry it's so early, but the storm was so bad, I wanted to call." Dean?

"It's . . . calmer now," she said.

"So you're okay."

"Fine," she said sternly.

"How are the trees?"

"The trees," she repeated dumbly.

"There was so much wind. I've been out already and there are a lot of downed branches on the roads. I thought of you and those tall cypresses . . ."

"I haven't been outside to look. I mean, I see needles all over the driveway."

He told her to take a look and gave her his number and said to call him if she needed his help. She thanked him, and he asked if she had taken down the number he had just given her, and when she said she had not, he gave it to her again. "Hold on a minute," she said, and she wrote the number down. She should have been excited to have his number, but his timing was terrible and she was worried about the garden. "Thank you," she said brusquely. And then they hung up.

Once the coffee was ready, she took a quick tour of the house; there were no leaks. Then she put on her wool hat and gray scarf and went outside to see what the storm had wrought. The flower beds were soaked, but for the most part, the plants had not been damaged. The gladiola leaves and the irises were bent shyly, but had not been broken. The dirt by the pond was water-logged; the ground was low there and the gopher holes just added to the low water table. The pond was full. And there was debris everywhere—cypress needles and little pine branches and pine cones.

She was walking along the pond toward the iris bed, and the clouds were peeling away like the skin of an onion to reveal the blue sky underneath. She imagined herself to be one of the birds twittering with high-strung excitement over the events of the night before. This was when she saw Einstein.

She was accustomed to thinking of the tree with a certain amount of disdain. It was not attractive, and it had not woken up this spring, and she had no idea what to do with it. Now, as it entered her vision, she could not at first understand what she was seeing, and time slowed as she narrated the scene to herself. The tree was down, but not the entire tree. Everything was all right. But it wasn't all right, because a much larger branch had felled two branches, and their extremities were entwined like clasped hands. The branch from a neighbor's pine tree had fallen, and Einstein had reached out in the middle of the night during the storm to grasp the pine to help it, and both branches had fallen, severed from their hosts. They had collapsed on the ground like those entangled lovers covered in ash in Pompeii.

The pine branch was substantially larger than the cherry tree branch, and her first thought was to disentangle the branches and throw them both away in the green yard waste bin in the front of the house. But she would need a chain saw to cut up the pine branch, and she had never used a chain saw and was not even sure if the old one was still somewhere in the toolshed or the garage; some time ago, her mother had moved the lawn mower and all "valuable" gardening items out of the toolshed, afraid that homeless people might come and steal them.

Then she realized that in fact two branches had been severed from the cherry tree, with a third one partly broken off, still connected to the trunk by a tiny bit of bark and inner flesh. She examined this wound: it was slightly green in color.

Then she backed into the house and called the Tree Doctor. "A branch fell onto Einstein . . . ," she began, nearly breathless.

"I'll be there in ten minutes," he said.

She had no idea where he lived—she had assumed it was deep in the valley—but he was, in fact, in her driveway within ten minutes. He opened the door to his truck and held a small bag in one hand, while fixing a mask into place over his mouth with the other. She was standing on the front steps waiting for him, and realized she had forgotten her own mask. Her hand shot up to cover her mouth and then she let her fingers drop. There was no point. He nodded at her bare face in greeting, then hurried to the gate that separated the front of the garden from the back. They dispensed with any customary pleasantries; he simply unhooked the gate himself. She wasn't sure how she felt about the fact that they had this familiarity now, and that he could let himself into her back garden when he wanted to.

He was heading straight to Einstein, and when he reached it, he fell to one knee as he had by the other cherry trees in her garden. Then quickly he began to separate the pine branch from the cherry wood, and when this was done, he opened his bag and pulled out a coil of black tape and a pack of Popsicle sticks.

"I guarantee if you look up what to do with a broken branch, the conventional wisdom will tell you to cut the branch off." His voice was slightly muffled through the mask, and she realized it was because he was breathing a little harder than usual. He wasn't exerting himself, exactly, but she knew, as a mother knows, that his breath had changed due to intense concentration. Her children had done this when they had begun to learn to draw.

"Can I help?" she asked.

"In a minute."

She remembered her first daughter's birth—an emergency C-section. She had insisted on staying awake during the procedure, in exchange for the doctor narrating what was happening to her body and to the baby. The doctor, a woman, had promised to do so, but in the end was speaking in a kind of code to two other teaching physicians, the baby's doctor and the anesthesiologist. She caught only glimmers of what was happening to her body, things like "That's not the head," or "Blood pressure is perfect," and later "Needs oxygen." It was like that now. The Tree Doctor was moving at a tempo known only to him, and he did not tell her everything he was doing. He seemed intent on seeing what part of the tree was still connected to the branch. "Hold this. Here," he said.

Obediently—it was her tree he was fixing—she held the two parts of wood together while he tore off strips of tape and attached them to his wrist. Then he took one of the Popsicle sticks and moved her fingers just slightly, so the stick could go against the torn branch. He began to wind the tape around the branch. This was an easy fix, he told her. The other was harder.

It had been only a few hours since the branch had fallen. Had they waited a full day to begin the procedure, he would have discarded the branch, but there was enough time to try to save it. He was going to do a graft, he told her, and this required exposing the part of the branch known as the cambium, the white tissue just under the bark where the juices in the tree flowed from root to tip. "This is the nerve center," he told her. The cambium was always shifting, moving outward, while making the branches and the trunk thicker as time passed. The good news was that Einstein still had cambium, which meant it was awake and not dead, despite the lack of leaves on what they considered its skull.

"Although you understand," he said again, "that the roots are really more like the brain. The head isn't the part that is sticking up."

From his bag he produced a towel and he spread this on the ground, then placed the tape and the Popsicle sticks on top off this. He opened his bag again and pulled out a knife, a small bottle of liquid, and a blue cloth bag, perhaps five square inches, and laid these on the towel. Then he unzipped the smaller bag to produce a terry washcloth. He unscrewed the cap on the bottle and spritzed some of the liquid onto the cloth—she could smell alcohol. He rubbed down the knife to sterilize it, and then began to cut the end of the fallen branch. He worked quickly, shaving the end of the branch at an angle so the exposed flesh was wet and green, and then he cut a wedge into the side of the tree the branch had fallen from. It took some time. He seemed to be preoccupied with how the inside of the tree was exposed, before he lined up the pieces and began—again with Popsicle sticks and tape—to bind the tree together.

At one point he was so silent, and his concentration so total, that she could hear him breathing hard against the mask. And then, holding the branch, sticks, and tape with one hand, he took a few seconds to release the mask from his face. He kept working.

She watched him fixing the tree for her and imagined him as a child doing something for another person—perhaps his mother. He would have tried to help her with dinner. Maybe he would have listened to her tell him about her day at work. He would want to be kind and would want to be protective and then occasionally, as he did with her, he would have some outburst in which he expressed his expert opinion, then thought better of such a display of egocentricity. It all endeared him to her.

After he had finished with Einstein, he walked around the garden to look at the other trees. Perhaps it was her imagination, but something about him seemed almost shy. He seemed to willfully prevent himself from smiling, as if to do so would draw too much attention to his mouth—to that marvelous lower lip—now uncovered by the mask. He had to know that his mouth was wonderful. He didn't look at her, either, though she knew he was conscious of her body next to his. They looked in the orchard at the apple tree and the plum tree, but neither had lost any branches.

"You should tell your neighbors that their tree came down in your garden. Homeowner's insurance should cover the cost of removing the dead branch."

"And paying the Tree Doctor?"

Only then did he smile, and it was a broad, wry smile. "It's true. I'm a professional. I'm a capitalist at heart," he said. "But I'm also the one who offered to come and look."

"I can . . . is a check okay? You can give me—"

He waved his hand. "Forget that."

His eyes reminded her of the Cooper's hawk. His gaze was awfully sharp for someone who had such gentle hands and who had so many elaborate tools fastidiously packed away in his blue backpack, all with the express purpose of mending an injured tree. To be predatory like a hawk must not, then, necessarily be a bad thing. A hawk was goal-oriented toward survival. The Tree Doctor's fingers had been gentle while he worked, and she could imagine being the tree, yielding to every cut from the sharp German steel blade, and giving up splinters just so the parts of it that were "working" could fuse together with the other parts and come together so it could continue growing. Was it always painful to turn oneself over to another human for care and for comfort?

"I wanted to know what you looked like the first time I met you," she said simply.

His eyes traced the contours of her face and she stood there and let him do this. It was not like standing in front of an X-ray machine, though surely a man who could splice together the wood on a sleeping cherry tree had the ability to see into other living things with a kind of precision that an ordinary man, say, an accountant, might not? "I was pretty sure I knew what you looked like," he said, taking her hand into his warm fingers.

She had had a crush on a boy but had been worried about her small breasts, and a girlfriend had told her that the man already knew she was small and didn't care. If that had been a deal breaker, he would not still be hovering there on the boundary of the conversation, waiting to see if it tipped over from flirting into contact.

"Do you have somewhere else you need to go?" she asked, practically.

"No," he said.

She let him hold her hand. He seemed to know that no one had held her hand for a long time, and yet she also suspected he was not the sort of person who would wait indefinitely for her to become accustomed to hand-holding. There was not really a gradual way—for adults—to go from conversing with masks, to holding hands, to actually fucking. Sex was not like putting red and blue paint together and then watching how the colors gradually morphed into purple.

"Shall we go inside?" her voice croaked. She could barely get the question out of her mouth.

Perhaps his voice was hoarse, too, and that was why he didn't answer. He drew her to him and he kissed her, but not for long. He began to climb the steps, leading her up onto the patio and into the house.

Five

It sometimes felt as though there were a story that existed outside herself—an overstory. She, along with everyone else, measured herself against this story all the time, knowing where she had or had not taken the correct steps and thus whether she was properly placed on the path to adulthood. By the time she was an adult, she knew it was impossible to mold herself to the story and that plenty of people were also dissatisfied with the story, but no one seemed to have any idea what to replace it with. The story spun on and on out there, like the planet Saturn whirling in the sky and bearing down on her life, one of those invisible forces the astrologers said dictated the very experience of existence. There were only a few pockets where one could acceptably deviate from the story's demands. Tragedy was one example. Sometimes people were marked by tragedy before they were *supposed* to encounter tragedy. Occasionally they got lucky and struck it rich. People liked to say that money didn't matter, but of course it did. It meant that the rules did not, in fact, apply. Tragedy, like great wealth, meant that a person could opt out of the overstory, at least for a while. That happened in novels all the time. Tragedy meant a man could say: "I'm sorry. It was not our time." It meant that even in *The Tale of Genji*, a woman could flee to a convent to get away from Genji, and that Genji himself, claiming to be afflicted with "melancholy," could fail to continue to pursue one of his heartbroken conquests, who would wonder why he had disappeared. Tragedy plus romance was particularly potent.

In stories, love was a thing that happened to young people,

and if it happened to older people, it was a surprise, like finding a bottle of wine in the attic that had been forgotten, and whose age turned out to have made it delicious and perhaps nearly priceless. In general, older love was not priceless. She supposed this was because sex between older people wasn't highly erotic, like pornography. Who wanted to look at old people having sex? A little old was okay. A *wabi-sabi* kind of older sex. But when people got too old, as even Genji the Shining Prince did, they have to be ushered offstage. There was a term she had once heard, "SORAS," which stood for Soap Opera Rapid Aging Disorder, and which referred to the propensity of soap opera characters to expeditiously grow from children (which happened mostly off camera) into adults, so as to quickly embark on the important project of falling in love. Even Lady Murasaki, like a modern-day soap opera writer, had SORASed Genji, aging him from a baby to age seventeen in chapter 1, before jettisoning him at the end of the book as though he were some fat old Elvis of a father, in favor of his young and beautiful son Kaoru. Genji's exit is accomplished in a chapter poetically titled "Vanish Into the Clouds" and marked by a blank page. Love, all the stories told her, was for the young.

Despite knowing this, she continued to look for clues about how to live outside this story. Part of her thought love ought to be possible. She did not want to be like the women in *Genji*, for whom love has faded and for whom life is a disappointment. Perhaps she should take inspiration from Genji himself, who repeatedly experiences the high of falling in love. She thought that Genji showed her what might be *possible*. To be a courtier in Heian Japan was to be obsessed with the arts, as all the men and women were, but it was also to engage in finding love and pursuing it and keeping that feeling throughout life. Why, she wondered, must it be so different for a woman? For herself? Why was it easier to imagine another person enjoying freedom—a man—than it was herself?

It had become so unsatisfactory now to watch the stories of young women earnestly pursuing love in films and on TV not knowing what lay ahead of them in old age. She had this feeling that the overstory did not expect her to have emotions anymore, though she found this preposterous. She was full of feeling and she wanted it to extend into areas of life beyond simply caring for others. She had been able to suppress this great emotion much of the time, but now, with the virus swaddling the globe and confining her here in the garden, her own desires had overtaken her capacity for self-suppression.

. . .

Are bodies like trees? she asked him.

What do you mean?

Can you wake up a body the way you can wake up a tree?

They love cherry trees in Japan because they say the cherries are like women. Some of the tree doctors I have met have treated those trees as if they were women.

She looked at his face and saw tears seep out of the corners of his eyes. They weren't heavy tears. Once, long ago, when she and her husband had first made love, in a tiny room in a rumpled bed, he had cried and she had asked him why and he had said he did not know. He told her that men cried sometimes during sex, when something in them was woken up. The Tree Doctor smiled at her, and she thought of wounded and bandaged Einstein outside with its exposed layers of cambium now attempting to transmit fluid across the barriers between them. The Tree Doctor had said to watch for signs of weeping.

Can I get you anything? she asked.

You can come here, he said, and so she curled into his arm

and smelled him. She liked his smell—she would not have had sex with him if she had not liked his smell. At least that was what she told herself. She smelled him and the scent made her relax. She felt so happy. She was quite sure that because of the sickness that was out there, strangers were not supposed to have sex at all, and yet he wasn't completely a stranger. How could a man who tended to wounded trees be a stranger?

Where are you from? she asked the Tree Doctor, as she lay on his shoulder.

Connecticut.

What is your last name?

I'm just Dean.

Just Dean?

For now, he said.

Not even the nursery knows your name, she said. I asked and they only said you were the Tree Doctor. She felt him tense up beside her.

He was uncomfortable with the questions. Not completely uncomfortable—just uncomfortable in that way of knowing that sex had opened him up and he did not want to regret this vulnerability. I like my privacy, he said. I just like it. People think they have to advertise everything about themselves . . . his voice trailed off.

Are you married?

Divorced.

Children?

Three. Two previous marriages.

Oh.

I'm better with trees.

I like your hands, she said, holding one of them. Why did you become a tree doctor?

Fell into it. Wasn't the plan. I didn't want to be a wage earner. I like plants. Plants gave me access . . .

To?

Life. People. Then, with tremendous feeling, he said, I'm going to save your tree.

. . .

Of course, he asked questions about her, and she told him the truth. In telling him the truth like this, she realized how much and how often she lied to other people. She had had five boyfriends and had lost her virginity at seventeen to a boy who was fifteen and had been much more experienced. Of the five boyfriends, only one had been anything close to abusive, and even that was mostly psychological. She had not had sex with someone new for twenty years, which was when she had first had sex with her husband. And she had not had any sex for six years, which was the last time she and her husband had managed, after a marriage counseling session, to come together. No one, not even her best female friends, knew any of these things. They thought she had written a novel, met a boy, and now lived happily ever after in Hong Kong.

"No, really," she insisted.

He didn't believe her. He was from a world—maybe a planet—where people had sex when they needed to. It was like breathing. She knew there were people like this and that they knew things she did not know. The minute she had seen him in the parking lot of the nursery, in his ridiculous shorts with his perfect legs and vibrant hands, she had known he was from a place where people always had sex. People like that couldn't imagine people like her.

"How does that work?" he asked her.

How had it worked? "Not everyone has sex."

"But if you wanted to?"

Had she wanted to? She cast back in her mind. There was so much history to cover. She thought of her first week of high school, and the girls who went to the keg parties on the beach and called, crying, to say that they had had sex. The term "date rape" in the eighties wasn't so well known. She had decided this would not happen to her.

"I mean, if you are the girl and you want a great guy, then you have to wait for the great guy and hope he notices you."

He disagreed. "We don't decide. Guys don't choose. *You* do."

She thought of all the failed crushes of her early adult life. "You have to understand," she said slowly. "I believed there was something wrong with me."

He stroked her hair. There was so much tenderness in his hand that she knew he was a man who understood how to console women. Perhaps he had a daughter. He brushed her hair, untangling it, and she knew he was doing this reflexively, but also to kill time while he tried to process what she was telling him. "How could there be something wrong with you?" he asked.

Her breasts, for one, she said. She read the comments in the tabloid sections of online magazines featuring a parade of celebrities in their bikinis. If they were skinny, a man might write something like "It's still a Rolls even if it's flat," or "Built like a boy." The last one was common. If the woman was fat, the comments tried to insist that the woman was "healthy" but louder voices prevailed that she was "thick." If she had had a boob job, and they often had, the cabal announced that she looked okay with the "bolt-ons."

"These are excuses. Sex isn't a picture," he said. "And you're . . . a professor." Then he apologized and tried to explain that he meant she was smart. "I tell my kids they should have as much sex as they can. Everyone should. You know this, right? Deep down?"

"Sure." This was what she was supposed to say.

"It's a lot of work to have two kids and a sick mom and very little support," he told her. "You deserve to have sex."

"I do," she repeated.

"Of course you do. You wanted to be here and you chose well," he told her. She did not want to talk anymore and kissed him so he would stop talking. He praised her. He told her how beautiful she was and what a shame it was that she did not appear to understand this, and that he would help her understand it.

All this time she had been composed of some kind of cold liquid, and now that he was next to her, her blood boiled. In fact, her blood steamed, like she was a prewar apartment in New York finally heating up on the first day of winter and clanging away so everyone could hear the racket. She could hear her blood hissing through her body. It rang in her ears and churned through her brain. She felt it pool between her legs, making her labia thick. She felt reconstituted. There was liquid everywhere—her legs were slick. How was it possible that she, a woman past the ability to get pregnant, had so much slime between her legs?

Her hands were hot. Her eyelids were hot. He put his tongue in her mouth, and she knew he tasted heat. Her own body was a repository of steam. He took her hand and put it between his legs and she felt how hard he was. "You did that," he told her. She smiled at him and understood that not all women could do "that" to the Tree Doctor.

"Should we talk about . . . the virus?"

"Which one?" He barked in laughter. "Bad joke. What do you want to talk about?"

"Just . . . they say we are supposed to be distanced—"

"I wear a mask at work."

"That's . . . good."

"You're my only sex right now," he said.

This was what she had wanted to know, of course, but his bluntness and the curious turn of phrase were so strange to her ears. She was his only *sex*. Put that way, she sounded like the answer to a multiple-choice question. Of course "my only sexual partner" would have sounded clinical. If he had said, "I want to be monogamous," that might have made things sound more emotionally serious than she knew they were.

"Oh. You too," she said brightly, as though informing someone that they were her "only sex" was the kind of thing to which she was accustomed. My God, she was so old! She had no idea how to date or tell someone about her sexual history anymore.

Much later, after he left, she wondered what he had meant when he said that she had chosen him. It wasn't like that. She was sure it was not like that at all. A woman could not choose a man. It was women like her who were on parade, and men chose one of *them*. It was the men who always held all the power. This was what all the stories told her.

. . .

He texted her that afternoon to ask if she was okay, and she assured him she was. She was and she wasn't. But she wrote back: "I'm great!" A thousand years, and this was what had become of Genji's morning-after poems.

When she went to urinate, she felt a pain between her legs. Well, of course she did. She wasn't used to having sex. But the pain felt like something more than soreness. "What have I done to myself?" She laughed out loud. No one was there to hear.

She received yet another text. "Can't stop thinking about u."

The "u" annoyed her. She didn't understand this need people had to not spell out words. So she wrote back: "I was just thinking of you too!" She could see the space after hers bubbling as he drafted a reply. Then the reply faded. She hoped he would reconsider all further "u"s.

She reread his line of praise. It was just one line. She reread it several times. How nice it was to receive a line of praise. How nice to be old enough to not need more than one line of praise.

Over the next few days the pain didn't go away, and she fretted over what to do. This was not mere soreness. She hadn't had sex in a long time, but she knew what this was. She had a UTI. Did this happen to other women who suddenly had sex after not having had it for so many years? She thought about her body, so tight and unused and suddenly forced open.

She put on her gloves and her mask and went to the grocery store and bought two large jugs of cranberry juice. She carried them, one in each hand, and then wondered if she was a walking advertisement for a woman who had just had sex in the middle of a pandemic and was now suffering from a urinary tract infection. So she found a shopping cart and put the jugs inside and decided to camouflage her purchase with other items. It was fortunately still early in the morning and the aisles were not yet crowded. She picked out a few flats of ground turkey and coffee and eggs, which had recently been limited to one flat per customer. She decided she no longer looked like a middle-aged woman with a UTI. She looked like she was stocking up. At one point she abandoned the shopping cart inside the store and went outside to look at the plants stacked along the wall between the exit and the entrance.

She hadn't thought of the grocery store as a place to buy plants, but there were petunias and geraniums, and then she saw, clustered all together, the vegetables. People had been here before her to buy tomatoes and beans—there were only a few of these plants left. But she could pick out cucumbers, squashes, and herbs, and she balanced a few of the tiny, flimsy plastic cartons in her arms and took them back to her shopping cart. For good measure, she added a bottle of wine and went to the checkout. The cart ought to look sufficiently camouflaged.

And all would have gone well except that the wine bottle caused the woman at the register to study her carefully and ask to see identification.

"Is that necessary? I mean . . . can't you tell I'm—"

"It's the law." It was early in the morning, and it was a pandemic, and the woman behind the register was humorless.

She did not want to produce her identification. She looked at the woman's name tag: Kate. Did she know any Kates? Had she ever known a Kate? It was possible she knew Kate. She pulled out her ID and the woman stared at it.

"I brought my own bags." She hoped to be helpful.

"Can't pack your bags."

"I can't—"

"I can't touch your bags. Next time, go through self-checkout if you want to use your bags. Although there is a limit on the number of items, and you have exceeded that." Kate handed her back the ID.

And then the woman asked: "Did we go to school together?"

"I . . . don't know."

Kate said her full name. "My married name was Fuller, but you might remember me by Kate Brighton."

She tried to laugh it all off. "I just got *carded* by Kate Brighton, omigod! So how are you? It's been, what. Thirty years?" Was it necessary for them to be having this conversation after thirty years?

"What are you doing here?" Kate asked.

She gave the most simplified explanation possible: mother sick, temporary job, family in Hong Kong. Sickness. Kate listened. But the simplified version sounded so simple and even a bit preposterous, and so she tried to elaborate, talking about how she had been flying back and forth to Hong Kong before the virus had come, although that wasn't entirely true, as Hong Kong had shut down before she had even made one flight back to see her children. "So what are you doing here?" she asked, in an effort to switch the conversation over to Kate. But as soon as she asked, she felt bad. "What are you doing here?" could be misconstrued as a criticism.

"Making extra money. My ex has the kids on weekends. I ring up groceries."

"Oh. Must be hard sharing kids during . . ." Suddenly she did not want to talk about children. She did not want to hear about Kate's children, because this would mean she would need to talk about her own. She knew Kate would not judge her for any of the decisions she had made, and the fact of this shamed her. She had been passing her days through the pandemic with no company but the garden, the birds, the virtual class, and the Tree Doctor, and she had unfairly affected a kind of superior stance about her hometown, which was, when you got down to it, sheltering her, and where people like Kate were kind and cared about her even after her many decades of absence. Kate wouldn't care about sex, about her marriage woes or her stalled writing career. They might develop some kind of friendship. She thought about how her parents had been so disappointed in their neighborhood, where people had hired consultants to help them decide what kind of grass to plant in the front yard, and of the Tree Doctor, with whom she had laughed about the neighbor unable to plant a rhododendron. She was a snob.

"Is it nice there?" Kate asked.

"Where?"

"Hong Kong."

"Oh!"

"Someone said you were in New York before that. I forget who told me. They said they heard you on the radio."

"That was a while ago."

There was, fortunately, another customer waiting with a cart loaded with groceries, and Kate nodded at that woman. "Be right with you."

"It's so nice to see you. The half of you I can see," she said brightly.

"Come by again," Kate said, turning her attention to the cottage cheese and loose locally grown artichokes now barreling down the conveyer belt.

And then she walked out, any further recognition obscured by the face mask. It was foolish to have worried or to worry. No one really cared whether or not she, a middle-aged woman, was having sex. My God, she thought. Anyone in the grocery store might be a person who had just had sex. She had never thought to look at other people this way. There were probably people in there who had also just had sex, and maybe people like her who had not had it in years and had completely given up.

But she also did not want anyone to know, because she was not yet sure who she was or how she should now present herself to other people. How could she know who she was now, after having seen the Tree Doctor just once? Maybe nothing about her had changed. She also neither wanted anyone's condemnation nor their approval; she wasn't sure she deserved either. She did not know if, in seeing the Tree Doctor, she was becoming someone new, or if she was simply developing a second self, the way some people are described as having a home self and a professional self. Maybe she would develop a lover self. Or maybe not. She didn't know. There were two types of poems in *Genji*: the exchanges between lovers, and the incidental poems in which a character suddenly expresses a feeling. Now would be a time for an incidental poem to help direct her thoughts, but what would she write?

As it happened, the cranberry juice did not cure her condition. She continued to feel pain when she went to the bathroom, and it wasn't pain from a vagina suddenly used with minimal lubrication; she had an infection. Ignoring the pain did not help, and by the middle of the fourth day, her body twinged consistently.

She made an online appointment with the nurse practitioner

who had administered a flu shot to her mother at the care facility in San Francisco.

The Filipino nurse practitioner, whose name was Evie, responded to her request immediately, and they set up a time to talk that afternoon.

"I think your mother is doing fine. She misses you."

"Thank you. I know. I miss her. Thank you for all you are doing."

"We will open the facility when we can. It helps when you call."

"I know. It's just . . . it's really hard over a screen."

"It *is* so hard." Evie was so empathetic. You had to be empathetic to work with dementia patients, she decided.

"I'm okay. I'm really okay," she babbled. She knew she should be asking about her mother, but really, what new information could they give her? At last she explained that it hurt to urinate.

"Did anything happen recently that makes you think you have a UTI and not some other condition?"

Here it was. "Yes," she said. "I had sex."

Evie was unfazed. "Did you use protection?"

"Yes."

"That's good. It doesn't completely rule out STDs. You should come and get tested when you can."

Oh, right. She heard this all the time in the news but had never quite applied the complexity to herself. Married people didn't have sex for fun.

"We need to test your urine."

"I'm one hundred and twenty miles away . . ."

There followed a discussion as to whether or not Evie could prescribe antibiotics without seeing test results (she could) and whether this was ethical (it wasn't), even though they were in a pandemic (allowances could be made). But Evie was not a gynecologist, and she really should see her gyno for any other conditions, especially given that she was having sex. That was what a gynecologist was for: a doctor just for female sexual organs. Evie needed to know if she took any other medication; she lied and said she did not.

"Please. I'm not twenty. I know about UTIs," she begged, and began to despair at how much havoc having had sex just once had brought to her homebound life (but wasn't sex always like that?), when Evie asked her for the local pharmacy's phone number. She also asked if she was going to continue to have sex and if it was consensual.

"Yes," she said.

"Okay. That's good. I forgot to ask in the beginning. Consensual but rough? Try some more lube next time? Personally, that's how it happens for me. I don't have sex, and then I do, and I have to remember to use lube."

"Right." Evie was talking to her like they were girlfriends! Talking about sex like it was a normal life occurrence!

Before the call ended, Evie asked for the date of her last period. It had been months, and she could not give a precise date.

"We only consider you to be in menopause after a full year without your period. So right now, we would say you are in perimenopause. Which probably means more lube is necessary . . ."

And then, at last, the prescription was called in. She picked it up an hour later and took the first pill in the car.

It took a few days for the medication to work and the pain to subside. During that time she and the Tree Doctor texted once or twice a day. While she waited for the infection to clear, she occupied herself with her teaching and with the garden, planting the petunias and other flowers she had picked up from her shopping spree at the grocery store. She learned, as she had as a child, that it was all well and good to plant plants; weeds would come up too. She could turn her back on a part of the garden, and a day later there would be more weeds. So she sat and pulled them out one by one, freeing the flowers so they could bloom.

. . .

May arrived, and the golden-crowned sparrows departed for Alaska, with the warblers close behind them en route to Washington State.

One morning, as she was sitting on the patio, she saw a cluster of juncos bouncing around below her mother's Japanese plum tree, gathering dead grass. When their beaks were full, they heaved into the air and landed in the wisteria tree and then, as though completing an obstacle course, carried the grass from one tree to another—the wisteria, the persimmon, the walnut—until each departed to his particular location to build a nest. Then they reversed course and came back for more supplies. Birds. They always knew what time it was!

Over in the bougainvillea, tiny kinglets clustered around the eaves of the house, snipping beakfuls of cobwebs. The hummingbirds did the same, though they retrieved the cobwebs while in flight. Some cobwebs had accumulated around the metal fire pit and patio furniture, and the hummingbirds seemed particularly to like the ease with which a great deal of silvery, tough web could be removed at once. It was only the females, though, who did this, building the nests from cobwebs so they would stretch as the babies inside grew. The male hummingbirds, those beautiful and showy creatures, only impregnated the females and did not do a thing to help with any of the work that came after.

Meanwhile, the crows flew from the tall cypress trees over to the dead branches of the cypress trees on the other side of the house and methodically used their beaks—and feet, if necessary—to snap the branches. Then, unlike the smaller birds, they flew in one long, lumbering stretch all the way across the entirety of the garden to the other trees, making no stops in between.

There were hours now when she stood in the yard, tracking the birds and watching them slip into the shadowy crevasses of branches. She had powerful binoculars, and yet even with those she could not see precisely where the birds went. Some secrets were kept only by the birds.

. . .

After the infection had gone away, and she and the Tree Doctor had finished a bottle of wine and had sex—again without lube, because she had forgotten to buy any—he asked her: "Did you come?"

There it was. The pressure and aggravation of that question. If it wasn't the size of her breasts, it was whether or not she could come.

"I don't want you to worry about that."

In the dark, she could feel him grow very still. "Have you ever come?"

"Of course!"

"Well, I don't know. I dated this one woman once, and she had never come."

"Like not even from . . ."

"Not even that. But you have?"

"Like I said. Of course." In the time between their first sexual encounter and that question, she had applied her scholarly mind to the internet's encyclopedic expertise on sex and orgasms and the multiple kinds of orgasms women had, and concluded that whatever happened to her body during actual intercourse counted as an orgasm even if it wasn't the same as what happened during masturbation. The articles made this sound completely plausible.

"You are sure?"

Well, no, she wasn't.

"Can you come if I touch you here?"

"Yes."

"But during—"

"I don't . . . We don't need to . . ."

"What is it? Tell me?" He could hear her distress.

And so she did. She told him that she knew he—men—needed her to come, and she did not want to address the complexity of making her come. It felt like a failure. She wasn't interested in failing. She liked sex and she liked him and it all felt good enough.

"It's supposed to be the best thing, though," he told her.

"That feels like pressure to me."

"To perform."

"Yes."

"Do you like oral sex?"

My God, of course she loved oral sex! She did not even have to say anything, and he slid down on the bed between her legs and began to lick her. The sensation was so intense, she put her hands over her face, then pushed his head out to stop him. She had not experienced such precision of feeling for years.

"You need to let me," he told her. He put a finger in her pussy and he licked her clit. She put a hand on his head and guided him and she could feel the muscles of her body clench down on his fingers when she came. He tried to put his dick in her then, but she had closed up so hard—like one of those sea anemones in a tide pool—that he could not get inside. She apologized.

"You apologize a lot," he told her.

"I'm out of practice."

"Did it feel good?"

"It did." And she told him about a dream she frequently had. In the dream she was aroused and she would tell herself it was possible to come in an orgasm. She had had the dream for years and woke up without having climaxed. She would wake up, on the edge, just before coming, and tell herself: "My body can do this."

He grinned. "It's just going to take lots of practice."

"Practice," she cooed. She sounded silly, cooing. "Fucking." This sounded silly too.

"Fucking," he agreed. He told her she was hot and she burst out laughing. "Is that funny?" he asked.

"No, no," she soothed. "It . . . I was . . ." "Come on," she told herself. "You cannot laugh at being told you are hot."

He looked uncertain. "I mean, you may be a professor, but even a professor wants to hear she's hot."

". . . you get to be a certain age . . ."

". . . bullshit . . ."

She thought about this. "I can't decide if it's stupid to want to be hot and old or normal."

"People are so fucked up," he said with impatience. "Sex is great. It isn't complicated." Then she realized he didn't like it when she analyzed his compliments. She was supposed to take them in, even if they were somewhat basic. So she nodded, as though what he was saying was obvious to her too. "Why did you stop having sex?"

He asked the question with an impatience she had not heard since the first time they had spoken on the phone and he had complained about the governor and the abundant water of California. She felt something was at stake in how she answered the question. Why had she stopped having sex? She had been so in love with Thomas, and so adoring of the shield of normalcy he had given her. She had been elated to have his daughters. Two beautiful babies had turned into beautiful girls and . . . "I'm not completely sure I know."

"You seem to like it."

"I do!"

"It was six months with my wife. My ex, I mean."

"You didn't have sex for six months?"

"I thought that was a long time. She said she had pains . . ."

"Did she go to the doctor?"

"That's what I said!"

"I'm sorry."

"Have you asked him why you aren't having sex?"

"It is hard to talk about. And then I guess it became easier to keep not talking about it." Why had she given up? The girls had been born. It had been impossible to sync mealtime and bedtime, and Thomas worked late hours at the office.

"You had sex before they were born?" he asked.

"At first. We had sex all the time. And then." He had stopped trying. She had brought it up a few times and Thomas had sniped at her: "Married people don't even have sex all the time."

She had tried to parse this sentence: "Don't even." Did he mean that even though they were married, it should not be assumed they would have sex all the time, as not all married people did? Or that being married shouldn't mean having sex? Whatever he meant, it was clear that her request for sex had been unwelcome. No, that wasn't the right word. Her request had been *inconsiderate*. Bad manners. That was how she had interpreted the statement, but then she thought about what one of her students had said when they were discussing *The Tale of Genji*. It was Henry who had declared: "Sexuality is a spectrum."

"What do your girlfriends say?"

"I've never told them," she said.

"What?!" In his world, girlfriends did not keep information like this secret.

But it was true. She had kept the information secret. Why had she kept it secret? She had been unable to publish a second novel, unable to inspire sex, and, most of all, unable to earn real money. Totally dependent on a man, and with two small children. It had all fit together. She had done the math without anyone's help. Something about her was deficient.

"But here you are. Solo in California during a pandemic," he said, with admiration.

"That was not the plan. It just happened."

"Something like this doesn't just *happen*," he said. "You were open to it."

She began to protest then that she had always been a rule follower, all her life. Always. She was not a cheater. She was not a person who lied on her income tax returns. This—the Tree Doctor—was an anomaly. And he listened while she poured her heart out to him about how unusual these circumstances were, how she had never cheated on a test, or plagiarized, or knowingly run a red light. "I think it was you," she said.

"Now, *that* is the biggest bullshit I've heard all night," he said, but he was grinning wildly. "Your husband say he misses you?"

"He doesn't complain about anything. About most things. Well, except for office politics. He wants a big payout."

"Does he drink?"

"Rarely."

"Work hard?"

"Very."

"Addict."

"I just said he doesn't drink."

"It's not always about what you eat or drink. You miss your kids?"

"Well, of course," she said.

"But?"

So she told him about her mother's first hospitalization, forty years ago. She told him how her mother had never become completely well, and how finding the right doctor and the right medicines had, over the years, become a family quest. When her father died, the job fell to her. "The last few years of trying to look after my mother and the kids and not being able to write and trying to take a family trip just to see something and go somewhere and then never having those trips materialize . . . The only time I've been able to go anywhere was here, to see my mother. And now I am happy to be alone," she admitted.

"Good girl," he said to her. He moved to suck on her neck and she let him.

Six

The nursing home had begun to send her daily photos of her mother smiling, or eating her food. She sent back photos of herself posing in front of the changing flowers in the garden. She began to watch the garden for flowers about to bloom, then stalked these blossoms and photographed them for her mother. The accumulated images on her phone—flower, bird, mother, selfie—all formed a kind of vision board. Was this what her mother had wanted her to do?

She felt like they were waiting for something. What were they waiting for? Was her mother waiting to come home? Were they all waiting for the sickness to stop? Was she just waiting to go back to Hong Kong? She would not allow herself to ponder if she was just waiting for death.

When the irises faded, she grew nervous that there might be no more flowers in the garden, but then, as if by magic, the foxgloves suddenly spewed out their weird mitten-shaped blossoms in white and pink. It was as though outside the normal communication of text messages and photos-by-iPhone, her mother was reaching out to her through the soil. "Look at me," they seemed to say. They said it to her with her mother's voice. "Look at me in the garden." They were making her look—they were controlling her, the way her mother's illness had controlled her too.

She should call her mother. She hated to call her mother. She wanted the virus to stop raging so she could go see her mother. How was it that not even a year ago, the most troublesome event in her life had been the search for a place for her

mother to live? After each hospitalization, she had been assigned a social worker, each one kind and well-meaning and
who had called her and called her mother, who had blocked their
calls. After each fall, another social worker was assigned and
the pattern repeated itself, until she finally understood the sig-
nificance of their presence in her life when one of them asked
her on the phone: "Can your mother feed herself?" Wasn't her
mother feeding herself while she was gone in Hong Kong? But
then when they were together, she was spooning the pasta or the
rice or the curry into her mother's mouth, as she had fed her
children. She had started to cry on the phone. No, her mother
could not feed herself.

How had she not known until then that in every neighborhood, there were places where residents who could not feed
themselves came to eat and sleep and watch TV?

"Do not ever put me in a home," her mother had told her over
and over. And yet, there they had been, at the juncture where a
home was necessary. She tried not to think about her decision to
put her mother in the home. She tried not to think of her mother
in the home at all and this was why she did not want to call.

. . .

One day when she was in the garden gathering a fresh supply
of asparagus, she heard a sweet voice and, turning to find its
source, saw a tiny bird on the ground beside her, eating newly
sprouted lettuce. His head was black and his body gold and she
realized it was a goldfinch.

And then her phone rang. Only half of her mother's face appeared on the screen; the other half was hidden, as her mother's
body had slouched down on the armchair on which the nurse
had propped her.

"Your mom, she feels good today!" It was Yvonne the nurse,
speaking to her off camera. "She wants to talk to you."

"Mom!" She loped back into the house to catch a stronger Wi-Fi signal. "I just saw a goldfinch! Remember? How I always wanted to see a goldfinch in the garden?"

Behind the glass, her mother blinked. She had not spoken to her mother over the phone for at least a week. She could see that her mother's face had become even more immobile, as though recently affected by a stroke, though she knew her mother had not had a stroke. They would have told her if her mother had had a stroke. In the house, the bedroom wall and the refrigerator were covered with photos of the two of them together in France, New York, and, most of all, Japan. Was this truly the same person now propped up in an armchair like a stuffed animal?

And then her mother spoke to her. The words were clear and enunciated, as though her mother were well again. "Before your father. Before. In Germany, there was a man. And he comes to see me every day."

They were conversing in Japanese. She and her mother had always had this private language between them, but not speaking to her mother for so many days meant that her language skills were rusty and she was unconfident. She felt like a child. In fact, they were both like children. She with her child's Japanese, and her mother, now being spoon-fed. All those milestones her mother had gained over the course of her life—eating, walking, driving—were one by one being taken away from her. Her mother could not bathe, walk, or eat alone.

Was there really a man from Germany?

"What is the German man's name?" she asked.

She watched her mother receive the question and watched her face tighten with concentration. It had been horrible to watch her mother, so beautiful and expressive, increasingly become this blank slate that projected no feeling except for pain and anger. She had been watching it happen over the past few years and had asked her mother's doctors numerous times if there might be something wrong with her mother's brain. "No," they had all told her. They had not noticed the reduction in her mother's language skills, because her mother, with her accent, had never spoken English fluently anyway. They could not notice the increasingly garbled problems with "he," "she," "a," "an," and "the," and the fragmentary nature of her sentences. Then, in the months before she had placed her mother in the facility, she had finally insisted on an MRI, and the doctors had diagnosed dementia. Her mother wasn't crazy. She was ill and had fought the illness and her diagnosis so they might be together as mother and daughter for a little while longer. Her own prejudices had caused her to join the cabal of judgment that had called her mother crazy.

"His name," her mother said clearly and in English, "is Carl Joseph." Was her mother getting better? She was speaking so intelligibly!

"Carl Joseph," she repeated. "And he is there?"

"Yes. And I want you to see him." Her mother's face was illuminated. She looked "normal." The uneven expression—the sag on the right side—had stopped. She was a whole person for a moment, expressing this wish that her daughter see this man.

"Okay," she said. "When they finally let me visit you, I will try to see Carl Joseph." When she said this, her mother visibly relaxed, comforted. She knew, as the daughter, that she had a singular power to comfort her mother. She had known this since she was a child, and it was a power in which she took pride that made her feel pressure and irritation.

The nurse thrust her head back in front of her mother and filled the iPhone screen. Yvonne was smiling and seemed to almost be trembling with life. *That* was how it was supposed to look when someone was alive: they vibrated. Thomas's eye-tracking software would likely pick it up. The difference was like looking at the foxglove she had transplanted, which was drooping, and the one that she had left in its original place, with its roots digging into the ground and the flowers illuminated. "Okay, thank you!" the nurse said. "We have to go eat the rest of dinner now!" It was four p.m.

"Yvonne," she said. "Can I please come see her? Can you make an exception for me?"

Yvonne shook her head. "I still cannot do that. It's not fair for everyone else if I sneak you in, but not them." Yvonne placed her mother in the center of the screen again. But now her mother appeared to have retreated into blankness. "Say bye to your daughter!" But her mother refused to wave. Her mother was not better.

She waved. "Have a good dinner!" she said brightly to the screen. "Thank you so much for calling! Gosh, it was so great to hear from you!" she gushed, every happy note in her voice trilling with false giddiness. "Bye! Goodbye!"

. . .

She told Thomas about the strange conversation with her mother. When she began to recount the events, she wasn't sure if she should tell the story as tragic or comedic. She began matter-of-factly, but then as the reality dawned on her in the telling that her mother truly had dementia, she could not let the story become a sad one, and so she began, in a high-pitched voice, to tell it as though it had been amusing. "And then she said his name was Carl Joseph and that he had been to see her!"

"Well, that's okay," her husband said blithely. "Maybe she's living in Germany in her mind right now."

And this infuriated her. "When we traveled to Japan, she took me to see her old boyfriend, who she almost married. If there was someone else . . . I mean, my grandmother in Japan told me about the man she almost married. She carried his picture in her handbag and used to show it to me."

"Maybe she had a crush on someone."

"I don't think so. I think there must be a man," she said. "Otherwise my mother would not have told me there was a—"

"How can there be a German man going to see her every day when we are all on lockdown?" her husband asked sensibly. If this conversation were geometry, her husband's question would have been a straight line—the kind of thing you didn't argue with. She hated him for his rationality, even though it meant he wrote great code and was remunerated accordingly. But the rationality made him mean and precise.

Her daughters clamored around the screen. They looked tired. Not enough sleep, she guessed. "When are you coming home?" they asked in unison.

"As soon as the travel restrictions are lifted," she answered. She felt a pang at seeing them just on the other side of the screen. She felt them missing—like phantom limbs. Had her mother felt that way about her during their FaceTime chat? And then she began to sense how her daughters were feeling. The feeling was back! "How are you?" She knew the answer before asking, but she asked anyway. A difference between a modern mother, which she tried to be, and an old-fashioned mother, like her own, was that a modern one asked for feelings rather than dictated them.

"He's making us watch war documentaries," Sophie whispered into the camera.

"I thought you were watching Disney."

"We ran out."

"Impossible. If you add in the after-school TV shows, there is enough Disney to last you for at least a year," she said.

"He says we need to learn about real life. About what adults do."

"Put your father back on the camera," she instructed, and her husband returned to the screen. She was about to speak to him—sharply—about this diet of war documentaries, when something in his face made her stop. He looked exhausted. Stern and stoic, as always, but his eyes were wide and ringed like some kind of owl. She had not truly been paying attention to him, which was why it took her a moment to realize that she had never seen him like this before.

"Honey," she began.

"I'm doing the best I can," he told her immediately. "There is only so much Disney *I* can handle." It was then that she noticed a tuft of hair on the back of his head that had been gathered into a ponytail. She wondered if he had done this himself, or if the girls had. Most likely it was the girls, given that not all the hair had been put into the ponytail. He had never complained about being the father of daughters, but perhaps he had been suffering in a house with two girls more than she had realized.

"Can't you let them watch Disney and you can watch your war documentaries in a different room?"

"They are scared if I leave them alone."

"But . . . that's the point of watching Disney. It feels safe."

What was it with middle-aged men and the war and history documentaries? Was it that as they passed into some other stage of being a man, they needed to delude themselves into feeling as though they were one with those moments in history when men had been certifiably heroic? "I was there at Guadalcanal!" Her father had been the same way before he died. The couch had been ringed with books on the war in the Pacific, and every night he turned on the History Channel while her mother fumed and tended to the orchids. "Can you sit in the room with them and maybe put on headphones? And read? Or listen to a podcast?"

He nodded that he thought he could. He nodded that this would work, that it was just his body in the room that the girls required.

"I'm sorry I'm not there," she said this automatically, and they both knew she said it only because it needed to be said, because the moment required that she acknowledge her absence. To not do so would be bad manners. A part of her—was it a traumatized part?—noted how easy it was to solve their problems like this, at a distance, over the screen, not unlike the way she had listened to her mother earlier that day talk about Carl Joseph, while it had been up to someone else entirely to feed and bathe and change her mother's diapers that night.

She wondered how long the lockdown would last. She thought about these two experiences of watching her emotional life on a screen—her mother, and her children. She wondered if this was how it was for God, if there was a God. Did he look at everyone's lives through a pane of glass, watching the stories unfold, interacting as he chose, and ignoring and muting them when he felt like it?

"It's not going to last much longer," Thomas said.

"I don't know about that."

"Come on. This is not some movie where the virus wants to kill all of us! It'll just end one day. Soon."

"Thomas," she said gently. "I think we need to start to think about what we are going to do if it doesn't end."

The way he looked at her through the screen made it clear that the virus continuing indefinitely was not a mental pathway he intended to create in his brain.

"We might need to think of . . . other ways through this," she said. "I think you should consider bringing the girls here."

"I can't leave this time zone," he said.

"Right," she said. "We will wait a little bit more."

. . .

It was hard to remember now at what point she had realized her parents didn't have sex. Maybe it was something that clarified in her brain over and over again as she aged, like one of those rivulets of water brushing over a granite boulder in the middle of a stream, gradually carving an ever-deeper groove. "They don't have sex. Oh. They *don't* have *sex*." This fact had developed in the permanent architecture of her brain alongside numerous supporting stories. Her father had not complained about the lack of sex, because he loved her mother, and her mother didn't really care about sex anyway. Love was not about sex. Sex didn't even matter.

She was ten the first time her mother was hospitalized, and afterward, when her mother came home for the first of many long recoveries, when the family rhythm was centered on her mother's body, she had, without realizing it, gone from caring solely for herself to also caring for her mother. She had taken the small toy Liberty Bell from her room to her mother and asked that her mother ring the bell when she needed anything. The bell, which weighed no more than a pound, made a loud noise that carried easily for the twenty yards from one bedroom to another. But her mother had not been able to pick up the bell. She was too weak. And so next she had taken the small bell that had hung around the neck of a favorite toy—a lamb—and given this to her mother. The bell was small, light, and round, and in multiple might have made up sleigh bells, and her mother could easily ring this, though the sound didn't carry terribly far. She learned to be quiet in her room, the better to hear her mother's call for help.

Her mother could not have been this sick and weak and have had sex. She could articulate this to herself once she was a teenager. But as a child, what she had really learned was that the body was something over which to exercise caution and care.

It would be decades—now just over a year ago, in fact—until she managed to get her mother out on the patio one day after yet another hospitalization, and her mother would say: "I was surprised when I got pregnant. Your father was not good at sex."

She was shocked. There had been no preamble to this admission. There had been no softening, polite small talk. No nice Southern manners, Thomas had noted when she told him about the conversation later.

She and her mother didn't talk about sex. They talked about how tightly to bind an Ace bandage around her ankle, or how the lack of a nap made her mother cranky and thus rude to the latest cleaning lady, who had disappeared, as had so many others, or how the omelet in the restaurant *had* contained ginger, which had caused inflammation and thus pain, even though she had explicitly explained to the tense and frowning blond waitress that her mother was deeply allergic to ginger. This was what they talked about when it came to the body. And while they did talk about children—family is invaluable—there was little talk about the hows and whys of pregnancy.

"I thought you couldn't have sex because you were—"

"Is that what he told you?" Her mother had been propped up in the patio lounge chair, two extra pillows cushioning her tiny head and a wool blanket across her knees. She was so frail now, and after each hospitalization it seemed miraculous that vitality could continue to pulse inside that body, which, despite medicine's best efforts, continued to waste away. And that was the thing: she could feel this wasting away inside her own body. Her ability to feel that was a by-product of the intense bell ringing and listening training and all that had come after her mother's first illness. She could feel what her mother felt. If she ever wondered if her mother could feel what she felt, the question was overridden by the terrible fact that to be sick was to be in a condition of greater physical urgency than to be well.

"I tried to encourage him," her mother rued. "He would push and push and I would say, 'Good job. That is good. That feels good.' But he could not . . . what is word?"

"Orgasm."

"I could not believe when I was pregnant."

There are some things people do not want to know about their parents. Perhaps this was one of those things she had not wanted to know. Or perhaps it was something she did not want to know, but should.

"In the Hara family," her mother said to her slowly, "we marry weak men. Our women are strong and beautiful and clever. But the men we marry are kind and weak and die early."

"It might be worse to marry a strong man," she suggested.

"That is why we always find and marry weak men," her mother told her.

How like a late-blooming summer flower she had been, sitting on the patio that November, wrapped in the blanket but still basking in the seventy-degree temperature that was now autumn in California. "Over and over we find them. But that is also our opportunity." Her eyes pooled. "I have so much to tell you. Things you will need to know by the time you are my age. I am afraid I will not be here."

"I'll be okay," she said. What could a sick woman tell her? And yet as she had thought this, she glimpsed, over the horizon of her approaching fifth decade, the slope of a hill whose terrain she could not yet see, but that her mother had indeed traversed. The hill was coming closer to her, and when she visualized it in her mind's eye, she often went back to that afternoon on the patio as the moment during which she had first been aware that the hillside even existed. Whatever her mother had meant to tell her in more precise language, via the vision board, was related to this conversation on the patio. She was sure of it. The fact that her mother could likely not tell her what the vision board was for put her on the brink of crying. She would not cry. She would not topple over into the great sorrow that comes with not being able to speak to the dead, or to those who are on their way there.

. . .

Here and there in the garden at least a dozen bamboo sticks had been intentionally placed into the ground. They had been cut from the stand of bamboo that shielded most of the property from the main road. Their arrangement—at once purposeful but random—reminded her of the stick arrangements in *The Blair Witch Project*, but these were not sinister.

As spring went on, the meaning of the sticks became clear. A lily now sprouted beside each stick, and each shoot was in the shape of a spire, with all the leaves tightly compressed. As this spire rose, the leaves would begin to separate from each other like an accordion, and she realized that unlike the iris, which added leaves as it grew, the lily was born with everything it would ever need. Only the flower buds would emerge later. There were twenty of these lilies expanding now. Her mother must have put the sticks in the ground at the end of the season—perhaps last year—to remind herself where the flowers would emerge, and where not to plant anything else.

When she went for a walk in the garden that day—one of several—she saw that her mother's Japanese ume plum tree was ripe. The plums were strange—green with a splotch of red on one face, where the sun had kissed the skin the hardest. They were ready for harvesting, and if she did nothing, the plums would simply fall to the ground and rot, which was what had happened last year.

Or she could pick them.

The plums were intended to be pickled into a medicinal food the Japanese called *umeboshi*, which was so sour she had been unable to eat it as a small child. They were an acquired taste. They were the kind of food Japanese people liked to give to

Westerners to test their palate. Her mother had planted this tree to have her own source of *umeboshi* plums because it had become expensive—impossible—to bring home enough pickled plums from Japan year after year. Her mother had wanted a supply that would not run out. And this, too, had been one of those things she had found irritating as a child. Why must everything from Japan double as medicine? Why was nothing ever fun? And yet there was the recent news touting the idea that cultures that ate fermented foods, like these pickled plums, seemed to have lower rates of infection from the virus.

About an hour before her final class began that day, she took a basket from the pantry and went outside to collect a heaping pile of plums. She did not pick them all. It would be too much work to pick them all. The plums were warm to the touch, as though the flesh under the furry skin was alive with blood vessels. It was just the sun, she knew, but the weirdness of the fur and the sense that the plums were sentient made her feel obligated to turn them into pickles so they could fulfill their essential life's purpose.

In the minutes that remained before class, she leapt around from web page to web page, looking for an easy recipe.

In the end, all the recipes were simple, but they reminded her of one thing: she needed red shiso leaves. In the garden, there were vegetables whose names she did not know, but she doubted very much that there were any shiso leaves growing.

The alarm on her phone rang, bringing her out of the world of recipes in which her head had been immersed: it was time to prepare to teach. She looked behind her. When she first had arrived at the start of the sickness, the house had been fairly tidy. But now the view her students would see was of a mess— bulb pamphlets, a camera, binoculars, bird and plant books strewn all over the bed where she increasingly sat to work. She began to stack the books, but as the time before class began to evaporate, she simply picked up the blanket on which the mess had congregated and threw it into a corner, far from the prying eye of the camera. She made the bed quickly, and then ignited the Zoom link. Eighteen pairs of eyes were already waiting for her.

They had been spending these last few classes discussing Genji's great house, actually a remodeling project he finishes after returning to the capital when his exile ends. The Lady Rokujo has died and left him her estate, which he expands from one to four villas, each facing its own garden designed to encapsulate one of the four seasons. In chapter 21, he installs the women in his life who best reflect the particular season of each garden. The Lady from Akashi, whom he meets in exile and with whom he has had a daughter, lives in the Winter villa with a garden populated with pines, chrysanthemums, and silvery oaks. The Lady Rokujo's daughter lives in Autumn, surrounded by maple trees and a veranda that provides an optimal view of the fall moon. Another lover resides in Summer, a shady garden thick with bamboo, and Murasaki, naturally, lives in Spring, whose grounds are chock-full of plums and cherry blossoms and other spring blooms.

"He's like Hugh Hefner," Ravenna said.

"Hugh Hefner had no taste," Momoko countered. "Also, you can't tell Hugh Hefner's women apart."

The house, Rokujo-in, is the physical manifestation of Genji's exalted status, and for the next ten chapters or so, his life is one of beautiful bashes and pageantry. He hosts dances, boat races, and calligraphy contests, the kind of events that usually take place at the Emperor's palace and probably still do. But it is at Genji's Heian-era, Gatsby-esque party house that the coolest gatherings take place and where everyone wants to be. Meanwhile, Genji's son by the illicit affair with Fujitsubo is made emperor Reizei, and *he* learns that his true birth father is Genji! Instead of being upset by this news, Reizei is delighted and gives Genji the retroactive title of Retired Emperor. The gods have fulfilled their promise to raise Genji to greatness.

The house is fictional, though some have said it was based on a real-life villa owned by Minamoto no Tōru, a courtier who lived during Lady Murasaki's time. She had been to this villa and shared with them photos of a young geisha she had happened to see there in a cornflower blue kimono, posing for a portrait in front of a jade green pond.

She told them that Murasaki describes—and artists had painted—the elaborate gowns Genji designs and handpicks for his women. Museums had curated whole shows just around the clothes in these chapters! Artists also loved to paint the garden, and one of these—depicting the rolling of enormous snowballs in the Winter quarter—particularly charmed her, along with all the cherry blossoms in Murasaki's Spring quarter.

For two classes she had kept the conversation focused on the house and on the parties, and on the artwork they had inspired. And now at last she had arrived at this, the final class.

"What happens to the women?" Ravenna asked.

"Murasaki becomes a gardener."

"That's how she gets close to the Buddha," Momoko said.

"You mean the whole subplot about how Genji won't let her cut her hair and become a nun?" Ravenna asked.

"No," Momoko replied. "It's her garden. She makes her garden Buddha's paradise. Genji won't let her leave Rokujo-in, so she brings the Buddha to her."

She wanted to show them some photos of Katsura Villa, the architectural wonder and inspiration for Oracle cofounder Larry Ellison's residence in Woodside, California. But her class insisted on pushing through the later chapters of part 2. Genji's world unravels, and the cause is, as usual, a woman. Despite the personal happiness he has shared with Murasaki, he has always regretted not having a wife of status. And so Genji remarries.

"And that's his undoing," she told the class. Murasaki, long patient and tolerant of Genji's numerous affairs, becomes ill with grief. She speaks with one of the younger members of the imperial family, asking him to take care of her plum and cherry trees in the garden, and then, after a final farewell to Genji, Murasaki dies.

And then she read from the novel: "Elsewhere the single-petaled cherry blossoms fell, the doubles faded, mountain cherries bloomed, and the wisteria colored, but *she* had known precisely which flowers blossom early and which late, and she had planted them accordingly for their many colors, so that in her garden they all yielded their richest beauty in their time."

She imagined Genji, alone, watching as the flowers winked on and off. How lonely both he and the plants would have been without the hands of Murasaki, who had always tended to them both.

"And then?"

She steadied herself. "Then the novel takes over with his descendants. But the voice and tone are different."

"Like part two in *Wuthering Heights*."

"Sort of like that," she agreed. She didn't like part 3, finding it about as easy to care about Niou and Kaoru, Genji's descendants, as it was to care about Linton and Hareton in *Wuthering Heights*.

"I'm going to miss this class," Astrid told her.

"This class kept me going," Ravenna said at last.

Their emotions surprised her.

"I want to know what happens to the garden, though," Henry said.

"Me too," Astrid agreed. "What happens to the garden at Rokujo-in?"

"I don't know, actually," she told them.

"Genji's children live at the house. His son Kaoru—who isn't really his son—keeps the garden," Momoko said, but she didn't know much more beyond this.

"I'm sorry we've run out of time to read part three," she said. It wasn't the first time she hadn't made it through the entire book with her students. This had happened in classes in Japanese history too; professors in college taught up to the Meiji Restoration and then didn't really want to talk about the 1930s and the war and all that happened after. People who fell in love with Japan often wanted just to talk about what was beautiful and not to look at what was ugly. She, too, wanted to cling to the safety of her stock of images of cherry blossoms and gold-flecked shell-game boxes. She didn't want to go anywhere near the characters in part 3. Sometimes it was better not to finish a story.

She thanked her students for their work that semester and then watched as, one by one, their little boxes disappeared and the boxes that remained grew larger and larger until it was just her in her rectangle and Astrid in hers and then they, too, said farewell.

. . .

The Tree Doctor had stopped using "u" in his texts, and now spelled out all his words. He was still working in the garden once a week, and he had also spent some time with her in the evenings. They did not have dinner. Only once did they have sex again—a quickie, during which he did not seem concerned that she did not come and he left not long after.

One morning she had another text. He wanted to see her, on a non-gardening day. This time he added: "I could bring a pizza." A pizza. He sounded like Thomas, taking them all to eat pizza at Pizza Perfect Hong Kong, as though he were doing the family a favor by coming up with pizza as a solution to eating. Didn't men know there were consequences for middle-aged women who continued to ingest carbohydrates? Her days of eating French toast and dumplings and pizza with gusto were long over. All the same, she wrote back, as though she were thirteen: "Sounds great!" Moms did that. They seemed happy when they were not. He told her he would swing by around six thirty.

It was still warm, so she went outside and wiped down the patio furniture and shook the pillows free of cypress and pine needles. She placed the two chairs side by side. As she worked, she felt a vague pressure between her legs. Did she have a UTI again?

He arrived and set the pizza down with a thunk and turned his gaze toward the garden, stretching out his arms to release tension. She liked to see this. The Tree Doctor, who had been so carefully concealed during her visits to the garden store and during his initial gardening, was now a stretchier, looser version of himself, and she liked the feeling that, at least for now, she alone had his secret and unmasked essence in her presence.

He had brought paper plates and plastic forks, all from the restaurant in town, along with two blue plastic cups and a bottle of wine he uncorked with a wine opener attached to his keys, and divided the pizza onto their plates. All this triggered the memory of being in college, when a warm slice of pizza and the near-instant end to hunger it could bring had fueled her through late-night study and preparations for exams. In an instant she felt decades younger.

"I have something else," he told her. "Be right back." When he returned, he was carrying a cardboard flat of flowers—tall ones in shades of indigo and violet. In the slightly fading light, they seemed illuminated.

"They look like—"

"They look like foxgloves. Related. These are delphiniums.

Damaged stalks here, there." He showed her, and explained that customers did not want to purchase flowers that seemed damaged. "Thought we could plant them together. Now or tomorrow morning."

"How much?"

"They're damaged, so they're free. But I knew you wouldn't mind."

Indeed, she didn't mind. The delphiniums were short term perennials, and so would grow back for a few years, producing blossoms that would not bend or break. She thought of how her mother would have loved the gift of free flowers for the garden and would have approved of rescuing plants that otherwise would be discarded for their imperfections. They decided that before they ate they would quickly place the plants in the soil, and they knelt together, resolving where there was space among the other plants, and how it might be nice to place a delphinium beside a foxglove. They tapped the plants so each fell out of its plastic container, and they patted the earth around each transplanted flower, working together easily. When had she ever been in the garden with another human being like this? Not in years, not since she was a child, planting flowers with her mother. Then they washed their hands with the garden hose and sat out on the patio to eat the pizza.

"Thank you," she said. "That's the first time anyone has brought me flowers to transplant."

"It's nice to share with someone who will care." He scanned the garden. "People think of flowers the way they think of interior decor. They forget that plants are alive and individual like people. Now you'll remember me when those flowers bloom." He leaned back in his chair. "Sure is nice out here."

"In August we can sit out here and watch the meteor shower," she said. What was she doing, planning ahead like this, as though to engage in a different kind of relay race? With him. "I used to sit out here and watch the meteor shower with my mother. It'll get dark enough and we can lie back and look at the Perseids."

"Who is that?"

"The Perseids?" How could he not know? "Every year the Earth passes through the tail of the Swift-Tuttle Comet. The sky lights up with rocky ice. That's the Perseids, and if you are good," she said, as seriously as she could, "you'll see one a minute."

The Tree Doctor was looking at her with bemusement. "I wish we had a heat lamp."

"Nothing so modern and newfangled as that in this house."

"Is that a firepit?"

"It is."

"Where is the firewood?"

She pointed toward the line of cypress trees. "Stacked up over there. A lifetime supply from the one time my father trimmed the trees."

"I'll be back."

"I'll go with you."

"Too many gopher holes," he told her. "And you don't hold your wine very well."

This was true. He disappeared into the darkness and came back a few minutes later carrying five logs; two were balanced on one shoulder, another tucked under his arm, and two more locked tight in the other arm, which flexed so hard she could see his biceps. What had her husband carried the last time they had been together? There had been the time he had unboxed her laser printer—a new printer just for her, so they no longer had to share.

The Tree Doctor insisted on lighting the fire, though he turned out to be rather inept at this. It took only a wad of newspaper and the last remaining match from the Buddhist altar for her to get the fire going.

"Pyro, eh?" he said. "Anything else I should know?"

He brought both lawn chairs over to the firepit and placed them side by side. After they had been sitting for a few minutes, he put one hand gently over hers. "Do you feel guilty?" he asked.

"No," she said immediately, though in truth she had not taken all that much time to think about it. She had been curious about sex, and then they had had sex. She supposed she felt guilty, or might eventually, but she also felt certain that to say she felt guilty at this moment might mean there would be no more sex, and that was not an outcome she wanted. Her curiosity about him was still not satisfied. "You?"

He shrugged and his face looked startled, as though her answer had stripped away some protective layer he had been wearing. "I mean, it would be natural, right?"

"But do you?" she pressed.

He pursed his lips. Something about her answer now irritated him, which struck her as strange, considering that he had been the one to ask the question in the first place. "I'm divorced."

"But did you used to feel guilty?" she wanted to know. He was not a guy who had ever been faithful. Of this, she was certain. There was just so much ease in the way he had sex and about her body and about the idea of having sex. He wasn't a man who had at any point stopped having sex with multiple women in order to raise his family, or who was now flailing as a result of being separated from the anchor of domestic life. She wondered how he saw her. Did he see her as an essentially innocent person whom he was leading down a path that he knew well but from which he felt she should protect herself? If he had been down this path, why shouldn't she?

"And you are not." He grinned at her.

"I am not—?"

"Divorced."

"I think about it," she said, somewhat defensively.

"Tell me."

It wasn't really true that she thought about it. She did not actually want to get divorced. She had simply thrown this sentence out between them as though to try to equalize their situations, but now that she had said she had thought about it, she began to try to find a way—at least through conversation—in which this version of herself might be true. She began to present her hypothetical self who wanted to get a divorce. "I started thinking about it maybe five or six years ago, when my daughters were smaller than they are now."

He nodded. "I first visualized it when my youngest son was nine."

"The thing is," she said, "I don't even understand how having children changed everything, but it did."

His eyes gleamed suddenly. "It's a test. You learn what you value."

"I definitely do *not* want his family values."

"Which are?"

"When I met him, he was a programmer." It had been so . . . exotic! A programmer! A man who could always pay for a nice dinner! A man who seemed genuinely excited to be taught how to go to the opera and the ballet and who thought that getting married and starting a family was normal, and not a threat to his artistic impulses, which was what the last two men she had dated, both writers, had used as the reason for their breakup. So she and Thomas had married and she had even been given a platinum engagement ring with a real diamond. Never mind that the setting was a bit plain. Her hand sparkled. "Then he went into management and complained about not working on the product. Then he went back to product and complained about missing management. He's never happy." She paused. It had been years of gradual dissatisfaction with management, product, and his mother. "And his mother is never happy—"

"Divorce isn't for everyone. I don't know that it's right for you," he interrupted her sharply. "It's expensive in more ways than one."

She didn't like that he doubted her ability to do anything— even get a divorce—if she actually wanted to. "People do it all the time."

"Plenty of people avoid it. I belong to this club—"

"What club?"

"Just a club of high-functioning guys. And I'm always fascinated by the guys who go to therapy, or family therapy. They work so hard to keep their families together. You know." When he saw that she did not know, he added: "Because divorce is so *expensive*. If you have money. And, like I said, even when you don't. But especially if you do."

She didn't think of herself as having money. She supposed that based on the location of the house, she looked like she had money. People often made that mistake, looking at her house, unless they looked closely and saw how the rugs were threadbare, the orange linoleum in the kitchen was still there from the seventies, despite the current penchant for French country tile, and the showers and toilets were unchanged from the fifties. Only another Californian understood how it was to have a house that had skyrocketed in value, while nothing else about the homeowner's financial status had changed. "When it was just my husband and me, we were in the city and we had so much *fun*. And then we got married and he turned into his parents and he wanted our children to turn into him. That wasn't supposed to be the deal. We got together to escape our parents." She remembered how the first time she had met Thomas's mother, her future mother-in-law had complained about her own husband and how he had been a workaholic. She hadn't been anywhere in years. And look at Thomas now—a workaholic, expecting her to stay at home like his mother had.

"A man likes to set the tone for his family," the Tree Doctor said.

"Did you do that?"

"Her parents were both dead when we met," he said smoothly. "I'm not sure it's fair to compare."

"Maybe that's what it is." Her father was dead and her mother would be soon. And just like that, was her family not supposed to matter and his was?

"You close to your parents?"

"I was. I guess."

"Is he close to his?"

"I guess. Yes. It's just—it feels like because he makes more money, he gets to have the family he wants, and I have to—"

"The person with more money does win. You know this, right?" he said.

"I can't believe that's true."

"You get *one* life," the Tree Doctor said. "And you do get to decide how to live it. I personally don't want to live my life with so little—"

"Money?"

"I have plenty of money." He laughed. "I was going to say . . . *feeling*."

She imagined him moving among his trees, loving the trees, touching their branches and shaping their bodies and making them bloom. He would want humans to regard him with the same care with which he looked at the trees.

But he didn't talk about the trees. He began to talk loosely about the conventionality of marriage and how he considered it a sad institution that had kept Europeans tethered to their hovels and farming plots before they arrived in America and their imaginations were free to visualize other futures. He was making a connection between marriage and being an American that, to her, made little sense.

"This club I belong to—"

"What is this club?"

"Just some guys. No big dealy. Anyway, some of the guys say family is where you go and they can't kick you out. Or it's your legacy. Or it defines you. I heard someone say something once— that a family is a set of shared experiences. I like that. It leaves room for possibilities."

The conversation and the wine had her vaguely aroused. She started to understand that he was speaking not just of sex, but of the idea that life had many possibilities, that a person could have more than one self. It was a hard thing to imagine now, during the sickness, when no one could go anywhere. But he said that now, when they could not travel unless it was truly urgent, was the closest they would ever come to what life might have been like before the age of the railway, before the car and the plane, when fidelity and the family had been even more of a ballast than they were now. "This is how it was in the old country," he said theatrically. "This is why we left the old country."

She told him about her mother and the German, Carl Joseph.

"You think it's true?" he asked.

"I don't know. I know so little about her life before she got sick. I don't even know if she had sex before she met my dad. I know she had a boyfriend—she took me to meet him in Japan when I was a kid. I hated him."

"Because he wasn't your dad."

"Exactly. I wondered if she regretted coming to America and staying."

He rubbed her fingers. "I bet he's real. Wouldn't your mom miss someone who made her feel good?" One of the logs in the firepit shifted just then, sending up a spray of sparks, and she knew it was likely that the wood had burned down enough that part of the log had collapsed, but the effect was that for a moment the fire seemed to be listening to her. Or listening to him.

"We never had conversations like that." She stopped herself from saying more. It was hard to determine just how much they were going to share with each other. Sex implied intimacy, but it did not mean she had the right to burden him with the full weight of her emotional pains, and the pain of her mother's illness was a greater pain than that of her marriage. If she did that, she suspected, the sex would disappear, and she relished the sex.

He laced his pinkie in hers. His hand was hot, warmed by the fire, and the transfer of heat from his hand to hers sent a shock through her body. Then he smiled at her slyly, and she smiled back. "How are the trees?"

"Still growing," she said. "The branch you mended is still alive."

"You water them throughout the summer and you'll have some gorgeous blossoms in the spring. I just know it." He pulled her onto him, on the patio chair, and her mind charged ahead. How were they going to have sex on the patio? And if they didn't have sex here, how would they put out the fire before going to bed? "Relax," he said. "We aren't in a hurry. It's a worldwide pandemic. No one can find us."

"Just . . . the fire . . ."

He kissed her, and after a few minutes she relaxed. The fire was still lapping at the logs behind her, and when the smoke blew in their direction, they ducked and yelped like children. He kissed her entire mouth. He licked her teeth. He ran his tongue against the line of her upper teeth, as though to pierce the inside of her lip to her skull. He put a finger in her mouth and she felt her jaw click open while he rubbed her tongue. She had to relax so much to let his finger move between her teeth and his tongue. With his other hand he put a finger between her legs and grinned when he felt how wet she was. How much more open could she become? She stopped worrying about the fire and asked him just to fuck her.

"It's still burning," he whispered, and he flicked her clit with his hand. She heard blood whirring in her brain and her ears. He asked her to suck his neck—without giving him a hickey—and she did. He put her hand on his cock and she felt him grow hard inside his jeans. "This is my favorite thing in the world," he told her. She was by now so drunk on dopamine and wine and heat that she only barely registered that he meant sex in general. "But it doesn't always happen," he told her. "Must be a magic pussy. Best all around."

They fooled around like this until the fire died down enough that the logs burned red and then transformed into coals, and then, without a word, they both stood up, perfectly synced, and linked hands to go inside. Her legs were slick and she felt like a thirteen-year-old who had just masturbated five times.

But on the bed, naked, she said: "I need to tell you something." She explained about the new UTI.

A slight coldness that might have been confusion passed over his face. "So what are we doing?" The light was out, but the moon made his face gray and a bit hard, like marble.

Why had she told him this? "I just wanted you to know."

She could feel him looking at her. His face seemed to be computing something about her, perhaps assessing her behavior against the behavior of women he had known in the past. She felt frozen: the proverbial deer in the headlights. It had seemed right to tell him, and yet a part of her had considered that she shouldn't have sex before the UTI—if it was a new UTI—had healed. She had forgotten to ask Evie if she could have sex at all if the UTI came back. Wouldn't *he* know? How could she be this naive about sex in this day and age?

She was fascinated to be in this slight breath in time, with all that manly coldness surfacing on his face while he calculated what to do. How she enjoyed his heat, his coldness, and his heat again, the alternating current of his very male energy that was such a mystery, so different from her own.

His face changed in a way she had never observed before. His upper lip curled. It seemed to grow more plump, as though some inner thread had drawn it into a gather. His eyes looked past her and he pulled her back down on the bed. He put his hands between her legs to part her open again. His cock was huge. "Just be . . ." She wanted to ask him to be careful, but she saw that he was not going to be tender at all.

He pushed—not viciously, but firmly—into her body and began to fuck her. Only when he was inside her did he look into her eyes. He held her hands with his own, his mouth still curled, and he fucked her. It hurt and it felt fantastic. He let go of one hand, and stuck a finger partway up her ass. "Feel this," he said, fucking her until she cried, the pleasure and pain blending together. Deep within her, a current shuddered and charged down her spine and into her body. It was like giving birth to an invisible electrical charge. When he came, there was blood mixed with milky cum.

. . .

The matter of the shiso leaves continued to plague her, and she might have thrown out all the plums she had picked were it not for an encounter she had in the freezer with a plastic bag, into which was stuffed a folded-up Japanese newspaper. The newspaper seemed to be about the ongoing cleanup efforts after the earthquake in Japan, so the package was fairly recent. She unfurled the paper and found, at the center, a frozen mush in a familiar shade of purple. Could it be? She took the leaves out of the freezer and decided to go pick the rest of the plums.

She had just touched the handle on the sliding glass door,

intending to go outside for a walk, when she saw something in the backyard that made her stop. There were four fledgling falcons sitting on the ground. Three of them were arranged in a line in front of the pond, while a fourth was sitting on a rock at the back of the pond. They were large. By her calculations they could not have been older than six weeks.

They looked both ferocious and helpless. Each, she knew, was going to grow up to be a killing machine. But for now there they were, sitting together, blinking in the sun, and squeaking to each other.

The fledglings did not seem interested in hunting or flying. They seemed dazed. The air was filled with butterflies, and one large blue dragonfly skirted the head of one of the fledglings, and the young hawk flinched. She could see the universal look of incomprehension and fear in the hawk's eyes. One day, she thought, those eyes would be focused and alert, but today, this young bird was like anything else that was young and confused. She felt a tenderness toward the young predators. Then a shadow fell on the grass, a black form tracing a line across the backyard. The hawks, as a group, shuddered and looked up at the sky.

A blob of shadow appeared on the lawn again, larger this time, and she craned her neck to see what was flying. It came back a third time—a vulture. And then an adult hawk launched itself out of a tree, screaming, and dove for the lumbering vulture. The big black bird banked left, unable to outgun the hawk. The fledglings all jumped and two flew away into the higher branches of a tree, while the other two made for the shelter of the shrubbery on the neighbor's property. A moment later, the lawn was clear of big birds, and she went out to harvest the rest of the plums.

The fledglings returned often in the days that followed, while the plums marinated in salt and shiso. This was helpful in the practical sense that on the phone with her children, she could speak with animation about the young hawks, even if her daughters were only mildly interested, since they could not see the hawks themselves. Still, she shared their antics with her family.

Daily, she watched the hawks, and tracked the trees, and pickled plums, and marked the progression of the lilies. And on occasion, after again taking a round of antibiotics to cure the second UTI, she had sex. When she had sex she felt her body temporarily taken over, like she had been given an IV that left her feeling temporarily high and youthful. Other times—a lot of the time—she was exhausted.

There was nowhere to go, no place else she could wish to be, because everywhere was sick all at once. The fact of the sickness was a worldwide pressure, like a storm front, but worse. It had moved across the planet and was crushing everyone. When she visualized the virus on its microscopic but effective tsunami path, she felt a deep helplessness. There was no reason to struggle. There was, for her, no true reason to stay alive. She had never known an enemy like the virus. But no, she must not think this way. She was needed.

She examined the bookcase in the living room, which, along with her father's art catalogs, held copies of her favorite books from college. There were three translations of *The Tale of Genji*. There was *The Pillow Book*, written by Sei Shōnagon, Lady Murasaki's archrival. There were other books, too, that she had not looked at in decades—translations of diaries and of poetry, and then she saw *An Account of My Hut* by Kamo no Chōmei. She had forgotten about this book, written by a former poet of the court who had fled into the mountains to live in a hut. She cracked open the book. Why had Chōmei left the capital? "From spring through summer there was a drought, and in autumn and winter typhoon and flood—bad conditions one after another, so that grain crops failed completely. Everything people did became wasted effort. . . . After a year of such suffering, people hoped the new year would be better, but the misery increased as, in addition to the famine, people were afflicted by contagious disease."

When she had read these books as a student, the scenes of famine and illness had seemed like ancient history, as though getting sick were something that happened to people only in the past. She hadn't related to these stories. And now she did. She clapped the book shut.

Seven

At the start of June, the garden glowed with stargazer lilies, a bobcat trotted into the backyard and then disappeared, and the news heralded a possible vaccine. All this coincided with a decline in death and infection rates. A few businesses began to reopen. As more flights resumed, the price of tickets came down. Travel restrictions were at last loosened, and Thomas began looking for a good quarantine hotel with rooms available, while she researched flights that would take her across the ocean to be with her children. Her family could come to her far more easily than she could go to them, but Thomas still did not want to leave Hong Kong. She would need to test negative ten days before reserving her ticket to fly. While she awaited the results of her antibody test, she called her mother's care facility to see if it was possible, with the relaxed rules, to arrange a visit. Permission was granted.

She began to gather a small pile of gifts. Her mother had long ago asked her not to appear with presents of any kind. Still, she could not fight the impulse. She collected a dozen of the pickled plums she had made from the garden harvest and the frozen shiso leaves she had found in the freezer, and packaged these in a small glass jar.

On the day of her visit she went out into the garden and did two full circuits, picking enough flowers for a fat bouquet. She saved the bird-of-paradise for last, then lopped off five tall stalks. Her parents had once shown up with a dozen of these blooms in her dorm room in New York City, back when it was not necessary to explain to security in the small Monterey Regional

Airport that they were "for our daughter" in order to hand-carry the oversize bouquet onto a plane.

She had been embarrassed by this large bouquet. She had not had a vase large enough for something so tall and heavy, but her mother had immediately commandeered a janitor, who had good-naturedly strode off to find a suitable vase. He said he had taken it from the faculty lounge two buildings over, and then he had stood by while her parents assembled the bouquet—the vase and the birds-of-paradise—in her dorm room. Some workers at the school were currently on strike, and she was embarrassed that her mother had employed the help of the janitor—who was Black—because she did not think this was what one was supposed to do during a strike, but the man had not seemed to mind. In fact, he had waved to her on campus for her remaining three years. "Hello. How's your mama?" he would ask.

"Fine," she would say, not entirely certain she understood the precise details that now bound them together. It had something to do with her mother and the regard he now held her in, flying all the way across the country and carrying an immense bouquet of flowers from the garden for her daughter. Only many years later did she realize how much a bouquet made entirely of birds-of-paradise would cost in a shop.

She gathered all the blooms that she could, stuffed them into a vase, set the whole thing down on the floor by the passenger seat of the car, and secured it with pillows.

The road was quiet. She was in such a state of shock to be driving a car on the highway that most of her emotional energy was spent trying to process visual information at a speed to which she was not accustomed. For many weeks she had risen and walked around the garden first thing in the morning, taking in the details of the flower beds and the vegetable patch. The world had moved around her at the pace at which she walked, and at the speed at which flowers bloomed and died. Driving required a different kind of noticing.

When she made it to San Francisco, she was half an hour early for the appointment, and she parked in the designated spot outside her mother's facility, a building that was slotted between two Victorians, and that, while not a Victorian itself, sported a false olive green front with peaked windows that made it seem like it was. The daily news now highlighted the plight of families separated from their elderly parents and grandparents, as she was, but in those stories, adult children were able to drive by and wave to them through windows. The windows in the front of her mother's facility belonged to residents in private rooms; the only way to reliably see anyone in the facility was to go inside.

It was here, finally parked, that emotion swelled up in her body. She sat outside the facility and cried. Her brain once again took in the fact that her mother was not in her childhood home, but here in this facility, to which she had been moved for her safety. Was her mother safe? She should have come sooner. She had asked to come sooner. She had to remind herself that the virus had made this impossible and that her guilt was a reflex. She was living in the world of the virus, just as surely as she was living in a world with oxygen. The virus had flooded the world. The virus had brought death closer to everyone. The virus had made a mockery of plans like moving her mother into a care facility for safety.

She wiped her eyes.

Then she opened the door to the car and stepped out onto the street. She circled around to the passenger side and gingerly retrieved the bouquet, still in its vase; it had not toppled over. She grabbed the jar of plums, locked the car, and went to the front door of the facility, where she rang the bell.

The nurse who answered had on a mask. So, too, did the activities director, a middle-aged Frenchwoman with a loud voice and red hair that she had not apparently been able to dye for the past three months. Everyone else in the facility usually wore robin's-egg-blue scrubs, but the Frenchwoman was allowed her own clothing, and she generally wore something bright, as she was today—a pleated lime green knit skirt that fell below her knees and a white long-sleeved top. But the Frenchwoman seemed distressed and cut off from a part of herself—perhaps it was the mask. There were those who wore masks who felt oppressed by them. Maybe the Frenchwoman was one of them.

A Filipino nurse in scrubs said: "Welcome back." Then she saw the enormous bouquet. "Oh, wow." The Frenchwoman stepped in to help wipe down the vase with disinfectant.

A table barred visitors from passing into the building's interior; it stood in the entry hallway like a kind of altar. The nurse explained that the facility now had a set of actions every visitor was to take. She would move through a series of steps, from left to right, first disinfecting her hands with two squirts from a giant bottle of Purell. Next she was to disinfect her phone with a small wipe. After that, she was to chose a set of gloves, a mask, a robe, a hairnet, and shoe coverings. The increasing degree to which she was washing and covering herself felt ritualistic and familiar. By the time she was ready for the hairnet, she could see the diminutive figure of her mother at the far end of the hall, listing to the right and clutching a walker, as two other women— both nurses in scrubs—maneuvered her to the entrance. As she placed coverings over her shoes, the Frenchwoman positioned two chairs—six feet apart—where she and her mother would presumably sit and hold each other's audience.

Her mother shuffled toward her, and she felt emotion surge from her body as though she were the surf and her mother the shore. And at the same time, she felt the weird familiarity of going through all this disinfection. It wasn't just the Purell or the wiping down of everything or even the hairnet. Surgeons did this all the time. What she thought about were those shrines in Japan where she had washed her hands and rinsed her mouth and taken off her shoes before entering. In her earliest trips to Japan with her mother, when she had finally been old enough— perhaps five or six—to do something other than lie around in her grandparents' home and watch cartoons, they had begun their travels throughout the country. In those subsequent earliest visits to the shrines, her mother had explained that they must be clean before they entered the grounds. They could not wear their shoes, though occasionally then, as now, shoes were permitted if completely covered.

And so it was not as though her mother were the shore and she the ocean, now racing to reach home. It was as though the table on which all the articles of disinfecting were placed was an altar, and her mother some ethereal goddess emerging from the rear of the sanctuary, and she must purify herself before she could speak to her mother and hear her voice. It must have been like this in ancient Japan, she thought. There were so many of those shrines and statues and festivals dedicated to warding off illness or celebrating the end of plagues and illnesses, and these gestures—washing hands, cleaning feet—had become sacred acts. They were ways of keeping oneself clean so one would not get sick. They were ways of keeping oneself healthy so one would not get others sick. They were the physical movements of care.

They sat in two chairs. Her mother's voice was soft and slurred, hidden behind the mask. And because, very quickly, the Frenchwoman became bored and began to play the piano just inside the hall, it was difficult to hear what her mother had to say. In fact, her mother generally had to repeat herself five times. Sometimes six. When people cannot understand someone else speaking to them with an accent, they sometimes laugh, pretending to be in on a joke. She tried this now with her mother. "Ha-ha-ha. Yes!" Pre-dementia, her mother had despised such false actions, but surely she would not notice now. Instead, her mother fixed her with clear, uncomplicated eyes. Dementia might cloud the minds of others, making them vague, but it was sharpening her mother's, making her more direct. Her mother reached up with one of her mangled hands—her fingers could no longer work independently. Those beautiful fingers that had withstood so much arthritic pain to embroider pillows and make quilts and prom dresses now could work together only as a lever. She tugged down her face mask. "I said. Did you find. The German man."

The words fell into the room like pearls clattering from a broken necklace. "No," she said.

"Why not?"

She closed her eyes. They were in a care facility in the middle of a pandemic, and the first bouquet from the garden was now standing on the table that barred the entrance to the back, and all her mother wanted to talk about was some German man.

"I don't know . . . I don't even . . ." Sometimes it felt as though, because she was American, her mother expected her to be able to translate every facet of the culture for her. And in a way, this was not an unreasonable request. "I don't know where to start looking for him," she said.

"He was here," her mother told her.

She looked at the Frenchwoman. "Excuse me," she said. "Excuse me!" she shouted, and the woman stopped playing the piano. "Did my mother have a guest? A German man?"

The Frenchwoman cast back in her memory for a German man who had visited her mother. "No," she said. But then one of the nurses interjected: "Oh yes. I think so. A long time ago."

"She had a visitor?"

"I think he is someone's husband?"

"Maybe brother?"

She tried to control her temper. "I am sorry," she said. "But it is not as though we have all the time in the world, and if there is a German man . . ."

"We will find him," they assured her. They were soothing her. They were people accustomed to soothing. They soothed people like her—family members of those who had dementia. How was it possible that now, in her mother's absolute twilight, there should be this drama over whether or not a German man existed?

In school there had been girls who had squealed over the elderly almost the same way they had crooned over babies. "She's so cute!" She had not felt this way about babies or the elderly as a thirteen-year-old. She had wanted whatever might be the equivalent of riding dragons or growing wings like a fairy who could fly and cast spells. She did not find looking after babies or the elderly to be fulfilling, and if she were honest, she looked down on and even pitied those who did this for a living. Yet here she was, completely at their mercy.

Her mother was leaning forward and whispering to her with a sharp, conspiratorial look in her eye. "That woman lies," her mother informed her.

"Who?"

"That woman." Her mother was talking about the nurse who had confirmed that a German man had indeed visited the facility.

"Okay." She said this even though she wasn't sure she believed her mother. She felt small and relegated to childhood, wrapped in her mother's presentation of the world to her. There were just the two of them swaddled together. How many times before had she been here like this, with her mother insisting that the world was one way, while everyone around her believed it was another way? And yet, over the course of the past three months in the garden, the point had been driven home to her that the world *was* the way her mother had presented it.

"I have photo," her mother whispered. "In iPhone."

"Of . . . ?"

"Carl Joseph."

She caught the attention of the nurse again and asked for her mother's iPhone to be brought to the front of the facility.

"Your iPhone? Oh, okay. I can bring that. Do you want to give your daughter your passport too?"

Her mother, who did not disengage her eyes, shook her head.

"No passport?" the nurse asked.

Her mother shook her head again.

"Why do you not come?" her mother asked her.

Her stomach clenched. This was the question she had been dreading. "You know," she said slowly, "about the pandemic?"

Her mother looked at her blankly, one side of her face pulled down by gravity.

So she tried again in Japanese. She didn't know the word for "pandemic," so she asked: "You know about the virus?"

Her mother nodded.

"That's why."

"Other people had visitors," her mother told her.

When the nurse returned with the iPhone, she asked if it was indeed true that other residents had had guests. "No," the nurse told her. There had been no one. The facility was actually still officially on lockdown, and they were making an exception to allow her to see her mother. The nurse handed her the iPhone. The power on the phone had long ago run down, so she plugged the cord into the wall, waiting for the battery to bring the phone to life so she could at least see the photos inside. Another visitor had arrived—a woman—carrying a small African violet. She was now going through the same process of disinfecting and wiping down and covering herself by the entrance, and the

Frenchwoman was setting up another chair, six feet away from her mother. There was to be a second appointment. She wondered if it was like this in prison, too, with orderlies going off to find prisoners who had to remain behind glass in order to see their visitors. For how long would this go on?

She wanted her mother so badly. She knew that people died and that life changed once those people were gone. Her father had died and she still wanted to ask his advice. She still looked for kindness in men, because he had been kind. She had few chances left to ask her mother for help.

"Thomas and the girls are in Hong Kong," she said.

"They are coming?"

"He won't leave his job."

She peered into her mother's skull, as though looking into the small round window of a Magic 8 Ball moments before the triangular die inside floated to the surface through blue water with a clear direction: "Outlook Good."

"Stupid," her mother said.

They both laughed. Her mother was still in there! "I don't know what to do." She did not want to go back to Hong Kong. She feared being stuck overseas. She knew the nature of illness and knew how viruses could persist, and the only reason bird flu or H1N1 hadn't been more successful was because those viruses had been inferior. They had not figured out how to mutate in such a way that they could spread easily and hitch a ride on international flights. This virus had. And if it was going to stress and change the world, she wanted to be home in her own country. Thomas still thought the sickness was a bad cold.

"You fight." Her mother's lips stuck to her front teeth, so the *f* came out harder than usual. Her mother was fighting to say the word "fight."

"I have to fight?"

"If he cannot do, you do."

Do what? "He won't come."

Her mother began to slump to the right, like a pillow set on a sofa and losing its shape. She watched. It couldn't be that her mother could not straighten herself up in the armchair. Surely her mother would catch herself? And yet there was her mother, staring back as if she were unaware that she was slumping.

"Okay now, Mrs. ——." The Frenchwoman propped her mother back up.

Her mother seemed almost to smile, as if the entire episode of slumping and propping had been funny. It was nearly comical. But it wasn't funny at all. This was her mother, unable to sit upright in a chair.

The other patient in the room was healthy enough to be able to hold the potted plant in her own hands and hold it as she sat down. Why was that woman here in this home, if she were coordinated enough to sit while holding a plant? The other two women—resident and visitor—gossiped with each other, and they both had enough energy to smile a lot and toss their heads casually. To be able to gossip was, in fact, a sign of a capacity for wasted motion, something her mother no longer had. Her mother kept staring at her with that half smile—a kind of disturbing, childish smile. Clowns used half smiles like this to scare small children.

Her mother continued to repeat her sentences, not because she was prone to repeating, but because there was now so much noise with the Frenchwoman playing the piano again and the two gossiping ladies—one still clutching her potted plant—that her mother could not manage to raise her voice above the fray. A year ago, her mother would have been irritated to have to repeat herself so many times, but now she was patient, simply saying the same thing over and over.

"I said, because you are here, they cannot use this table," her mother said, referring to the laughing ladies.

Bing. The iPhone sprang to life and she picked it up to look at its face. "iPhone is disabled. Connect to iTunes." She heaved a sigh. She had no idea why the phone was not working, or indeed why it was disabled. She asked her mother for her iTunes user name, but her mother did not know it.

"In situations like this," her mother said slowly, in Japanese, "there is a problem."

"I need to take the iPhone home," she said.

"Carl Joseph is in there." Her mother lowered her gaze to the phone. "I want you to see his face."

"Sure. I'll check the photos. I will."

She fought the urge to be irritated. Here they were, in the sunset of their time together, and she was tasked with finding photos of a man from her mother's past who was from Germany, even though they were here in San Francisco. The phone had locked in the secrets of his face, if there were indeed any photos at all, and if there really had been such a visitor. It was infuriating to hold the phone in her hands—the phone with its data containing the images of her mother's last five years—and know that she could not get it open. As was the phone, so was her mother, she thought: a decaying artifact holding on to its potential expression. She felt overcome with frustration and sadness.

She wanted to ask her mother one more question. "What should I expect now?" Was it only illness that awaited her?

"I have another question," she said loudly to her mother to establish that this was their space to communicate. She wanted to claim the space away from the ladies with the African violet.

Her mother looked at her with bemusement. Her mother understood what she was doing. There would never be anyone else in her life who could read her body language or the slightest change in facial expression or her vocal cues like her mother. When her mother died, no one—except perhaps one of her daughters—would ever know her this well again. "Okay," her mother said.

"The Einstein tree," she said, so loudly that the Frenchwoman looked up and stopped playing the piano. "You know. The cherry tree." She held up a photo on her iPhone. "It isn't growing leaves and it isn't dead. What do I do?"

"Nothing," her mother said and shrugged the half of her body that could still shrug.

"What is it? Did you plant it?"

Her mother's face was a grotesque approximation of what it had once been. It was a Picasso portrait of illness, all flattened planes intersecting at the wrong angles, eyes wide and round and the mouth pursed in what art historians called an archaic smile. "It came," her mother said.

All her life she had hated it when her mother uttered phrases that were supposed to sound like profundities, but that were really bad fortune cookie fortunes. "I don't know what that means." Or was it the dementia?

"It came," her mother said again.

The Frenchwoman and the nurse were hovering nearby, as if they were ready to intercede if this conversation required any kind of intervention. Dementia patients grew agitated easily.

"What do you mean it just came?"

"It . . ." Her mother searched for the word. Her eyes tracked back and forth as if scanning the interior of her brain. It was painful to see all the nerves working together just to form this one word, nearly forgotten but still in her mind. "Volunteered." Her mother said at last. "It volunteered."

"You didn't plant it."

Her mother shook her head.

"But it's in the perfect location, just in the bend by the irises. Right where that patch of dirt curves. It couldn't just have landed there by accident."

Her mother was immovable.

"It's a volunteer tree."

Her mother nodded.

"You know it isn't grafted. I've learned about the difference between grafted and nongrafted trees, and that one isn't grafted. Einstein is a whole tree."

Her mother nodded again, and then beamed: Pleased, it seemed. Pleased that the tree was a volunteer tree? Or pleased that she finally understood why that funny tree, of all the trees—that scraggly Einstein tree, which was so old and didn't have the luscious Chia Pet head of the other cherry trees—was so beloved. It was a volunteer. It had wanted to be there and had simply grown.

But that was not the end of her questions. There would never be an end to the questions. "One more thing," she said. "I found a piece of paper. It said 'Vision Board.'"

"Vision. Board."

"I found a note in your handwriting. Did you make a vision board?"

Her mother's eyes drifted.

"Mom." She called her mother, and her mother's eyes snapped back to her face. "Did you make a vision board?"

After several seconds, her mother nodded once.

"Where is it?"

Then her mother's face took on a kind of pained expression. The question was hard and the answer even harder.

"Did you start to make the board and then stop? Or is that note all there is?" There were so many possibilities, including that her mother had never even made a vision board in the first place. After so many years of translating America for her mother, she could not fight the urge to generate stories so her mother could choose the one that fit, and then the two of them would know why there was a piece of paper that read "Vision Board."

"Maybe you made a vision board? Maybe you were collecting images to put on the vision board?" She tried to ask dynamically, like a fisherman throwing bait into the water, but her mother did not bite. Instead, her mother slumped, to the left this time, like a marionette that had been set down after an hour of activity and was now slowly letting gravity take control of its body. Her mother, she realized, was tired.

"I made umeboshi," she said, and held out the jar, which the nurse immediately swept up to sterilize with wipes.

"I am proud," her mother said. "I will eat. I will get well." She could see her mother believed she would get well. The denial her mother had wielded for decades—that she was not sick, did not need a nursing home, and had no dementia—was intact. She wanted her mother to have a chance to get well. She was afraid of crying, so she said: "I am going to let them have this table. I mean, the ladies with the African violet."

Her mother nodded. It was a very Japanese thing to notice that someone else needed their space.

"You will come again?" her mother asked. The tree and the vision board were forgotten, and she was focused now only on the prospect of being abandoned in this facility.

"Yes," she said. "I promise. I will come again." She did not say when she would come. She could feel her mother asking her for a precise date, but she would not give it. She did not know when she could travel again, and she didn't know if the roads would be open or if she would be going home to her daughters. She wanted to go back to the garden—her mother's garden. She wanted to wait there.

A nurse followed her outside. "We made you this birthday card a little while ago. She made it."

She had completely forgotten her birthday, but her mother had somehow remembered. She took the card, which featured glitter and kittens surrounded by pansies. It was not at all in her mother's taste. It had been bought from a local drugstore, but her mother had managed to write "Mom." Someone else had written "I love you." Weeks ago, on her birthday, the staff had helped her mother remember the day she was born.

"I should bring her home," she said to the nurse.

"A lot of people say that right now," the nurse told her. "But you should let us care for her. We know what to do." And with that, the nurse left her alone on the sidewalk.

Back in the car she cried again. Perhaps in two weeks she would see her mother's death. She felt panicked by the speed at which this fact rushed toward her. But her mother would not die quite so soon. She would not die in two weeks, or even two months.

Why wasn't her mother with her? She could take her mother back home with her. She could pick her up and take her home. They could be together in the house. They could see the garden together. It was possible. She could do it. She could change the diapers and puree the soup and spoon it into her mother's mouth and keep her mother from choking. She only thought the work seemed hard. It wasn't hard. Other people did this for their parents. She could do it. She ought to.

She drove home despite the crying. The drive after this visit took one hour and forty-six minutes. It had been predicted to last an hour and fifty-three minutes, but after crossing the Santa Cruz Mountains and descending into Moss Landing, the minutes evaporated. Soon she saw the wide-open stretch of Monterey Bay. This was her home. How many times as a young woman had she come back here, landing in the tiny airplane that putted from San Francisco to the two-runway World War II–era airport in Monterey, craning her neck to see her parents on the viewing deck, waving to her as she landed. That was before her father died, and before she had learned that, one by one, they would all die, and that the lights in her life would wink shut.

There was no one here now to welcome her. And her mother was never coming home again. She remembered the drive from the house up to the care facility, and how for the last half hour of that drive—which she had timed to minimize hitting rush hour, but which had still taken three hours—her mother had groaned and whimpered and asked, "How much farther? How much farther?" She had promised her mother they would visit the house once she was well, but her mother was not coming home.

What happened with trees that could not bloom? Did they feel this pressure too?

. . .

She wanted comfort, and the computer, the videos, masturbation, ice cream, a phone call. But none of these things would really help. She wanted sex, and she called the Tree Doctor to ask if he was free. She explained that she did not look her best, but she would like a visit.

He brought her more flowers for the garden—a hodgepodge of zinnias, leftover rhododendrons that would not bloom until next year, and tomatoes that had gone unclaimed. They planted them together, the urgent but gentle gestures of digging and patting the ground giving her reassurance. Then he showed her that he had brought her a bottle of wine—chilled rosé, he said. It was some label she didn't recognize, and she dismissed it as probably being cheap and local. But after a few sips—they were out on the patio—she realized it was good. "Hey, this is good."

He smiled, maybe a little sadly. "You thought I would bring you some shit? It's from France."

"I don't know much about rosé." The rosé tasted like its color ought to taste—light and sweet and sorrowful. She imagined the liquid settling into her veins, riding in her blood like a halo. Her body had a pink halo.

"I asked my mother about the Einstein tree," she said. "And she told me it's a volunteer."

He nodded. He was looking at her intently. When he focused like this, he was an incredibly good listener. That is, he knew how to appear to be listening, at least for a certain length of time. Some relationships were like this. Cyclical. A man paid attention to a woman when they were together and not the rest of the time, but when they were together, they were each other's focus. A good lover was like that. A good lover, she knew from *Genji*, wrote a poem for his lover, something perfectly suited to them. And in the poem, he left space for his lover to write back, so the two poems would fit together neatly.

Despite the wine, she felt like there was a barrier between them—a boundary of convention she couldn't cross, even though she knew it had been crossed before. And then he made it easy. He clenched his jaw. His face changed before her, and he wasn't the man who had brought wine and was listening to her cry about her mother and the still-dormant cherry tree tucked in the crook of the arm of the raised iris bed. He looked almost cruel. Predatory, perhaps, and she was a little bit frightened, though she told herself she should not be. She had called him.

"We are lucky, right? To get through the pandemic because of the plants?"

He took the glass out of her hand and set it down on the table, and his face looked stern, like he had decided something for both of them, and whatever he had decided had tired him. Then he smiled at her with his lips pressed together, and he looked kind, the way he might look when he asked a shop clerk at Macy's to please put his items in two separate bags.

He stood up and stretched and she looked at his body. Was she really going to be close to that body? She had been close before, but right now he looked far away. He was California casual—shorts and sneakers. His feet were so large, as though they were in sneakers a size too big for his height. It was a small imperfection that amused her and made him seem human and fallible. She felt tenderness for him, and this small surge of emotion in her body made her feel closer to him.

He put one hand on her face. He was touching her cheek and then he slid his hand into her pants and she did not respond. She did not mean to resist. She had called him, and she knew this, but getting over to the other side where they were going to have sex was something with which today she needed some help. She felt childish and stupid that she needed some help, but she could also see that he knew this about her. This was part of being lovers. He put his hand between her legs and rubbed her clit. She smiled at him—her first hard smile of the day, and then he squatted and kissed her, still with a hand in her pants, though this was an awkward position.

They needed to go somewhere with more space—the bed. How to transition to the bed. He stood up and took her hand.

In the bedroom he lay down on the bed and propped his arms behind his head. "Take your shirt off," he told her, smiling.

This had not happened before and the request felt like a missive from another world—a dominion where men asked women to take off their shirts. "Why?" she asked.

"I want to see you take your shirt off," he said.

So she started to take her shirt off. As she did this, she realized she didn't really think she was all that much to look at or that anyone could be excited if she took her shirt off. This was what she thought. Taking her shirt off would disappoint him. But he was smiling on the bed and asking her to take her shirt off, and a grown man would not show up in the middle of a pandemic for sex, only to turn away when her shirt was off. She hated that even now, in this situation that she had willed, she was certain something in her body was defective. She wanted to cry. How had she failed to learn how to stand in front of a man and take off her shirt in a way that would add to the evening and add to the sex that was to come? Every time she read a book, the character in the novel either had no sex, or the author avoided the sex, or the character was "in control" of having sex and knew what she wanted and had an assortment of dildos and porn and vast experience from which to draw that would inform how she was supposed to act. And she didn't have this. She could not make up for the time during which she was supposed to have learned how to be liberated. And never having been liberated—or at least not in *that* way—she couldn't go back to that earlier, liberated self, and pretend she was recapturing her youth just for this moment in the evening with this man, in the way people in novels did these things. There was no way to regain the lessons she was supposed to have learned about what to do now, and she had been hiding this fact and it was impossible to fix. She burst into tears.

It was so deeply embarrassing—so existentially embarrassing—that she couldn't even figure out where to go. Running dramatically away into another room would, of course, have been a very theatrical thing to do, and she didn't exactly feel panicked so much as ridiculous. She was deeply sad—for the person she was now, who had always behaved so well that she was not sure how to function, and that she was crying. So she stood there, and it was as though all evening, music had been playing and now the track had stopped and they were quiet, waiting, just waiting, for the music to start again.

"I am not into making people do what they don't want to do, so . . ."

"That's not it."

"Did I misread . . . ," he began.

"No."

There was a pause. "It can be hard to tell what's going on because of—"

"You are operating without all the information."

"—the masks," he finished.

Then she went over to the bed and sat down, crossing her legs. There was so much wrong and irregular in the world and she didn't know where to begin. He continued to lie there on the bed, observing her curiously—almost bemusedly—and she could feel that between them there had accumulated enough trust that he was not about to flee the room. One thing about being older was nice, she thought. She wasn't overcome by youthful emotions like desperation or a frantic desire to comprehend something. Her wires were just crossed. She just needed to express herself properly.

"It's been a while," she finally said. "Before you. I mean, in general."

"So?"

So she suspected it had *not* been a while for him, but then why should this matter? She would have worried about this when she was younger, but it really didn't matter to her now. Some people had more sex than other people, but then some people knew absolutely nothing about the Kano school of painting.

"What are we doing?" he asked her directly.

The problem was not what they were doing. They were in fact doing what they appeared to be doing. She wanted him to know precisely where in the story he was located, which was that despite her online appearance as a teacher of aesthetics who had written a novel about an exchange student in Tokyo who traded sex for a Hermès handbag—which had never happened to her—she was someone who didn't really know how to take her shirt off in front of a man. And that was embarrassing because a woman was supposed to know.

"What happened today?" he asked.

She hesitated. She just wanted uncomplicated sex. A nice

moment of health. She wanted some version—but better—of the sex they had already had. She wanted a reliable ride. She considered lying. If she told the truth, it might all get too complicated, and it wasn't as though they had met on a dating app where they had matched for identical spiritual and lifestyle goals. "You know I saw my mother," she finally said.

"And?"

"It was . . ."

"When was the last time you saw her?"

"Four months ago." When the world was healthy. Or rather, when everyone had thought the world was healthy and had believed in the solidity of a structure that had even then been crumbling. Her mother had appeared healthy because she had been hiding the fact that she was eating instant ramen. The world had actually been harboring the virus. She thought of those videos she had seen on YouTube of people caught in the waters of a tsunami, unable to break free of the surge even when someone on the shore had attempted to reach out and help. They were all riding such a current now, and no one had any way of knowing if the current was throwing them close to the seam between the world of the living and the dead. So much of her life had been spent worrying about this boundary and attempting to keep her mother on this side of it. She felt a kind of gleeful and desperate freedom in knowing that everyone else now saw how vibrant the boundary was. It was right there! You could die. "He mourned that nothing could detain someone destined to go," she remembered reading in *Genji*.

The Tree Doctor patted the spot next to him the way you might invite a cat into bed. She climbed into the spot, sitting on her haunches, still with her shirt on. He looked at her, curious, as though he had never been in exactly this position before. Without asking, she climbed on top of him, straddling him, and leaned in to kiss him, and his lips parted. He made a small "oof" sound when she leaned against his stomach, which told her he wasn't entirely prepared for her to do this, and then suddenly everything was easy.

Some men liked some clothes on, but she wanted hers off. She had always believed she looked best either completely naked or fully clothed; in between didn't do much for her. In or out. She was in. She was kissing him and pulling off her jeans and then her underpants and then balancing on her hands, still kissing him while she took off her socks with her feet. He was trying to help her with the jeans, but she was much faster than he was at removing her clothes—motherhood had done that. Motherhood had made her a queen of multitasking. The light was fading quickly so she didn't bother about the blinds and, anyway, the neighbors weren't going to pay attention, and she found, in the moment when she considered how she might feel if they did pay attention, that she didn't care.

There was blood ringing in her ears. It sounded like water. The blood was rising in her body like a tide. The blood was going to carry her. Sex was not a thing you did or did not do; it was not something you could read about in a book and then perfect. It was a current you rode. This was what she wanted from him. She wanted him to put her back in her body.

She had not looked at his penis closely. She had seen maybe five or six penises in her life—seven, if you included the years of childhood when she had showered with her father, until that had, without any discussion, stopped.

She helped him with his pants. He was sucking in his gut so it did not pop out over the top of his shorts, and so he could, in fact, get his shorts unzipped, and the boundary—the shorts and the waistband—made his body look bisected. It was a touch of vanity that many men had, buying a pair of shorts into which they could just wedge their abdomens. Once the shorts were down around his ankles and there was only his underwear, he looked like one continuous continent of hair and flesh, and the way the dark, wiry hair swirled on his chest and down to his stomach and gathered in a whorl before disappearing beneath his underwear thrilled her, as though it were traveling along a current into this pattern and the current were connected directly between her legs.

His shorts were around his knees, and she was in the process of pulling down his underwear when he lurched up; he wanted a condom from the pocket of his shorts. As he tore the package open with his teeth, she pulled down his underwear until he was naked with her. Everywhere she touched him and he touched her, there was only skin and a little bit of hair. It felt glorious. It felt like melting. Skin was the most exquisite substance in the world. They could make silk sheets and latex playthings and fishnet stockings and heat-producing vibrators and none of it would ever feel like this. Like skin. Like the pulsing of life itself. She was passing through her skin into his. She felt herself unfolding and in her mind she thought of water running, of tree sap oozing out of a crack of bark. She thought about the olallieberries strung up and fucked by bees, and the hawks on the tree fucking and eating dead birds while the mates of the dead cried, and she thought of the irises slicing out of their green skins, of the poor cherry trees and their pink flowers rammed deep inside the silver bark and unable to come out.

His mouth felt good. It was wide because of the angle of his jaw. His bottom lip was thick, but this was hard to see because of the way his jaw hid his lip unless she was completely level with his face. She liked that he had this secret density. She wanted his mouth open and wanted him to open hers. He ran his tongue over her teeth and she felt her legs grow hot. She wanted his tongue in her mouth and his dick against her clit and she wanted to feel both spaces in her body stuffed. Full.

"I want you inside."

He stuck his hand in her mouth. "Inside where?"

She had only ever had a man inside two places. "Everywhere," she said.

"You're brave." He said this like it was a fact and not an assessment.

It was a strange word. She didn't feel particularly brave—she just felt wanting.

"Do you have lube?" He was holding her off his dick with one hand and rolling the condom onto his penis himself with his other hand. She pressed against his hand on her chest. She liked the resistance. It was like a game, him holding her off his dick. She pushed hard and felt him push back.

Oh God. She had forgotten the lube. *Again*. Was there any lube in the house? When had her mother last had sex? Or her father? It was a house of decades of illness where people worried about things like hospital beds fitting through the door and ramps over staircases. No one was thinking about lube. "I doubt it."

He licked his finger and wet her pussy. Then he stuck two fingers up her vagina. His fingers went up inside her and pressed forward, against the front of her vagina, and her body responded like a bass string humming when it is plucked. He took one of her hands and cupped it, and cupped her hand around his dick. He had on the condom and so they smiled at each other for a few minutes and then he pulled her on top. He did not fit.

But the Tree Doctor was not a man who would stop just because his cock did not fit inside a woman he wanted to fuck. So he rolled her over onto her back and put three fingers inside her body and she tried to relax. She tried to tell herself to relax. Her body had so little idea how to actually accept a man inside it anymore, even though this was what she wanted, and when he began to slide inside her, it hurt, and she told herself it did not hurt.

She didn't want to be a person who needed lube. But a middle-aged woman, midway through menopause, needed lube. He licked his finger and wet her again, and then he slid inside her and tears seeped out of her eyes while he put his hands under her ass and fucked her and she wondered why she had been trapped inside her body like this, as if it were she who was sick and not her mother. She had behaved as though it was her in that facility and not as though she was only a little bit past pre-menopause, with a thinning, drying vagina. They were both supposed to be fucking like this and they were both supposed to have orgasms because to do so was as normal as a plant secreting a leaf from the ground to the outside to show what its essence really was.

Afterward, when he was asleep and his clothes were piled on the floor, she willed herself to get out of bed. She told herself she needed to fold both their clothes in the interest of tidiness, so no one would trip over a mound of socks and underwear in the middle of the night, should they need water or the bathroom. She folded her underwear and her shirt first, in case he woke up and saw her. "Just folding my clothes," she could say, while his lay in a wad. But he didn't stir.

So she folded his clothes next, beginning with the socks and then the underpants and his T-shirt and finally the shorts, which were heavy because their pockets were laden with the things a woman might carry in a purse. Keys. More condoms. Change. His phone and a wallet. She briefly considered charging his phone so when he woke she could say that she had seen it and had worried it would die, but then there would be questions about what else she had touched in his pockets, and it seemed best to just fold the shorts, phone and wallet and all, so as to look as though she had done so casually and out of consideration but not because she was snooping. Even if she managed to explain away something like charging a phone, it would still border on snooping.

Then she flipped open the wallet. It was fat and nearly papier-mâchéd with receipts. Chevron showed up a lot, as did Lucky grocery. Both were in the mouth of the valley, on the way to the nursery, so it made sense that he would stop there. She resisted the urge to examine his cards except for the one piece of information that she wanted: Dean Mason. Card after card confirmed it, as did his driver's license. He was Dean Mason of Greenwich, Connecticut, a town she had never visited. There was so much more she could investigate, but with his name and hometown, she could do her sleuthing later. She put the wallet back in the pocket and stuffed the phone in on top of it, then folded the shorts casually. When her first attempt looked too tidy—the result of many years of her mother schooling her to neatly fold and pack everything—she tried again, and then again until the shorts looked as though they had been tucked away by someone thoughtful but not too intrusive. Then she crawled back into bed and got her phone to look up Greenwich, Connecticut. And all at once the complete exhaustion from the activities of the day overtook her, and she fell asleep, still clutching her phone.

. . .

When he left, early in the morning, she felt a kind of terror, as though something had just vacated her body. She was alone inside a husk. This must be the kind of terror that women around the world felt when they had sex and then their lover, who was not tethered to them, left. Murasaki, Aoi, Rokujo had all felt it when Genji left them and went to another lover. It was the panicked terror of being a child who has been put into bed to sleep alone one night and who worries that in the morning their parents will not be there. It was a feeling of being completely alone, a reminder that she was, in fact, alone, even if she did not feel alone. It was a kind of second wave of grief after leaving her mother, who was even now leaving her, drifting further and further away from her, as the many wires in her brain ceased to fire. Was her mother feeling this now in the facility? Her relationship with her mother was the closest she would ever be to another human being, and the night of sex with the Tree Doctor had not lessened this pain but exacerbated it. She had to sleep. She had not had enough sleep, and if she slept and woke up into the bright optimism of sunshine in the garden with its birds and flowers, she would feel better.

There was a bottle of Tylenol PM by the bed and she downed two pills, then staggered to the bathroom and back. Her pussy hurt. She hoped she would not get another urinary tract infection.

Her mind wandered.

Should she bring her mother back?

This was followed by the thought: Would her mother make it till the vaccine?

She needed to detach from this question. Her mind would never give her the answer. She touched herself. Her pussy hurt. Good, she thought. Hurt.

Eight

The internet turned up only one Dean Mason from Connecticut. The name appeared in combination with others—Tommy Dean Mason, Robert Dean Mason, and even, confusingly, Carol Dean Mason—and the little network of Dean Masons lived in many other places. Only one, however, actually appeared to live in Greenwich, Connecticut, right now. To learn anything more about him, she would have to become a member of the service that retrieved his information in the first place, but she knew from past stalking incidents with male students that she wouldn't truly learn much. There would be information about extended family—the wife or wives—and the children and their children. But she wouldn't get the answer to the real question she had now, which was "What are we doing?," with "What will happen?" coming in a close second. She was only dimly aware that she ought to ask what it was that she wanted.

She was not a devotee of social media, despite having a Facebook account, and though it took her several tries, she was able to log on to her page. There was an accumulation of alerts and messages, and she ignored them; she knew from experience that they would simply take up hours of her time, whose closest corollary she could think of only as the two times of the year she removed mildew from the tile of her shower. Instead, she typed "Dean Mason" in the search and looked at the results, of which there were many. The imprecision of the Facebook algorithm gave her many more results than Intelius, although, to be fair, on Facebook she couldn't search with the aid of a geography filter. She learned that there were quite a few Dean

Masons in the British diaspora spread out from Hong Kong to New Zealand, though there was also a painter and a rather well-known Los Angeles deejay who posted a few throbbing videos featuring the taut rear ends of young women she guessed were his groupies, and whose ease with unmasked proximity looked dated in this time of the great sickness.

She scrolled through names and profiles; there were a handful of Dean Masons who did not use actual profile photos but relied on images of yachts at sunset, or dogs embraced in burly arms. Each man, she thought, must have been sure that his yacht and his muscled arms embracing a dog was a unique way to display, in a single image, the essence of himself. She didn't put it past her Dean Mason to think similarly, though she wanted to believe he would be a bit different from those others.

And then after about ten minutes of clicking on profiles, she found him. He had not logged on in the past two years—or at least the most recent public post on his page was from two years ago. And for the three years before that, there were only a few photos visible—each time he changed his profile picture or background photo. At one point he had clearly changed the privacy settings on his account to limit what a stranger like herself could see. But he had not been thorough. The photos and posts from five years ago piled up with no apparent distinction between what was personal and what was for the world. And, as she thought about it, five years ago, when things in the world had felt ever so much more hopeful, if gluttonous, there had not been a need to hide what was private from what was public—the two went together so easily. And there they were—his pictures of his wife and his family, though mostly he posted pictures of three boys who were already teenagers.

She could figure out the wife's name and view her profile. The wife, Sharon, had fewer recent posts, but there was one dated six months ago, from Christmas. There they were—the three boys, the wife, and Dean. They were dressed for Christmas. The wife was petite but a little chunky and blond and wore a red dress and sequined shoes that she recognized as having been featured that winter in a J.Crew catalog. The boys each wore a tartan necktie in a different color—red, green, and blue—and Dean was in a suit. They were standing in front of a darkly stained chestnut fireplace. The wife had labeled the photo "Cotton Club, Xmas 20 . . ." Another club, though probably not the mysterious club with the men that he had mentioned. They were smiling together, as a family, and it was supposed to be the kind of upper-middle-class holiday portrait that fancy people took, and she could feel how hard the wife was straining in her smile to give the right impression. There was Dean with his hands and his disregard for formality, smiling, certainly, but exuding sex and a kind of possessiveness; he had his arms around two of his sons, and seemed to be pulling them toward him, into his body.

The photo came with multiple likes and comments. "Beautiful family," "Gorgeous." And then she read: "Wonderful, father, husband and Tree Doctor." She stopped snooping for a moment while her stomach pooled with acid.

She flipped through the family photos, running into a whole series of pictures posted by the wife with Dean's name attached. There were photos of cats wearing tartan ties, and the pictures were dated from various Christmases past. Dean had a wife who went to such lengths to make Christmas happen for the family that she even dressed up the cats. She was a good wife. Facebook attested to this. There was not one birthday that was not celebrated with a tall, intricately frosted and individually themed birthday cake. Every holiday was precisely decorated and cataloged and photographed. According to social media, Dean had an exquisite family life—and on occasion he even showed up for the photos that were, naturally, taken by the wife. Dean's wife would not depart in the middle of a pandemic and leave him with the children.

She went back to Dean's page. She knew she was not the only person to have felt as a child that her own childhood had passed quickly, only to discover as an adult that other people's childhoods passed quickly. All childhoods were short. So it was with these three boys on the internet. She could scroll back through their gummy smiles and gelatinous faces and then fast-forward, spinning the mouse, to recent photos where their jaws had lengthened and their strong teeth had come in and their smiles had expanded. It happened so quickly online. It was happening to her family, too, she thought.

What was she looking for?

He seemed to switch locations in his posts. He traveled regularly from California to Connecticut, and then down to Florida, and then back to Connecticut again. Many of the photos were of trees. There was an unsophisticated precision to how he displayed his life. Now family, now trees, now family. But there was also something calculated in how the pictures were presented, work life alternating with home life in a way that was so regular and so clearly considered; the photos were not just the product of a man who happened to log on occasionally—or at least for a good decade this was not the case. The photos had been updated every couple of days, as though he had intentionally blurred the distinction between his life online and life as it was lived. He was living to present himself. "All influencer all the time." He did present himself. There was a photo with Larry Ellison and a pine tree in a garden that she assumed was at Ellison's private residence, a reproduction of the Katsura Villa, the Japanese imperial palace in Kyoto. There were photos with half a dozen silver-haired men, all of whom were actors she recognized. They were pictured with their trees. For whom was he presenting himself? He was just a tree doctor. Just. She chided herself for the snobbery of the word "just." What was it like for him to be in proximity to such wealthy people?

She went back twelve years. She looked for patterns, clicking on the photos and examining the comments and the likes. She saw that five years ago, a woman named Suzanne had given each photo a heart. And in the beginning, Suzanne had left comments like "Too cute" and "So adorbs," comments that made her stomach clench at their sweetness and predictability. She clicked on Suzanne's profile—she had also shut down most of her public access, though Suzanne, too, did not have full command of her privacy settings, which made it possible for her to see that she lived in Seattle and had one son and mourned a dog who she believed communicated to her via pigeon feathers she found dropped on the six-by-four deck of her condo. Suzanne had, at about fifty (she was guessing Suzanne's age), gone to Cancún, where she had posed in her bathing suit on a horse and posted the image, and a great many people had given her hearts and thumbs-ups, including Dean. But back on Dean's profile, Suzanne had continued adamantly leaving Dean comments, and after assiduously responding to the early comments, he had suddenly stopped engaging. She had continued to leave him hearts but stopped commenting, and then their interaction trailed off. A new woman named Barbara, who lived in Denver, had begun to like Dean's photos. Barbara—a trim blond who had ever-so-slightly-overdone filler and Botox but had a great body for her age, due to what appeared to be a consistent tango regime—veered less toward the perky and more toward the easily spiritual. Half of Barbara's own Facebook page, which was still publicly accessible, consisted of reposted Alcoholics Anonymous memes, and the other half of interpretations of astrological phenomena. Every now and then Barbara dropped a hint about how she had not expected, as an adult woman, to still like spanking, which elicited the "ha-ha" emoticon from her followers. But Barbara, like Suzanne, had also dropped off Dean's profile after some nine months of interactions.

Was his social media life actually that easy to interpret?

The more she looked, the more the story filled itself in for her. Aside from Suzanne and Barbara, there were others—Helen, Candace, and Tracy—who popped in and out like migrating birds appearing when the season called them forth. There was always someone new in his feed, along with some primary person who loved his pictures and told him so, and whom he would declare in the comments was his best friend, before whatever it was that had drawn them together cooled, and the woman disappeared. None ever seemed to disappear entirely, though. Suzanne and Barbara seemed to reappear most often in short spurts—often around holidays—and sometimes he even responded to them and kept up little conversations with them in the comments section of his posts, before they drifted off again. He was, she realized, that thing she had only ever read about or perhaps glimpsed in the distance at the robust family-style restaurant that slightly moneyed lawyers and doctors visited in Carmel with their families, who would then slink off to the bathroom to send a text or perhaps make a phone call. He was a womanizer.

Given the geographic spread of the women, he was a good one.

She wondered where the many women came from.

How was she supposed to feel? How *did* she feel? If she had been younger, and chiefly concerned with falling in love, she would have been horrified. She was in shock. She was also sort of fascinated. It was like picking up the scent of a trail that had gone cold after a decade. What had he been like when he was younger? His wife's Facebook told her a tiny bit. There was a visible tenderness between the couple. He was younger and fitter and wore his outdoorsiness alongside hers. They were both in exercise gear, but somewhere around the second child, she became plumper and wore more knits and stopped smiling for the camera. By the time the second baby was crawling, she wasn't in any of the family photos, likely because she was the one taking them. And he was wearing gardening clothes, and his face had hardened. He was going to care for trees—his trees—whether or not the family approved of him flying around the United States to check on precious cherries and conifers. What kind of a man traveled the country because he had a certain way with plants? Who paid him to fly from Maine to Seattle and Denver and Los Angeles to look at trees during the day, while he saw Suzanne or Tracy or Barbara at night?

A friend had once said to her that sex with a womanizer was the best kind of sex to have. "They know what to do with you," she had said, sitting with excellent posture in a black corset, her boobs spilling out over the top like the froth of a shaken 7Up erupting out of a can. Her own tits had never done this. She had interpreted this moment to mean: "If you have tits, you will know deep secrets about sex," and so had assumed she would never know those secrets. But now, on the other side of decades of dating and mating, she was catching the men who had survived and who could still fuck.

"You chose well," he had told her. But she hadn't chosen anything.

. . .

The Tree Doctor continued to bring her things from the nursery. When they planted flowers together—or he showed her how she would need to clip the wisteria and the fuchsias that autumn, or when they planned for some aspect of the garden's future—it felt as though they had been lovers for a long time. It was almost like a second marriage. He understood her home and garden and thus a facet of her childhood self—the person who had grown up here—so well.

What was true and what was not? Why had the Tree Doctor lied? She made up stories to explain his behavior. But she didn't care about the lying. No, she did care. At the cellular level now, her body was disturbed. Maybe what she felt was envy. It was perhaps biological that she felt envy. Her skin felt thin. She had, after all, let him into her body. Wasn't envy the reason why a few of Genji's lovers died when they found out about his other women? It was natural, she felt, that her skin was thin. She wanted the story they were in together to resume the correct course—the course on which it had been until now. What was that course? She knew better than to really believe it was a love story, but a love story was the one story she knew. Wasn't it? Perhaps a meeting between a man and a woman did not have to be a love story. What did she want?

When she was younger—decades ago—before she got married, jealousy had occasionally highjacked her body in an ugly, alien-possessing-human, B-rated-horror-movie kind of way. In a Lady Rokujo–possessing–Lady Aoi kind of way. She had wondered if everyone felt like this when in the grip of envy—so insanely concerned with what others were doing. Most of the time when people talked about jealousy, it was to say loftily: "I don't get jealous." People didn't talk honestly about the intense disorientation of jealousy. She wondered if she was abnormal. But women were always being compared to each other, which encouraged envy. Even scholars ranked the women in *The Tale of Genji*, awarding the character Murasaki "best overall" in Genji's collection of women.

There was a quote she had kept tacked above her computer for years. It came from chapter 25, when Genji, after insulting a group of women for reading novels, declares: "I have been very rude to speak so ill to you of tales! They record what has gone on ever since the Age of the Gods. The Chronicles of Japan and so on give only a part of the story. It is tales that contain the truly rewarding particulars!" What might those particulars be?

She thought of a moment, about two-thirds of the way through the novel, when Murasaki is informed that Genji will be taking on the Third Princess as his wife. Murasaki, learning this news, pretends not to care. But she knows what it means; Genji loves her, but the Third Princess has a status in the world that she never will. It is almost as though this new marriage is designed to remind Murasaki that her body is inconsequential. "Hers was no doubt a heart without guile, but of course it still harbored a dark recess or two. In secret she never ceased grieving that her very innocence—the way she had proudly assumed for so long that his vagaries need not concern her—would now cause amusement, but in her behavior she reexamined the picture of unquestioning trust." Later she thinks: "I am I."

She thought of her mother, living her life as a mother, but perhaps all these years secretly hiding away the memory of a German man in her mind, an image that now supposedly lived inside a phone she could not open. Googling had told her she would need the help of a technician, but even this might not unlock the phone. And anyway, did she truly want to open the phone and learn that her mother had had a lover?

One night she awaited the Tree Doctor, who was arriving yet again with a pizza. She wished he weren't bringing pizza. She knew there was only so many things a person could pick up to eat in the middle of a pandemic, but she wished the pizza would stop. She stood in front of the mirror, naked after her shower, and looked at her skin, which had started to dimple. She was getting fat. It must be the pizza, and yet it must also be her age. She got dressed and went outside.

When he came through the gate, bearing the pizza aloft—comically, like a cartoon character carrying a pizza on his fingertips—she was amused and she laughed but she could also feel that the humor was forced. Wasn't it out of laziness that, after all these weeks, they were still eating pizza out of a box? Maybe it had always been laziness and she hadn't noticed, because she had been so entranced by each of the flowers and shrubs he had brought along with the pizza. But wouldn't a man who truly cared about her come up with something new to eat? Nevertheless, she pretended to be delighted when he set the pizza down with a flourish, and twirled his hands balletically. Then she helped him serve the pizza onto the plates she had brought out.

They began the evening as usual by talking about the garden. At one point, she stopped eating and went to pick plums from the tree; they were sweet and ripe and she ate three. Then he stopped eating, and went to check on Einstein, returning to the patio to tell her that the cherry tree appeared to still be alive despite the lack of leaves. "I'm curious what it will do this summer," he said as he licked his fingers, and she thought about how weird it was to see him licking his fingers after touching the tree. He often licked his fingers after he touched her.

"You think it'll bloom?"

"Might. If you read about cherry trees in history, you'll see they show up like this. Some new varietal just starts growing."

"Like a virgin birth."

He wiped his hands on a napkin and began to eat the pizza again.

"How does the tree . . . ," she began.

"No one really knows. They assume that there was some cross-pollination. Some seed gets carried and then one in a million of those seeds turns into new trees. That's how we have the Kanzan. It popped up one day in an orchard in Tokyo and was grafted and sold around Japan and eventually here."

"Couldn't Einstein be a Kanzan?"

"I doubt it. Kanzan only do well here in California as a graft."

"Why do you know so much about them when you are a co-nifer person?"

He took a plum from her and she hoped its sweetness would make her question seem innocent. She was asking too many questions and she could feel the delicate math between them. If she asked too many questions, she might not get sex. She needed to hang on to the sex. On the other hand, now that the travel restrictions were lifted, and she had been to see her mother, and the semester had ended, she was starting to make plans to leave California and return to Hong Kong, and she would, in all likelihood, never see the Tree Doctor again. So what did it matter if she pressed beyond the tacit boundaries of their relationship to ask a few more questions than usual?

"You look different," he said frankly. "New eye shadow? You change your hair?"

She thought about stalling. "What do you mean by that?" But he would know she was stalling. His frankness was one of the things that was so attractive to her.

"No."

"Something has changed. About you."

"Just older." She tried to laugh. Did he suspect she knew he was still married? Or something else. And the way he framed the statement—*something* had changed, but not precisely *what*—meant he was prepared to parry. "I'm just—" she said and her breath quickened. "I'm tired of the . . . sickness. That's all. I miss my kids."

"It's natural," he said.

"I can't believe I'm really going to see them soon. I mean, I'm excited. but it's also weird . . ." Her voice trailed off.

She wondered if he believed her. He wouldn't look her in the eye, even though she was staring right at him. She should not be afraid to ask the questions she wanted to ask. She should not be afraid of him. Finally, she said: "I want to know why you know so much about trees."

He set his piece of pizza down on a plate. "You know how there are some hairstylists who fly around the world cutting hair?" By the way he asked the question, with such authority, she knew it was a line he had used before. Maybe with Suzanne, Barbara, and Tracy.

"I've heard."

"I'm like that. But for trees."

"How does *that* work?" She meant: What network of people existed in the world that one man—the Tree Doctor—would be so favored to cure and care for trees? Even here in Carmel, which was a very fancy town, when people hired gardeners, they hired Mexicans, with a few old-timers using Japanese gardeners. How had Dean put himself in this position of flying around the country to plant a conifer?

"Just part of the extended network of people I know. For instance, my buddy owns the nursery in Carmel Valley, like I said, and I was just going to stay for a few weeks. I was on my way to Malibu—"

"Malibu?"

"Business," he said. "Another buddy has a nursery attached to his estate. He collects plants and needed my help. Anyway, he wasn't quite ready for me, and I was passing through here. And then the virus . . ." He trailed off. "Do you know how the cherry tree came to America?"

"Through Washington, D.C.?"

"Washington wants you to believe that." He smiled at her. "It was wealthy Californians first. Down in Southern California."

"You mean like Huntington?"

"See? I like how smart you are, Professor. Yes, like Huntington. He's the most famous, but there were others. It's because of men like Huntington that we have fuchsias. Palm trees. All kinds of plants we take for granted now in California were naturalized in that man's nursery. In those days—I'm talking 1915—you had to be rich and special to get one of his plants. I mean, now anyone can get a fuchsia. But you look around and see who has a fifty-foot-tall magnolia or an old camellia, and it will only be people who had money and access to someone like Huntington."

"So you know people like that. People who want new and amazing trees."

"Special people always want special things. For a long time, only very special people could have their own cherry tree."

"You mean rich people."

"Rich people are special."

"But they can't plant their own rhododendrons . . ." Did he not remember laughing with her over the software designer who couldn't plant his own rhododendron?

"They don't need to. They can hire me."

"I thought—I thought you didn't care about rich people."

"Only a rich person says that."

She couldn't figure out what to say in response to this. She was not rich. She lived in an expensive house, but that was not the same thing. She felt uncomfortable and out of control and suddenly diminished.

"Did I answer all your questions?"

"Oh, sure . . . I . . ."

"What are you going to do with what you know?"

"Mostly I just like to know things. That doesn't mean I need to do anything." She felt mildly panicked.

He appeared to be thinking this over. "People usually can't help doing something when they think they know something."

"Nothing really has to change," she soothed.

He nodded curtly, mouth turned down. And then he started to kiss her.

Maybe it was all her questioning or the fact that she would

soon be leaving California that prompted the Tree Doctor to be even more amorous than he had been in the past. He did not ask her to take her clothes off, as he had been asking recently, but as she crawled across the bed, he grabbed her pants and pulled them off in one motion, so she was momentarily startled. She was also curious. Had he been this strong all along and hidden it from her? She doubted he would hurt her, but then one never really knew.

He told her what to do. "Suck my nipple," he said. "This one." And while she did it, he began to stroke himself. It was so markedly selfish, her sucking on his tit while he jerked off, but she could see that he was enjoying himself, and hadn't he made her come so many times over the past few weeks? She sucked his tit and fingered it when he asked.

"Come and look," he said to her at one point. He was standing in front of the full-length mirror in the bedroom. "Come here." He wanted to fuck her from behind and look at their bodies while he did it. She let him. While he fucked her, he whispered in her ear: "Look at how good we look together. And we look completely different than we did at the start. Ten years younger." She saw that he wasn't looking at her, but at himself. She looked at him too. And it was true. Despite the pizza and the lockdown and the lack of very much exercise, he looked younger.

Then she tried to look at herself objectively, but it was impossible. The power of it—the total opening up to him and of watching herself get fucked in front of a mirror—made it impossible for her to criticize her body at all. She looked twenty-five years old—okay, maybe thirty-five—with her hair slick from his saliva and his pre-cum all over her and her back arching to let him inside her even deeper. He had de-aged her.

Abruptly, he stopped what he was doing and fished some lube out of the pocket of his pants. She noted, as he squeezed the lube onto his fingers, that the bottle was half-empty, and she thought he was going to fuck her, but he pulled her onto the bed and flipped her over onto her stomach. "Relax," he said and inserted a finger up her ass.

She flinched. "Wait."

"Relax," he said again.

She was scared but also excited, and he slid in another. She became quiet. Docile. When he put his cock inside her, she cried out. "Please don't hurt me. Please don't hurt me."

"I won't." He muttered as a man does when yelling at his hammer missing a strike and bending a nail. His focus was on himself and his cock and not on her at all, but she was helpless in this position. She felt cracked open when he slid inside her, and when she cried he pulled back out so only his tip was inside her. "Okay. It's okay," he soothed, as though she were a puppy. He felt her muscles with his cock and he rubbed his hands through her hair to calm her and he slid in slowly, slowly.

She let him. She told herself to be calm, just as he was telling her to be calm. They were both telling her—her ass, really—to be calm. And when he was inside, he leaned over and began to whisper into her ear, his voice hoarse and his breath hot, so it was like he was fucking her ear too. What he said was not important. It would sound foolish to write it down now. He said: "I am the first man ever to be in your ass," which was true, and which, when she thought about it later, sounded preposterously arrogant, but which she also knew was meant to sound intimate, and she knew that she was to feel pleased at having let a man inside.

She split in two. One part calculated how much pain she was feeling while acknowledging that yes, in a way, it was pleasurable, as it is to feel the tension of needing to defecate and the extraordinary release that comes after. The other part observed her, the woman who had not had sex for six years and who was now in lockdown with a cock up her ass. They worked in tandem, these two sides of her, and their sole goal was to keep her body intact and safe through this experience, which was nearly like having sex again for the first time, not knowing how it was all going to turn out and how she would feel after.

"That's enough," he said with authority, and when he came out of her, relief rushed through her body like a sudden fever. She turned her head and gazed up at him. She had never in her life been so physically close to anyone before, and just the fact of that weakened her, so she only wanted to be close to him again. She cried. He smiled at her, seemingly charmed by her crying, and held her, and when she did not stop crying, he excused himself to wash his hands and his cock; he was fastidious, he said, about germs. "If you have anal again, make sure you both wash afterward." Then he came back and fucked her quickly, missionary-style, and then they were spent and he slept.

But she could not sleep right away. She had just learned what her body could do and what it was for and what she could make with another person. She might have gone her entire life not knowing about sex that was this pleasurable, if fucked-up. She wanted to wake him up and ask him to do it all to her again. And then she began to cry, wondering what else she did not know. She had that terrible hollowed-out feeling of having been close to him, and knowing he would leave in the morning and go out into the world, where the virus was waiting. She would go home to her husband. To her children. This was how it was. But she did not want to go back into the prison of her unloved body.

He had said he was a tree doctor, but really, he was what was once called a lothario, or a gigolo, or, in the time of Genji, a lover. It was his profession and he was good at it.

. . .

Perhaps two days later, she found a little amaryllis on her front doorstep in the morning, and she knew he had left it; it could grow on the patio during the months she would be gone. The house would be rigged with an alarm, and she had arranged for someone else, recommended by Juan, to cut the grass. She began to pack and made an appointment to drive up to see her mother again.

But all the time she was making these plans, the infection rate was rising. She went to sleep on a Tuesday clutching her iPhone, whose news alerts across channels informed her that worried officials were considering renewed restrictions, and then she woke the following Wednesday to read that Monterey County had issued an alert announced online by a large red exclamation point. What freedom had existed—haircuts, masked dining at tables on the sidewalk—was now to be retracted. The virus, that stealthy, brutal taker of lives, was on the prowl and the county was obliging by shutting down more activities. She sat on her bed and read and reread the text.

Hong Kong and Japan were the first to close their borders to all unnecessary travel, with France, Germany, and the Scandinavian countries following in rapid succession. Australia and New Zealand had never believed in the dip in the first place, and had never reopened.

Perhaps a day later, Thomas called to tell her that because the borders had closed again, her flight had become difficult. Not impossible. But difficult. And again, they revisited the idea that he and the girls might fly to see her, but Thomas had balked at the thought of abandoning his office, getting on the airplane, and traveling across the ocean, and said, "I still think we will get this under control in a couple weeks. It's just another couple weeks."

Very quickly, all nonessential travel was halted as the world strained to contain the virus. It was on the news everywhere: "World Travel Ceases." She was trapped. Bound in place. She felt awful. They were all helplessly adrift on this sea of virus. She had been planning another visit to her mother and then a reunion with her daughters, but actually, all forward momentum had to stop. It was not just her mother, with a compromised immune system, who might fall prey to the sickness. She might too. She felt ill, as though she were experiencing the emotional equivalent of motion sickness.

The Tree Doctor must have seen the news, too, because he texted her and offered to bring her a pizza. "Unless you've left?"

"Thank you for the amaryllis," she wrote back. "I'm still here."

When he arrived, they did not even pretend to be hungry or in need of the pizza, whose fate was to cool on the floor in the hallway where the Tree Doctor set it down. She met him at the door and he crashed into the house and then they were on the floor in the hallway with his hand up her skirt. "You *thought* you were leaving," he said. She realized she was crying as he fucked her so hard she had a rug burn on her spine, and afterward, during an interlude in bed when he coated her back tenderly with Neosporin, he apologized.

In the evening light, his face took on deep shadows and she saw how his thick lips broadened into a wide smile.

"You could've gone on to Malibu," she said in a small voice.

"I'm not ready for Malibu," he said. He spread her legs apart and began to fuck her again, gently. "You tell me if I hurt your back," he said. He put his hand on her clit and rubbed it, and then inserted a finger inside her pussy, pressing up, and when she began to cry out, he did not ask her why or what precisely was eliciting this noise or if anything was hurting her at all.

In fact she wanted him to hurt her just a little bit. She thought he ought to be capable of hurting her. Not too much. She wanted to feel, though, that he could hurt her, because she wanted to feel how much smaller her body was in comparison to his. "Hold my hands," she said. "Down." He seemed to understand. He had held her hands before, during sex, but now he flexed his arms straight, so she was fixed into place beneath him as he fucked her. She was constrained. She felt herself loosen and being pried open while, stroke by stroke, he took pleasure from her into his body. She felt herself giving in to him and watched his eyes grow wildly round, as though his irises were spinning. And then it was not like he was wearing a mask, but as if she were seeing through his skin and down to his bones, as though his face had become one of those Day of the Dead skeletons. Maybe she was seeing underneath his flesh. Maybe the only way to see what was under the flesh was to be bound like this, giving up everything in her body to someone else. She wanted him to take everything. She wanted him to fasten her with the sheets or perhaps her clothes. Some twine. Bind her so it was clear how paralyzed she could become, while he could orgasm hard, thanks to her complete immobilization.

. . .

So she had missed the tiny window during which it might have been easy to return to her children. She had to adjust again to being here in her childhood home. Daily she woke and reminded herself to look in the garden and to look at the birds for solace. And her class on *The Tale of Genji* would soon begin again—on the computer. She had received an email just a few weeks ago asking if she would be willing to teach it, and she had agreed. She would be happy to have the money deposited directly into her account, and she thought she could probably teach the class half-asleep. Certainly she could be half in pajamas.

The week before the first class, she received emails from Astrid, Momoko, and Henry, asking to attend a second time, because they missed the discussions so much and wanted to go through the text again, and they wanted to do it with her. They were annoyed with the college for keeping them remote—Astrid had taken the term off. But the three of them wanted to re-read *Genji*. "This time," Astrid wrote, "could we get to part three?"

"Honestly, I don't really know part three that well," she wrote back.

"I read ahead," Astrid told her. "I think you could teach it. I think the students would benefit."

She allowed her three former students to join, but drew the line at starting the book in the middle, protesting that she was not prepared to lead discussions in this manner and that she didn't really have her materials prepared for the latter part of the book. But she promised to try to speed through parts 1 and 2 this time around, so the class would actually get to read part 3. So it was that she started off September once again sharing what she knew about the Shining Prince, who "revealed such marvels of beauty and character that no one could resent him." She was prepared for the discussions about rape this time, and acknowledged that, yes, Genji did kidnap and groom Murasaki and that there were modern-day feminists in Japan who deplored this behavior and *Genji*'s status as a classic, while also emphasizing that this should not be a reason to avoid *Genji* completely.

"This is why I hope we get to part three," Astrid said, despite having promised not to speak in class. "I think that whole chapter is a repudiation of parts one and two."

She decided to read part 3 on her own in advance of the class to try to prepare for discussions. She remembered the basic outline: As in parts 1 and 2, there are two brothers, Kaoru and Niou, who compete with each other over the attention of women. Kaoru is believed to be Genji's son, but is actually the product of a liaison between Genji's wife the Third Princess and another man. Kaoru doesn't know this in the early parts of part 3, but seems to sense that something is amiss, as he is plagued by an unspecified self-doubt.

"Sometimes he felt as though there must be something wrong

with him, and that thought, too, started anguished reflections." It is the musing of an insecure man, far more doubtful and lacking in self-confidence than Genji ever is. Kaoru has the sense, from his youth, that his world was an illusion.

Reality is also an illusion for Genji, who according to the gods would have been emperor but for the jealousy of others. So the gods conspire to make his life the glorious experience it should have been. The same luck does not befall Kaoru.

Both Kaoru and Niou eventually fall in love with Oigimi, who, unable to choose between the two men, starves herself to death. There follows a brief period of mourning and confusion until the author introduces Ukifune, the last great female character of Lady Murasaki's tale. Ukifune has the good (or ill) fortune of looking nearly identical to Oigimi, though Ukifune, at least, is clear that she loves Kaoru. The sex between them is powerful enough to confuse Ukifune, because she no longer knows whom she loves the next morning: Good sex could do that to you. Eventually Ukifune is so distraught, she attempts to drown herself, and it is this act that is often referred to by readers as an attempt at "agency."

And this is where she usually stopped reading. Oigimi's suicide and Ukifune's attempt at suicide, in such short succession, depressed her, though this particular evening she read on to the part where Ukifune is discovered alive by a passing group of monks and, in the manner of all good soap opera heroines, she has no memory of who she was and how she arrived in her spot in the shade of a tree.

. . .

Sometime in early September she began to see ads on her computer from Holland Bulb Farms, which was having a sale on bearded irises, and when she clicked on the link, a web page opened to a spread of dozens of glorious irises fanning out their plumage, like a peacock fanning its tail over its head. She ordered the irises liberally.

The subsequent email that landed in her inbox told her that the irises would ship as soon as it was the correct season to plant irises in her climate. She realized she was planning for the following year. She was behaving like someone who did not plan to leave. Would she ever leave?

The website had additional instructions. Every fall, the iris bed would need to be cleaned. An iris did not grow from a bulb, nor from a seed, but from something called a rhizome. Certain plants like ginger, turmeric, and the iris sprouted off an underground stem; the part of ginger that people ate was this subterranean stalk.

On a warm but not-too-sunny day, she put on her gardening hat and took her clippers and went outdoors to address the thick and tangled iris rhizomes. The rhizomes were beige, somewhat like a tube of ginger, only the papery skin that covered the flesh was wrinkled. They looked like desiccated penises. The rhizomes were flaccid and some had expired, and she snipped those off and threw them away, then saved the young, fleshy tubes and covered these with dirt. She wondered if there was therapeutic value in seeing an iris bed as essentially an exercise in salvaging the parts of the penis that still functioned best.

Some of the rhizomes were very long, and she threw away six inches of discarded tubing. In other areas, the tubes had shoved up against each other, forcing each other out of the ground, their necks flexing like the rippling and interlocking serpents and limbs in the statue of Laocoön, carved by an unknown Greek.

She felt something gazing at her while she cleared up the rhizomes, and when she looked up into the holly tree, she saw the bright yellow Townsend's warbler watching her with intense birdlike curiosity. He was lemon colored, and his eyes were covered with black spots, so he looked like he was wearing a little mask.

"Hello," she said, like she was some kind of Disney princess who could communicate with birds. He hopped away up into an oak to eat some bugs. She hadn't seen the warbler since the spring—he must have migrated back from the Pacific Northwest. Fall would be here soon.

. . .

She could feel the days growing shorter, and the loss of sunlight and the ever-darkening color of evening elicited a small panic in her throat. She wanted to hang on to what had sustained her without fail during her sheltering: nature. She began to go for walks in the canyon near her home. She had not been in the canyon in years and she found it unchanged. Her body responded instantly to the obstacle course of brambles and gullies, and she relished the feeling of plunging down into the wild wood. She knew that the first part of the path was crowded with poison oak and berries; her childhood in Northern California had made it easy for her to distinguish between the two leaves. One kind of leaf was shiny and the color varied from green to red. Berry leaves were a similar size and shape, but matte, owing to a coat of fine down. She had to avoid the poison oak.

The path in the canyon turned left—south—and she stopped in the middle of a bridge to see how much water was in the creek below. There was only a glimmer, but enough for the birds to have a bath. She passed the felled trunks of pine trees. It used to be that after winter storms in California someone always had to check and see if any trees had fallen, and then the forestry crews went in to remove anything that was unsafe on the path. Some of the fallen trees she remembered from childhood and some were new.

She walked on. The path curved and she recognized a bench

where she and her American grandmother had always stopped to eat their lunch. The bench was in a strategic location: in the spring, the area around it would be illuminated with nasturtiums of all shades of orange. They had died back now, and in their place was a faint impression of green, and here and there a late-blooming blossom that had not kept up with its kin.

The light grew golden just up ahead. It was coming down strongly from the southwest, but filtered through the oak leaves. The oaks never lost their foliage, though spring would bring fresh, slick, bright emerald leaves and the old ones would fall off in turn and accumulate on the ground in a matte shade of gold. The loss of the old leaves and the emergence of the new were so perfectly choreographed that most people referred to the oak trees as evergreens. The first time she had seen fall on the East Coast and learned that she was looking at oaks, she had been astonished by the palm-wide span of thick leaves and how they turned such strong shades of red and yellow. Nothing like that happened on the West Coast.

She paused in the golden light and looked up at the tree. It was alive. Small, masked birds jumped from branch to branch and drew her eye in to their activities. It was the warblers. She could barely keep up with its flittering motion from branch to branch, as it ate the dried flowers left over from springtime.

A jogger ran past, and he pulled on his mask when he saw her. "Woodpecker?" he stopped and asked her, panting.

"Warbler," she said.

"What's that?"

"A yellow bird."

He looked up and she could tell he could not see the bird at all. He saw only a tree. There were half a dozen woodpeckers squawking higher up in the branches, and she watched as the jogger craned his neck to see those birds pounding at the flesh of the dead pine tree and jockeying for position to get at the insects in the wood. She decided she did not care if he saw the warblers or not. She could tell he did not care either. She saw how he made the decision that he had paused only for the woodpeckers, after all, and she watched the muscles in his face relax as he decided that the woodpeckers were all there was to see. He resumed his run.

She remained there in this splash of golden light and studied the birds. Their yellow color was so strong, she wondered how anyone could miss them. She supposed they were sort of camouflaged in the sunlight and in the trees, flanked against the hillsides with the yellow grass. She admired the intelligence of nature.

The canyon wasn't very big—thirty-some acres—and it was situated between two housing developments. Despite that, it was home to many more birds than she saw in the garden. Even just standing there, she knew this to be a fact. There were perhaps fifteen of these little yellow birds flitting from branch to branch.

Wren-tits popped up out of the brambles beside her and made an atonal screeching sound. She heard something repeatedly digging in dried leaves and figured it was a towhee. At one point she heard the air whip, and six crows flying in formation sliced their heavy, inky feathers through the air as they angled around the branches—and each other. Other birds flew with discipline and strict geometry, but the crows never seemed to miss a chance to fly and move with irony. One chased another midflight, while another playfully brushed past a woodpecker, and then they were gone. The forest continued to rumble. Not too far up, a woodpecker stuck his head out of a hole in a tree. A moment later another woodpecker emerged.

She could hear the woods breathing. As intently as she was listening to the sounds of the forest, she knew the entire forest was listening too. The birds knew she was there, and they knew where all the other birds were in relation to themselves. She had, for now, become a part of the forest with them. She had never before paid such keen attention to trees.

From the direction of a house above the canyon, a dog began to bark. She had no indication of what had set it off, but it barked at regular intervals, and almost instantly the birds stopped moving. All around in the trees she could feel silence cover everything. It was not only the birds that had stopped moving, but the trees too. Silence affected all motion. The trees, she thought, also heard the dog.

A warbler was resting in a branch just over her head. It reminded her of playing hide-and-seek as a child, and the way two people might see each other in their hiding spots and telegraph through their eyes how close or far away "It" was. The warbler looked at her over his shoulder, then straight ahead, and then at her again. She stood perfectly still in an effort to join in the great waiting of the forest, while the dog barked.

When the dog finally stopped vocalizing, the little warbler shrugged, as though waking from the drug of sleep. He began to eat the tiny dried blossoms on the branch above him. Then he leapt to another branch just a few feet forward and batted at the leaves to get at the blossoms at the end of a twig. Around her, all the other birds began to move again and engage in the coordinated movement of foraging.

She continued her walk through the canyon, occasionally stopping under other oak trees, or alongside a grove of redwoods, but nothing had the same magic as the cluster of oaks where she had paused before. "The forest was more alive there," she thought.

About a mile from home, she saw a Cooper's hawk sitting on a telephone wire and she knew from the way the bird was surveying the ground that he was in hunting mode. She watched. Sure enough, he abruptly hurled his body off the wire and down into some brambles, emerging a moment later with what looked like a towhee in his talons. The little brown bird was prostrate like an offering.

She went to sleep that night greatly comforted. For once, her body didn't feel hollowed out and empty. It must have been the forest air. As she drifted off, she heard the trees begin to thrash in a sudden wind, and idly thought that she would need to use the pool scooper to clean debris out of the pond, so the fish could have clean water and enough oxygen.

Nine

In the middle of the night, she awoke to a fever. She had a cup of water by the bed, and she drank it, but then she needed to go to the bathroom. Then she went to the kitchen and ate two peanut-butter-and-jelly sandwiches, which put her in a stupor, and she fell asleep again on top of the bed. She woke up one more time when the fever passed and she was cold and she went under the cover, thinking that it ought not to be so cold in September.

She had overslept. The clock on her iPhone told her it was nine a.m., but the light coming in through the slats of venetian blinds was dark. It was normal for it to be dark when it was foggy. But this was not the dark gray of fog. It seemed to be . . . red.

She sniffed the air but smelled nothing unusual.

Cautiously, she climbed out of bed, then twirled open the slats on the blinds.

There was the world outside, bathed in red. It was a world she had never known or seen before. It was a world transformed, as if blood had seeped out of the orifices of every animal, plant, and rock.

She moved through the haven of her house. She walked gingerly, as though there were knives on the floor. She didn't understand what was happening. Someone had lifted up her safe and comfortable home while she had been asleep and flung it somewhere else where the world was red, giving the lie to the idea that home was a safe place.

From the kitchen window, she could see that the front garden was red too. Only here there were red flowers blooming—dahlias.

Their color had been pronounced yesterday. The bulbous brown sugar dahlia, which bloomed in a ball, was growing next to a scarlet poppy and beside a maroon anemone dahlia. But in the morning light, the heavy red color smothered their differences. They all looked the same shade of red.

She made herself a cup of coffee and stepped outside onto the driveway. Then she smelled the smoke. A bit of ash fell into her coffee cup and she fished it out and dropped it on the pavement. Then she walked through the garden like she did every morning. For weeks she had drawn comfort from her morning rounds and from noticing the minute changes in the garden. But just a few minutes outside now made her throat hurt. And it was cold. It was a strange kind of cold—not due to fog or dense clouds. It was cold because the sky was too dark and had been too dark for too long. The only time she had felt anything akin to this eerie kind of cold had been during a full eclipse, when she had stood in the path of the moon as it crossed before the sun, and the world had gone dark and cold. The birds had become silent, just as they were now.

She felt irritated and unsafe at once, and went inside.

All day she waited for the red sky to clear and for the temperature to warm, and they didn't. The news online at least informed her of what had happened: last night there had been something called dry lightning, which had ignited twenty-five separate fires in California; three were burning near her home. Because her town and community were small, the bulk of the media attention was focused on a fire now tearing through Napa Valley, and two other fires located on either side of Silicon Valley. If she looked at a satellite map of her state, she could see the smoke pouring up into the atmosphere, and in some cases, smoke from the three fires mixed together. The pollution was starting to accumulate. Her own part of California had gone from "green" air to "red." Closer to the epicenter of the largest fires, the air was maroon; the news predicted worse air would arrive in her town soon.

Idly, she remembered the golden-crowned sparrows she had fed this past spring, when the sickness had first started, and who had departed all at once for Canada. They usually arrived back to her home by the end of September; she knew fall had come by the arrival of the sparrows. But the entire West Coast was now coated in heavy smoke, and she could not imagine how it was that flocks of tiny birds could navigate through the air to reach her.

It never warmed up that day and it never brightened. Late in the afternoon she closed the blinds so she wouldn't have to look out at the sickening red sky—the color of a wound. She got into bed and pretended it was just dark outside, and she read and she slept, her body heavy. She was like the birds exposed to too much darkness; her body was confused.

. . .

She woke up groggy.

She knew where she was, but her mind was not clicking into action the way it usually did in the morning. It was the smoke. Her house had been poisoned by smoke. She had a friend who had died in a house fire. Not because of the fire, but because of the smoke. That was why in school when they did fire drills, they taught you to stuff towels under doors, and to cover your mouth with a wet towel if you had to escape a burning building. But there was no place for her to escape to. The smoke was everywhere.

She opened the linen closets and found her mother's old towels, carefully folded, and she crammed those against the cracks along all the windows in the house. She began to limit her movements to only three rooms. She remembered that in addition to all the other medical equipment her mother had purchased—the walkers, bed guard rail, blood pressure monitors, and humidifiers—there was an air purifier. She set up the machine in the bedroom, then lay down and waited for the air in the room to clear.

She lay in bed and slept, and when she woke, her head hurt and her throat hurt. She found her mother's anti-nausea medication and she took this, and then she crawled back into bed and began to refresh the online air-quality map, zooming in on her specific portion of California.

Over the next few days, she found increasingly sophisticated maps that did things like show how the air quality from one fire affected the air quality of another. For a time, her part of California only had one blanket of smoke, but then the winds mixed together three large blankets of smoke and the air above her home was dark gray and angry. The birds did not come to feed, except for the hummingbirds.

Of course she heard from her family, who were alarmed that for once her air quality was even worse than in Hong Kong, a fact they could not imagine. And she told them she was doing just fine, because what else could she say to the little group of three, who were incapable of assisting her in any way had she not been fine. But she was not fine. She was alone.

She watched the animals trying to survive. She donned her mask and went out and diligently refilled the feeders if they appeared to be even partly empty. She didn't know what else to do for the animals. She noticed that each time there was a slight improvement in the air quality—when it went from maroon to red, or the air quality index fell from 250 to 150—the birds knew it and left the trees to eat, before huddling back in the branches.

The maps told her the direction of the winds. She had always thought the wind essentially blew in one direction—from west to east—but the reality was, like so much else, far more complicated. The wind sometimes blew south, sometimes blew east, and sometimes blew in a circle. The weather forecasters now paid attention to the fires, the smoke, and the direction of the wind; the poison in the air would end only when it rained or the smoke was pushed elsewhere in the country.

She texted with her mother's caregiver. They were surrounded by smoke, too, they told her. They were running air purifiers. They told her not to worry. She worried about her mother—and she didn't. She was exhausted from worry. She couldn't even flagellate herself for failing to bring her mother back here to be safe. Here was not safe.

The rest of the time she watched the progress of the fires. One of the three was in Big Sur, an area so wild and rocky that the news warned it could be many weeks before the fire was even 10 percent contained. The other two fires were more worrisome for her. These fires were located to the west of her—one in Carmel Valley and the other in the Salinas Valley—and separated from her by hills. She calculated that one fire was thirteen miles away and the other fifteen. The best fire map was made by NASA, and it showed where the fires had already burned, and where they were burning that day. The county in which she lived updated its virtual maps of evacuation zones, and this was when she learned she was in zone 21, and far away from the fire; there were currently mandatory evacuation orders for zones 1 through 7. She determined that the nursery was located in zone 14.

There was only the one road into and out of the valley that connected directly to the highway. She wondered how it would be possible for everyone in the path of the fire to escape quickly.

The fire on the Salinas side of the hills was marching toward the coastline; surely it would be stopped? But then here, too, there were only so many roads out of the peninsula. In fact, when she stopped to think about it, there was only one road out of town to the north, and one to the south. Highway 1 was the road out of Carmel Valley, and it did eventually catch up with Interstate 5 deep in the Central Valley, but the fires had long ago cut off that road. The fires seemed to have an intelligence; they had already trapped the residents of her town by reducing their escape routes from three to two. The thought chilled her. The planet did not need humans at all. It could rid itself of humans as easily as a virus can highjack a body and consume it. She longed for the slightest reminder that the world could and would still be beautiful.

She sent the Tree Doctor a quick text: "Are you okay?"

"Watching the maps," he wrote back.

There was really nothing to do but wait. In the eerie silence, she heard sirens—fire trucks and ambulances. She napped, woke, and hit "refresh" on the air quality maps, then napped again. She checked her social media. And then she saw the many childhood friends whom she had not encountered in person for years, but whose photos of graduations and birthdays and anniversaries occasionally populated her feed. They lived nearby and had been close the whole time she had been sheltering here, though she had not communicated with any of them. They were posting which evacuation zones they lived in, and as the hours went by, and the wind stubbornly refused to stop blowing to the west, the fire grew, and the chances of their zones burning increased. She found herself worrying for them—worrying for herself—and any remaining shred of thinking of this house and this garden as somehow removed from nature and the world was now gone. If the fire came for her childhood friends, it would come for her too.

. . .

The following day, evacuation orders were issued to zones 7, 8, and 9, but one of her former classmates—a man named Kurt—

refused to abandon his home and posted photos of himself standing next to his son with their hands on their hips. They had a dream house, and he would defend it with his garden hose. His house was on a cul-de-sac. She was not to know his fate for another forty-eight hours, when she saw him on her screen again, a changed man. His house was the only one remaining on his street.

But by then, the fire had marched on toward zones 10, 11, and 12, and residents in those neighborhoods were forced to evacuate. She decided to cancel her class until the air was clear again.

Her brain, so slow these days from the smoke, tried to scan her memory for the locations of items that would make up an emergency kit. Thomas called three times from Hong Kong. The girls urged her to leave the house.

"Can't you go to San Francisco? Or down to LA?"

"The air looks bad everywhere," she said. "And they've told us not to drive on the roads unless we absolutely have to. Plus, where do I go?" Abruptly she began to cry. Everything was all wrong. It was so much more all wrong than just the pandemic and the enforced separation. She couldn't begin to tell Thomas all the ways in which it was wrong.

"Honey," he said with a touch of exasperation. Her emotions were an inconvenience. But she was so upset, she could not stop crying. "I'll . . . I'll buy you a ticket. Why don't you just fly here . . . ," he began.

Only now, she realized, would he spend money to buy her what would surely be an expensive ticket. "It is so much easier for all of you, as citizens, to fly *here*."

"But my job . . ."

"Fuck your goddamn job!" she screamed and hung up the phone. She continued to cry alone for a while, and the next time she and Thomas spoke, it was as though her outburst had not happened. He did not mention paying for her ticket again. She did not mention her discomfort in the smoke.

She began watching the official fire bureau updates on her computer. These were live streamed on Facebook, with several thousand people tuning in to watch every time the adults congregated in their masks to share the latest news on the behavior of the fire. This was how she thought of them—as "adults." They were the sheriff, firefighter one, and firefighter two.

As the virtual appearances carried on over the days in their weird choreographed ways—grown men in masks and firefighting uniforms—she found herself profoundly moved by human beings. People could, in fact, take care of other people. The men on her screen were ordinary humans—not celebrities, not the high-earning attorneys and physicians who now lived in her neighborhood. Each one came to the microphone before the camera, removed his face mask, and began to talk about the state of the fire. They used words like "dozing," "agricultural," "cleanup," "sensitive area," and "incident." By the third livestream on the morning of the second day, someone had blown up a paper map of the county and had drawn little red marks where the fires were, and these, along with the evacuation zones, made the map look like a battle plan.

The men—the sheriff and the firefighters—had become increasingly adept at explaining what they were doing. The fires, they said, were being propelled by the winds. The lack of crews and equipment meant they had to focus their energy on only certain fronts, which they were trying to do. They lamented the loss of twelve homes so far. The sheriff spoke sternly about the need to evacuate if an order was given.

She was fascinated by the men. They wore black and spit out facts. The state of being in an emergency had removed the need for spin, and replaced it with men who spoke the language of action. Why couldn't everyone communicate like this all the time? Why, in the middle of the sickness that had swept over the country, were there not more adults? In fact, it was the adults who were going to pull them out of this mess. It was the only possible way to feel something good again.

On the fourth morning, she woke to find that, despite everyone's best intentions, the fires had merged. The new, larger fire had swarmed to the top of a hill and was now pushing toward the highway and down to the village in the valley.

Her childhood friend Kate put out a simple request on Facebook asking if anyone could take her chickens. Kate had found a home for her pony, and the rest of the animals could travel with her to a motel. But the chickens needed a place to go, unless she left them in the coop during her evacuation, or turned them loose to the wild, which some of her neighbors recommended.

They had not spoken since the meeting in the grocery store, but the emergency of the fire removed the need to go over their shared history, and to bring their shared story up to the present.

"You can bring your chickens here," she messaged. "I have a caged vegetable garden in the back."

Kate fretted that if the chickens went into the garden, they would eat the cucumbers, the beans, the growing squash, and quite possibly the blueberry bushes. There would be nothing left to harvest. It seemed in that moment far more important to take care of the chickens. This was not a fate she had expected for her vegetables; then again, she wanted very much to do something helpful for someone.

And this was how, thirty years after they met, and more than twenty weeks after seeing each other again at the grocery, Kate arrived at her home with five chickens in two cat carriers, and hastily deposited them inside the vegetable garden. Together they cut wire and screwed the door into place so it could not blow open. And then Kate departed to care for the pony. There were five more hours left to completely evacuate zone 13.

. . .

That evening—still experiencing nausea and a headache from the ash and the poor air quality—she checked the news and saw that a crew from Israel had landed at the airport and was on its way to the valley. Another crew had left the Bear Fire, in Southern California, and was arriving with fire trucks and bulldozers and was heading into the valley. The air outside did not reflect this good news. A fire, she learned, could sense the weakness in human society, much like a virus could. She wondered if nature's essential quality was aggression. She had once learned that the old gods of Japan were powerful—but neither good nor bad. Perhaps this was, in fact, the case. The Buddha had compassion, and maybe only humans were capable of care and then only sometimes, when they paid attention to the Buddha. What was goodness, anyway? The firefighters had dug a trench along Highway 68 to prevent the fire from crossing it. If they were not careful now, the fire might cross Highway 1 to the north of the peninsula. And if this happened, there would be only one road out of town.

She was still processing this news and the possibility of an impending further loss of freedom when the Tree Doctor wrote to her: "Evac order. Can you help?"

The message was characteristically curt. "Anything. How do I help?"

Little white bubbles percolated on the screen while he tapped out an additional message. "All roads to Salinas closed. Can't get to the warehouse. Can you just come here?" He explained that her house wasn't too far from the highway. They would perhaps be able to make two, maybe three trips in the truck, packed with trees to dump on her driveway. Could she come and load up her car with some of the more expensive small plants?

"Yes," she wrote back immediately. A moment later Thomas wrote again to ask if she was still okay, and she ignored the question. She had things to do.

A slow but methodical stream of cars was now exiting the valley, even as she was going in. The houses she passed were dark; the paddocks had no horses. Everyone who could leave had departed or was departing from the valley. Near the nursery, on the lefthand side of the road, she passed a group of firefighters. There were two trucks and a patrol car and she could see the men craning their necks toward something, but did not have time to process their activities. The road rounded a corner and soon the men and their lights were out of view.

There was a sheriff's car at the nursery. Its lights flashed and from her car she could hear static and a voice mumbling from the radio blaring out into the dusty parking lot. Workers were loading a van with trees. Someone had parked a van alongside the main building and she pulled up behind the van, leaving some space for the rear doors to open easily. Then she clamped on her mask and got out of her car.

She was unprepared for the heat and the static in the air. Hot fingers stroked her head and she realized it was the wind, singed by the fire. She looked around. She had enough animal instinct to know that the fire was somewhere nearby, crouching in the yellow air on the horizon. She heard men shouting, and the voice of the Tree Doctor crystallized. "Go! Let's go! It's time to go!" he was shouting. She picked up a few plants and opened the back of her car and began to load it with flowers.

The Tree Doctor saw her and came up to her. He was wearing a bandanna over his mouth. The men, who had all been working in the building, now came out of the nursery and piled into their cars and trucks. Where had they all come from? The Tree

Doctor was steering her by her elbow. "You need to go," he said. "I'll meet you at the house."

She felt foolish to have come all this way to the nursery to help, only now to be driving back out. It had taken her too long to get there. She started her car, looped around the driveway, and joined the caravan of cars now exiting the valley.

Her heart rate accelerated. It was impossible to dissect precisely what out of the dozens of sensory signals she was receiving so alarmed her, but she was very much aware that it had been her own perhaps irresponsible decision that had brought her into the valley, and that she was leaving now because everyone was leaving. Again she felt a kind of weight—a pressure that came from collective action. Perhaps it was the situation that made her feel the sudden grip of terror; she really couldn't be sure. There was the flight from the valley, the yellow smoke, the heat outside, the weird wind, and now, as she came around the corner where she had seen the fire trucks on her way in, there were sparks. The air was lit with fire.

In the time it had taken to go into the valley and to turn around, fire had consumed both sides of the road, and she was acutely aware that there was only this one road out. Sparks dripped down onto the road, and when she passed under a tree, it was burning, too, emitting yellow smoke and shedding sparks like a flea-infested dog shedding pests. Any of the sparks might ignite her gas tank or those of the cars up ahead; she wondered if the nursery van ahead of her was stuffed with fertilizer.

Her heart began to pound like a machine disassociated from the rest of her body. She didn't need it to beat so hard; she was driving a car, she told herself, and had to stay steady, but she was lightheaded and she began panting.

There was nothing to do but to keep driving, following the cars in front of her and hoping that whoever was at the front of the line was moving forward, because somewhere farther along the road, the fire ended. She tried, as she had been taught, not to drive over the parts of the road covered with burning timber. Once or twice she passed cars that had stopped by the side of the road. She didn't know why they had stopped.

"Please stop," she said to the fire. The fire did not listen.

She glanced to the side of the road and saw the fire racing past at a terrific speed. She had seen videos of tsunami water raging toward land; that was what the fire was like now, except it was flames, perhaps five feet high, alive and breathing like a beast, with wind coursing through the chambers of its fiery body and breathing life into it. New waves raced over the hill, propelled by the wind, hurtling into the trees and the chaparral. None of this had been burning when she had driven past perhaps thirty minutes ago, and now all around her was hell. She had to get out of the valley. That was the main thought in her mind. Even if the fire followed, she could get out of the valley and head to the ocean.

The car that had quickly darted around her, as though to pass everyone else, stopped. Then all the cars in front of her stopped. They had come into the dark. Day abruptly turned to night. There was so much smoke and so much debris flying into the air and she had left the day behind. Her body was now wired to everyone else on this road, every action now dependent on everyone else's. She would not be able to move until everyone else moved. She wondered if it was the case that when birds flew in migration, they were so tuned in to hundreds of tiny sensory details that they were able to fly, in concord, from one location to another.

She saw that the sparks were thick and that the fire, which had been the color of a low-glowing coal, was now a bright yellow. The air was a blizzard of sparks. She could see the wind in the form of sparks, as it pushed them in waves across the pavement, the way the ocean makes little half circles on sand. She could hear the fire, too, roaring through the trees, capturing the pine needles and singeing them instantly so they ignited and glowed like electric wires charged with heat.

The cars behind her stopped. One driver in an SUV attempted to go off the road for a few feet and into the brush, before they, too, stopped; that way was also burning. They could only wait in the valley.

She was alone. Just a mind hitching a ride in this one body. If she died here in her car, she would be alone. She would also be surrounded by the other people like her, all trapped in their cars. Why was she in this valley? She began to cry and pray to God. She thought her crying most likely sounded ugly, hysterical, and mewling, and this only made her cry harder. She picked up her phone to call Thomas and the girls, but there were no satellite bars on the phone. There was no way for her phone to connect to the phalanx of satellites overhead, and still the phone winked at her, all glowing blue lights, an eerie balm against the dark and the red outside.

She watched the shadowy form of a woman get out of her car and begin to run into the brush on the side of the road, even though the grass and the shrubs were burning. The woman was coughing, and she made it onto the grass and began to try to run through it, before the heat—she guessed it was the heat—made the woman turn around back onto the asphalt road, which was also hot. If she, too, got out of the car and searched for an escape, she would look like this. She would look like a woman trying to escape.

The car next to her had begun to pump windshield fluid onto its front window, and so she did the same. Then she turned on the air conditioner. Maybe she could trick her body into thinking it was cool. The air was showering sparks and they fell like hot rain on the window. Each time one fell, she was afraid it would melt the glass or ignite her car. How long, she wondered, until the windows burned?

In the stories of the great fires she had learned about in Japan as a child, monks always carried out statues from the main temple—statues and paintings that had been made hundreds of years before, so even when the roof burned or the rooms filled with smoke, the treasures for which the temple was known would survive. The rescue of the statues had always been carried out by some unnamed monks, and she had pictured them fleeing the burning buildings with statues wrapped in fabric or perhaps not wrapped at all. She wondered if they had felt panic.

Smoke was starting to enter the car. She could smell it. She had on a mask because of the sickness, but even that was failing to keep the particles from the smoke out of her lungs. How could the air be even worse than it already was?

She began to regret that she was here in California. It had all been a whim. In fact, everything to do with the Tree Doctor had been a whim. But, no, she was here because of her mother. Her mother. What would her mother do if she died here in a fire?

They were in such darkness now that she could not make out more than one car ahead of her. She turned on the headlights and closed the vents and ran the filtration system, trying to keep the smoke out. It was hot outside and she watched the temperature of her car begin to climb. Then, just like that, the car ahead of her inched forward. The spectral form of the woman who had been wandering around outside climbed back into her car and its lights came back on. She put her car in gear.

Inch by inch they nosed forward, and she followed the line of cars now pressing through the valley. They passed a bulldozer and for a moment she was able to take in what had happened: a tree had fallen across the road and the bulldozer had moved it out of the way. There was a car on fire, and a bulldozer was in the midst of pushing it to the side of the road. She could not see if anyone was injured or needed help, and a part of her thought she ought to stop, but she did not. She followed the cars out. Her heart was pounding and the blood in her body rushed through her ears. She felt lightheaded from hyperventilating and from the smoke and she told herself she needed to stay conscious to get out of this patch of fire. "A little more, a little farther," she told herself. It was all too easy to see how and why a person might, in such a moment, succumb to stress and pass out before making it beyond the line of the fire. She had to make it out of the patch of fire.

It was almost like passing through a solid wall when they punctured the smoke and were out of the valley and into the sky. Here the air was not clear, but it was at least yellow and she was closer to daylight. Almost immediately the cars spaced themselves the way cars do when emerging from the bottleneck of traffic. A few roared away; some pulled over to the side of the road. She continued to drive, though she was crying at the same time and wiping her eyes. She took the mask off her face—it had started to suffocate her. The air still tasted acrid, but it was not as bad as it had been back in the middle of the fire. She aimed not for the beach, but for home. She pulled into her driveway and sat in the car, waiting for her body to be strong enough for the walk into the house. In the time she had been gone, someone had dropped off half a dozen trees. She was still sitting in the driveway when the Tree Doctor arrived a few minutes later.

. . .

She wouldn't understand for several more days what had happened in the valley, though she knew vaguely that the fire had been pushed in a direction no one had predicted, and that a small branch of the fire department had gone to the base of the hill in case the fire came over it, which it had at such an alarming rate she was lucky to have escaped. Her part in this escape was minor—the driver of the bulldozer, which had been borrowed from the lot of a house currently undergoing renovation, was later commended for his help, which included digging a trench ahead of the fire to stop it from advancing into a senior citizens' community, but this was only after they had removed the tree and the burned-out car that had initially impeded her journey. She couldn't really imagine the damage done except when she read in the news, later, that at its fastest rate the fire had consumed the equivalent of eighty football fields in one minute, and that visual—a football field incinerated in one second—had given her some sense of how fortunate she had been to survive.

When she eventually got out of her car, the Tree Doctor got out of his car too. It was dark now, and she didn't bother taking the plants out of the back of her car. He came and stood in front of her. He said he needed a shower.

"Why did you ask me to come?"

"Figured we needed all the help we could get."

"By the time you texted me, it was already too late to evacuate very far. You must have known that."

It was clear he had already anticipated that she might say this. He had a slight smile on his face—the one that looked as though he were indulging a small child. "They stopped it."

"We almost didn't get out. You can tell they never intended it to get over that hill back there. They never intended for the fires to merge. For all I know, it *will* get here."

"Not your zip code," he said as he took her by the elbow and began to steer her toward the door of her house. "Let's go in. The air is bad out here." Was he trying to have sex? Again she felt sick from the smoke and the events of the day, and she knew that even in the house she would not feel safe and that the house would smell on the inside. She knew that there was, in fact, no place to ever feel safe.

"You live around some of the wealthiest people in the country," he told her. "They—"

"The fire does not care." She shook his hand off her elbow.

"I'm sorry." He said it like a man who had been trained to say he was sorry when a conversation with a woman reached an impasse. At that point, she could almost hear a therapist's voice instructing him: "You must say you are sorry." "I'm sorry I called. I thought there was more time to evacuate more stuff. Okay? Now can we please go inside?" She didn't like this whining little-boy side to him. What a time for him to reveal himself to be petulant. Another version of herself—a younger self—would now be trying frantically to reimagine the window dressing of this conversation so they were not arguing over his phone call to her, but were instead escaping the ravaging fire and seeking solace—and sex—inside the house. She could see in his eyes that he was asking if she might assist in this version of events. She was not quite sure what she would do, but she realized that the power, in fact, rested with her.

"I've been running the air purifier in the bedroom," she said. And they went in.

She said she needed to make sure all the windows were closed and she wanted to take out the trash, but she also wanted the space to think alone. It was a trick married people knew—look like you are doing household chores when you are really buying time to be alone. She showered by herself, and as she dried off her body, she could hear him in the kitchen making slightly too much noise as he assembled a pot of coffee. What was all that racket? He lurched the refrigerator open and knocked over at least one Tupperware container while retrieving the ground coffee. He turned the water on too hard and he clinked the spoon against the glass container too loudly when measuring coffee into the press. When she went into the kitchen, she approached him just as he pivoted with the pot of coffee in his hand, and, startled to see her, he bobbled and she put her arm out instinctively to steady him.

"I'm just . . . I'm not . . . Not right now," he said.

"Not right now" she shouldn't steady him? Or "not right now" coffee? Was the coffee not for her too?

"I mean, I might be in the mood later," he said.

She had meant to steady his balance and had not touched him out of a desire to communicate intimacy or sex. Surely he knew this, and this nonsense about not being in the mood was some way to retain control over their remaining time together.

"Do you want sugar?"

"You know I don't take sugar."

He poured out a cup and handed it to her. She held the cup in one hand and then pulled her phone out of her pocket with the other. She called up one of the air-quality maps and waited for it to populate with the wind currents. All of California was bruised maroon, and some parts, like her hometown, were nearly black. The air outside was poisonous. She called up another map—this one from NASA—that was supposed to show the fires in California in real time. This map always took at least a full sixty seconds to load, and there were so many layers of information, she wasn't entirely sure what she was looking at. She could choose to see what had happened over the last forty-eight hours, but also the last twenty-four. What she really wanted to know was whether or not the fire had finally crossed Highway 68, or if it had been kept to the east. Was it marching toward them, or had it been contained? That was all she wanted to know. Were they hiding in her home in vain?

"Did you sign up for emergency alerts from the county?"

"Yes," she said. She had signed up after watching the very

first fire update on Facebook, but had never received any text messages after that.

The coffee wasn't helping. It was late in the afternoon—later than she would normally drink coffee, but all the platitudes she had about coffee keeping her up late at night seemed ridiculous. The caffeine was no buffer against this tide of exhaustion now coursing through the tissues of her body. She felt powerfully sleepy from the shock wearing off and her body relaxing in her home, even though logic told her that her own home might not be safe.

"I need to lie down," she said, and she left him in the kitchen and went to her bedroom, the phone still in her hand. She put the coffee on top of the headboard; it wouldn't be within reach there, but she realized she did not intend to drink it. She once again held the phone in her hands, as one might clutch a crucifix, and fell asleep.

. . .

She woke up in heavy darkness, and he was gone. She had no idea what time it was. She hoped it was the middle of the night and that she might have slept enough consecutive hours for it to count as a night of sleep, even if it was now 3:00 a.m. and she would be wandering around her house, an insomniac, waiting for morning. She checked the phone, still in her grip: 9:37 p.m. Her heart sank.

She had that heavy, chilled feeling she always got when she woke up at the wrong time. Her body, rested and alert, did not want to be lured back into sleep. She could even feel the juices of her body pricking her awake: her blood was coursing, and she felt like one of those ridiculous balloons that a clown in a park might blow up, before twisting into the recognizable shape of some animal. A moment ago she had been sleeping, and now her body was infusing her into shape.

The conventional wisdom was that one should not look at a cell phone if one wanted to sleep, but she clicked hers on anyway. The bright light of the home screen spread a selection of applications across its face, like a tray serving glowing candy. She flicked through the apps, then checked the one for air quality. It was worse. She did not feel as sick as she might have, owing to the air purifier still running in her bedroom.

She got up and stood by the bed. The coffee was cold, but she drank it anyway.

This had been her parents' bedroom. The house was rambling, in the California ranch–style way, and her childhood bedroom was at the other end of the house. As a child, it had felt so far away, but she had managed the distance to reach her parents when she had woken in the night from a particularly troubling nightmare. There had been periods in her childhood when her nightmares had been plentiful, and when she had, with increasing trepidation, gone to wake her parents for assistance with the bad dream.

The solution had seemed simple to her. She should sleep with them. All together in the bed, bad dreams could not press inside her skull. She had marveled, as a child, at finding her parents asleep in bed. It was almost impossible to imagine that they needed sleep—they were her parents and they dwelled in the land of the gods. Her mother, mumbling, would throw open the covers and invite her inside, where it was warm. Her mother, a disciplined and passionate woman, could open the bed up like that, without fully succumbing to waking, but it was different for her father. He found some kind of moral offense in her desire to crawl into bed with them, and, after a brief argument with her mother, her father would take her back to her room.

It was as though he didn't believe her dreams should lead her to need their company the rest of the night. Now here she was, sealed inside the bedroom with the air purifier. She had read stories of people who had been ordered to evacuate during a fire, but who had stayed in bed in their homes, speaking to a dispatcher on the emergency line. There was nothing that was actually safer about being here in this room in bed, but she still imagined it as the room of her parents, as a haven with the magic force field that had emanated out into the space just beyond the door, where she had cowered in her sleeping bag, hiding from a nightmare.

She thought about how it was common for many of the people in her circle to refer to family and to having children as a form of narcissism. It seemed like bad manners to point out to these people, who were otherwise scientific in their thinking, that it was difficult to know what a child was *for* unless one had a child. She did not think she had had children out of a desire to replicate herself; her daughters were so different from her.

She had simply wanted children. Wanted a family. It had overtaken her in that tugging way that she suspected birds felt when they traveled somewhere with lots of seeds and nice trees for nest-building. Was it possible to break down the urges of nature to such a precise point that a person could articulate it all through language?

She thought of what the Tree Doctor had once said to her: "A family is a set of shared experiences." This had struck her as so strange at the time. He had not spoken of legacy, or comfort in old age, or responsibility. He had made it sound as though family was the chance to join a sitcom with a permanent cast. But wasn't this, in fact, what a family was?

She checked the air quality. Still purple. She went into the kitchen and assembled a meal of cold cuts and bread and sliced carrots. She could not bear the thought of turning on the stove to cook something; even the slightest bit of extra steam or smoke made her recoil. She retreated into the bedroom with the one air filter and closed the door.

When she was a child, sick and home from school, she would sit in bed like this all alone while her parents went through the movements of the day in the outside world. They had both worked mostly from home, so she would hear them moving around outside, but still she would feel alone, and when her mother came in, harried and irritated, to take her temperature or bring her a cup of orange juice, she often entreated her to stay.

"As soon as you feel okay, you must go back to school," her mother would tell her.

She had felt so tired and weak and somewhat vulnerable from whatever cold she had, and the words had always sounded harsh, though as a parent, she now understood them. It took years for children to grow up. And in the meantime you were supposed to spend all this *time* with them, and prevent them from falling, or breaking anything, or getting sick, or being on the computer.

She wanted her mother, but could not have her mother. She wrote, instead, to her mother's nurse again, to ask if the facility was still safe, and to please let her mother know that she was running the air filter. She conveyed only reassurance and what she hoped was a breezy confidence. Then she settled more deeply into the bed.

A family is a set of shared experiences and memories. She sat in the bed, waiting for news of the fire, flipping through her memory bank and tabulating the shared experiences that were in the past and that would never happen again.

Ten

The fire didn't last. Once again there were enough firefighters and there was enough water and there were enough machines that the fire was beaten back, though not before a record twelve thousand acres and thirty-two buildings had been scorched. She spent three more days at home, watching the news on her phone and emerging from the bedroom to feed herself, before retreating back into the somewhat clean air of the bedroom, and while this felt restrictive, she knew that she was also fortunate to have this haven. She heard from her mother's nurse that all was stable in the facility. Kate eventually rescued the chickens, and her childhood friends returned to their lives, and the Tree Doctor sent Juan from the nursery to take back the plants that were in her car.

It took perhaps ten days, but one morning at the end of September she looked out the window and saw three brown blobs: golden-crowned sparrows eating grass. The earliest members of the flock had arrived, undeterred by the fires.

A few times she spoke to her children on FaceTime. It was really only Sophie who spoke to her now. Pia had adjusted to being on her own, though she waved at the camera—"Hi, Mommy!"—as though it were the most natural thing in the world to have a mother who lived within the twenty-seven-inch screen. But Sophie knew better. Thomas hardly spoke to her—they had slid into some kind of mutually unacknowledged but agreed-upon decision that if they never discussed anything, then there was nothing to discuss.

When her class resumed, and they finally made it to part 3 of *Genji*, she amplified their reading with material she had never taught before. She assigned portions of *An Account of My Hut*. While Lady Murasaki had lived during the Heian period, around 1000 CE, and had been able to enjoy its beauty, Kamo no Chōmei had watched as the Heian period changed into the Kamakura at the end of the twelfth century. The world into which he had been born had simply evaporated.

"I heard that the fire broke out in Higuchitominokoji, in a shack where a dancer lived. Then, spread by the wind, it touched place after place, until finally it reached everywhere, like the unfolding of a fan. Houses far off became engulfed in smoke as those near the center were caught up in swirling flames. The brightness of the fire was reflected against the solid cloud of ashes blown up in the night sky, a deep red at the center, which, as the wind had flames leaping 100 to 200 yards, kept shifting. People caught in the middle gave up all hope." Such destruction was followed by famine and illness, and when the men and women who had surrounded the emperor were unable to fight off the challenges of a rougher species—the warriors—the old ways that Murasaki had described simply faded as power was transferred to the samurai. There had simply been too much instability, illness, and destruction for the way of the Shining Prince to remain dominant. "Sometimes," she told her class, "things change too much."

Did Lady Murasaki have an idea about how a person might live after the time of the Shining Prince had ended? She was starting to think that the change in style late in the novel had less to do with a possible change in authorship than with something simpler: age. In part 3, the distraught Ukifune, who tries to drown herself after accidentally sleeping with Niou, is discovered under a tree. She then succeeds in doing what the character Murasaki never could: Ukifune enters a convent.

"Sort of like Jane Eyre when she leaves Mr. Rochester," Astrid said.

"Yes," she agreed. Except that unlike Jane Eyre, Ukifune does not end up reunited with her Mr. Rochester by the end of the novel. Kaoru finds Ukifune alive, but she will not see him.

Curiously, the chapter in which all this action is spelled out is called "Writing Practices." She had never truly paid attention to this detail before. But throughout the chapter, as Ukifune recovers her memory and heals from her heartbreak, she writes incidental poems as a part of her practice. And it is through the writing of these unanswered poems—for they are not love poems—that her sense of self begins to emerge again.

"Do you think it's autobiographical?" Astrid asked.

"I definitely wonder," she said. Perhaps the entire first part of *The Tale of Genji*, with its assertion that the world was a beautiful place with gardens and poems and dancing, and where some women suffered, was, after all, just an illusion.

"And then the book just ends," Henry said.

"She's never reunited with Kaoru," Astrid added.

"It's the perfect ending," Momoko said.

"Some say there must have been additional pages," she told them. "Maybe Kaoru reunites with her after all?"

"That would not be a better ending," Momoko replied. "It is better to leave her in the convent, writing her own poems."

She nodded. "She doesn't need anyone to answer her poems."

"She's not worried about who to love."

. . .

One day at the end of September, she was suddenly struck by the way Sophie peered at her from the computer screen like an illustration she had once seen in a children's book of a baby owl gazing beseechingly out from inside a dark hollow in a tree trunk. The book had been about a young owl searching for his mother, and asking, as various other animals stopped by the tree, "Whooo are you?"

If she thought back to the previous months, Sophie had always had that watchful, prepubescent, birdlike way of watching her, but now it had intensified, and a new leanness seemed to make Sophie's eyes strain from inside her head. It was a look of hunger. Sophie was hungry for her.

"Tell me," she tried to say brightly, "what you and Daddy did today."

"Nothing."

"Did you watch a Disney movie? Did the war movies stop?"

"It's hard to find entertainment suitable for all of us. We watched Aristocrats again. Daddy was on his phone. That's twenty-three times I have watched Aristocrats."

"Did you go out for a walk?"

"It's still the second wave. Daddy goes out for groceries and I make him shower as soon as he gets home."

She sat back in her seat. She understood then that Sophie was doing what she, as the mother, would have been doing if they had been together as a family. Sophie was watching her from thousands of miles away. What was she looking for? She was so young, she likely couldn't even articulate the questions that had accumulated over so many months of separation. But one question surfaced repeatedly across her daughter's brow. She could see this question as clearly as she had learned to see the minute changes in the garden, like the leaves on the wisteria on the southern slope of the garden turning yellow before the larger vine just a little higher up. The question was "Who are you?"

Sophie was desperate for her mother, and for her comfort. In the intervening months, during which Sophie had sent her father out for food, then reminded her father to shower when he returned, then comforted Pia, Sophie had started doing the work that the adults were supposed to do, and while Sophie understood that the world had been flattened—equalized—by the sickness, Sophie wondered if there was not, in fact, something that her mother was doing that had contributed to this situation. If her mother were there, then perhaps they would not need to watch *Aristocrats* twenty-three times. She would not need to worry if her father used enough soap in the shower to make sure no infection had been brought back from the grocery store.

Could a gaze go through the glass and land on Sophie and comfort her? She had been about Sophie's age when her mother had first become ill, and when she, too, had had to step into a role that children did not assume in the model family. She could see, in Sophie's careful observing of her through the screen, a shadow of herself, watching to see if her mother was breathing heavily and might need her inhaler, if they were about to have an argument over whether or not her mother needed the inhaler, if she was going to have to administer the inhaler when her mother waited a few seconds too long to use it. This was the intense scrutiny with which Sophie was watching her now.

"Sophie," she said. "Is Daddy around?"

Sophie sprang up as though she had been startled by a sound behind her. "Yes."

"Let me talk to him."

It turned out that Thomas had not been watching the graphs and the numbers as closely as she had. He didn't know, as she did, that there appeared to be a pause in the number of infections in his country and in hers. "If we plan now," she said, "you and the girls can come here."

"I don't want to leave my office," he said, so tiredly that she wondered if he meant it or if it was, in fact, a statement generated by a perfunctory piece of programming lodged in his brain.

She reminded him that the strict immigration laws in Hong Kong meant that even Americans like herself who had residency cards were not easily let in. Her ticket would be expensive, as would her quarantine. The United States, on the other hand, had, as a land of freedom, done a poor job of controlling the infection, which also meant that Thomas and the girls could get in without a special visa. As citizens, they were not required to quarantine in a hotel.

"It's still the second wave." How like a child he sounded, parroting what Sophie had just said.

"There will be a break," she informed him. "Pack the essentials and watch the news. I'll watch the news too. And when the numbers dip, I will book the tickets." From where had this newfound iciness come? It didn't matter. She needed to reunite her family. "I will book the tickets." After all, she did have her own credit card, even if she barely earned any money.

While she waited, she thought about the surfers she had seen all her life, hanging out on the California coastline. They would perch on their boards and stare at the horizon, watching the water swell and break until one particular wave looked large enough that it was worth the effort to try to catch.

But Thomas was not doing the same. She realized this when, in the conversations that followed, she tested him on his knowledge of the numbers just as he had once tested her on the latest headlines. He was too far entrenched in his Twitter feed. And though she thought of him as one does a hamster, running and running for no reason other than to keep a wheel spinning, for once she did not regard him only with disdain. She felt a kind of understanding, as a parent does when watching a young child learn to apologize. She wasn't angry. She was *comprehending*. Then she did something else. She purchased three airplane tickets.

The four of them gathered around the computer early in the morning, Hong Kong time, and she told them their tickets had been purchased. They would have a week to pack. "You'll come here," she said firmly. "I've made the reservation."

Three pairs of eyes were watching her, as if she were some exotic zoo animal suddenly capable of human speech. They were fascinated, confused, but also, perhaps, relieved.

"I'm combining all the confirmation emails into one PDF and will email it to you," she told her husband. "You'll print it and bring it with you. You'll all need to wear masks. You won't be able to take them off until you are in the car with me. Do you have extra masks?" When no one answered, she asked: "Sophie. Do you have extra masks?"

"Somewhere," Sophie said.

"Honey. You'll need to collect all the masks in one place. Wash the cloth ones so they are clean for the flight."

"I was thinking maybe we could . . ." Her daughter hesitated. Why was her daughter hesitating?

"Maybe what?"

"Well, sometimes people here wear these face shields?"

"It's a long flight," she agreed. "Thomas, you need to buy face shields for all three of you."

"I'm not wearing a face shield."

She sucked in her breath. "We have been living as a family over this computer for nine months. That is long enough. I have purchased your tickets to begin to put us back together again. And if Sophie and Pia wear face masks and you do not, and if you get sick and make them sick, I want you to know I won't ever forgive you. Ever."

His face very quickly became hard, as though he'd been slapped. And for the first time in her life, she felt a delicious indifference. There welled up inside her a coldness, now mixed with purpose.

"Sophie." She spoke to her eldest daughter. "I will be ordering face shields and sending them to you. Try them out when they arrive and make sure your sister can wear one—her head is smaller than yours."

Sophie nodded.

She looked out at the garden and then she said: "For fuck's sake, Thomas. It's a face shield. It's a twelve-hour flight. In a year, you won't even remember."

. . .

She had always remembered the near drowning of Ukifune as an uncomfortable story about a woman trying to commit suicide. But reading the chapter through with her class that fall, she noticed something new. Ukifune recounts to her rescuers that she had not succeeded in drowning herself, because she had been saved by a mysterious being—a man—who had intercepted her at the riverbed. In fact, when she was discovered, she was sitting under a tree and far away from the river. There were disagreements among scholars as to who had saved her—the Buddha, an evil spirit, or Kaoru himself. But the explanation she liked most was that it had been some kind of supernatural force and most likely the tree itself, and its tree spirit, who had found her on the edge of the river and brought her to shore to rest until others found her.

If a tree had rescued a woman, who had then rescued herself by writing, what happened if a woman rescued a tree?

While she waited for her family to arrive, she prepared the garden for spring. She planted bulbs that had arrived in a box so heavy the UPS deliveryperson had left it at the foot of the walkway, rather than carry it to her doorstep. She split the box open with a pair of clippers, then began carrying handfuls of bulbs around the garden and sinking them into the soil. The gophers would likely chew through half of them before the winter ended, but she hoped at least some of the more intoxicating varieties—the parrot petals, the black tulips, the pink daffodils—might survive the subterranean pests.

Then after the bulbs were planted, it was time to go retrieve her family. On the way to the airport, she saw that people were trying to prepare for the holidays. Even her neighbors only a half a mile up the street had put an inflatable Santa and his sleigh on top of their roof, along with one reindeer. She had a mound of lights in the living room. They were piled together with the ornaments and the boxed-up fake tree her family had used year after year. She would give that job to Thomas. She would tell him to plug in the chain of lights and throw out any strands that did not illuminate, and then they would dress up the house for the children. She would tell him this calmly and he would do it and they would keep the holidays intact for yet another year.

She had set aside a story to read to the girls tonight. It was a chapter from *The Long Winter* by Laura Ingalls Wilder. It was the part of the series where Laura makes presents for her family members, who all rejoice to receive a handmade apron, or slippers, or a scarf. She planned to let them know that Christmas could be special even without the glamour that had been inflicted on them in years past in New York, Paris, and San Francisco, where they were dragged from party to party and forced to eat too many cookies and go to *The Nutcracker* in velvet dresses. Not that there wouldn't be cookies. She had the ingredients for those prepared too. She planned to usher them all into tasks involving lights and sugar and walking to get them through this dark time, when the sickness was swirling everywhere like a blizzard.

And just like that, they were in her house. They were at once strangers to each other and strangely familiar. She found she was even a little happy to see Thomas. After so many months apart, she enjoyed his familiar presence. She could read so many emotions in his face: he was relieved to see her and delighted and shocked that he had managed the transfer from Hong Kong to California. She realized he had been scared. It was perhaps the first time in their relationship that she had been the brave one. She was grateful that they could quickly settle into a domestic routine, without unearthing everything that had happened in the months they had been apart. They could go about the business of re-forming the family and talking about the children and schooling and setting up Thomas's home office, and the practicality of these discussions, while somewhat shallow, was also soothing. This was what domesticity was for. It was a blanket under which she could crawl and warm up.

They did not have sex. This did not bother her. Sex, she knew, was something she could get when she required it. The decision was not up to someone else.

The girls were bigger, and she could not stop telling them they were bigger. They wanted her to touch them and hug them, and they followed her everywhere, and yet they looked bashful about it. Her daughters baked cookies. They were clumsy with the measuring spoons, unused to the joy of baking and its precision. She walked them through how to make the cookies the same size, and how to spread them out on the Silpat the same distance apart. She was trying to fill them quickly with the sense that all was stable, that the holidays were coming, and that nothing unusual had happened since they had been parted. But she knew that Sophie knew that she had changed and did not know why.

Thomas took over the sofa in the family room, where he sorted through lights. He was so patient about it—sorting them while watching sports and the news on TV. She stood in the doorway of the den and watched this man, the father of her children, dutifully checking every single Christmas light, and trying to isolate which bulb had burned out, rendering the entire chain dark.

It dawned on her that he was sorting the lights only because he thought she wanted him to. "I think there are better ways to spend our time. We can order new lights online. Instead we could . . . play a game together?"

He turned and looked up at her from the sofa. For a moment she thought he was going to remind her that he had precious little free time and that his job required that he work. "Monopoly?" he asked, throwing all the old lights into a paper bag.

"I hate that game," she said. And a little while later, they began to play a civilized round of Pictionary, and by the fifth cartoon, they were all laughing. She bought a heat lamp for the patio, and every now and then, Kate brought her children by to play Pictionary with her daughters too—always masked and outside, because California, it turned out, had been quick to adopt the mask and did not label it as a sign of being uptight. California was always surprising her. And, twice, Pia and Sophie went to see Kate's chickens and the pony. Friendship, she realized, needn't be hard. Sometimes she even Zoomed with Astrid, Momoko, and Henry, who, grudgingly, she began to think of as friends.

She asked her daughters to FaceTime with her when she spoke to her mother in the facility. Her mother was unable to talk now, but she could listen. Her mother could see that they were all together in one place, on one screen. This is the only way she will see her mother again. The hospital where her mother will be transferred will allow no visitors. When the virus finally comes for her mother a few weeks later, at least her mother will know that she succeeded and that the family was now together.

Sophie asked: "Why does the note say 'Vision Board'?"

"Your grandmother wrote that. I still don't know why."

"Was she making a vision board?"

"That's my guess."

"What was supposed to be on it?"

She told her daughter about the seed packets. She told her

about the trees she had planted and the flowers that bloomed and faded that summer, calling up the photos she had taken on her phone. She left out a lot. She told Sophie about pruning and weeding, about the joy of selecting plants, and the bulbs she planted. She told her about the birds—the hawks, the gold-finches, and the hummingbirds. It was now the brief winter of California, and the birds mobbed the feeder every day. She made her children fill the feeder. At breakfast they sat together and she asked them to tell her the names of the birds.

Only once did she hear from the Tree Doctor. Twice, if you counted the hyacinth.

She received a text, so breezy and childish in its deliberate attempt at casualness that she was annoyed. "Hey? U Good?" She hated that he had forgotten. Surely he had been texting other women who liked shorthand. She did not write back.

One morning everyone was still in bed when she rose and twirled the blinds open. Everything was as it had been for weeks: the pond full of rainwater, the Japanese maple trees bare, the grass green. But there was something on the patio. It was a small plant, whose container was no larger than a half-and-half pint. It was a pale blue hyacinth, pushing out tiny buds in the shape of miniature grapes, and it had not been there the night be-fore. There was a white bow tied around the pot. She leaned out into the glass window box to get a better view of the garden. The tips of the tulips and daffodils protruded from the earth; these bulbs were attuned to the hyacinth. It was like the hya-cinth was a clock—the timer by which to set spring. New flow-ers would bloom soon.

. . .

The sickness isn't gone when springtime arrives. In fact, it re-sumes its assault on the world, having changed shape just enough to find new ways to locate the weak. She knows now that the sickness is like the ocean. It comes in waves, like a tsunami, and her job as the protector of her family is to look for times when the tide is receding. In those spaces between waves, they can move and act, and then when the tide returns, it is her job to keep her family fixed in place in the house, the safest place she knows. The only thing she can protect is her family, and she knows that even this protection is not guaranteed. But they are managing, and they are fortunate. Even Thomas is excited to have found a potential medical application for his software that may allow physicians to track the eye movements of patients during online visits.

There are rumblings that the vaccine is closer to being ready. It almost doesn't matter that there is the potential for good news; everyone is exhausted. Springtime, however, does not care. Spring in the garden feels like skin being pricked by needles. It is tense. Her mother had once told her that in Japan, spring is associated with a rise in madness. She sees how this is so. In winter, they had been swaddled and cocooned in dullness.

She thinks of the stories of prisoners who are freed, and then long for prison. When spring comes, it is welcome in the same way as freedom is. It drives them all mad. The days are growing long and the leaves are doing violence to the bulbs in the ground, the silver bark of the apple tree, and the azalea branches. The green is cutting through its casing and flooding the garden with the flesh of leaves.

One day Sophie is standing in the garden with her when she realizes with a sharp elation that Einstein is still alive. Throughout the winter they had tugged on its branches to see if they would snap, as the Tree Doctor had told her they would if the tree were dead. But the branches never snapped.

Around the garden, things begin to leaf and bloom as they did the previous spring, when she had been here alone. It is in a way even better this spring than the last season, in particular, because she is with Sophie who looks out at the garden every day and wonders what it is that her mother sees.

Bit by bit the green emerges, only this year there are even more daffodils and narcissuses, owing to her feverish fall planting. And there will be tulips in all colors, their blossoms swelling like Easter eggs. Most mornings, she rises before everyone else, and puts the water on to boil and makes a cup of coffee. She walks the grounds, as she has done all year, and stares at the soil, waiting to see if anything is puncturing the dirt and starting to emerge. She can recite the order in which things will arrive.

The plums blossom first: there are the two in the front, and the one in the back by the rosemary bush, which the goldfinches continued to eat all winter long. The azaleas, having been watered all year, are almost zealous in blooming. The blossoms are large this year; she takes Sophie out to look at the bicolored one she planted, but most are white. The maples are bare for months, then one day their extremities seem blurry, as though in looking at the branches, she has begun to lose the clarity of her eyesight. But it's just leaves. She sees the delphiniums, the zinnias, the begonias—all the flowers she planted with the Tree Doctor. And she does think of him, as he promised her she would. She thinks of sex with him. Her body still remembers him.

She is with Sophie one day, walking through the garden, when they both see the same thing: the tips of Einstein's branches bursting with tiny buds. This year, the tree plans to flower. There are hundreds of dense blossoms on the bark and the clusters fill her with excitement but also with alarm. It's like looking at a tree with a sudden rash. She can feel all this potential energy, this tension straining to get out of the tree, and it seems impossible that any one structure could hold all that energy inside. She touches the tips of one branch that the Tree Doctor mended. The tape is still intact, but the branch doesn't really need it anymore. One end has gripped the other and they have decided, together, to guide whatever chemistry and whatever juices are required to push the soft white-pink petals into the buds at the end of the branch.

"Mommy," Sophie says. "This tree has been cut."

"No," she says. "We taped it." She did not mean to say "we."

It takes her a minute to realize they are having perhaps three conversations at once. The tree was cut and mended by the tape. But it has also been freshly cut in three places. The branches that were broken by the storm last year have healed, but there are new wounds: three branches have been sliced off with a knife. Whoever cut off the branches did so recently; she can see the cambium, still green. "Who would cut the tree?" Sophie asks.

"I . . . don't know," she says. Why would anyone cut the tree?

In a day, the first little blossoms pop open, and they are so darling and soft and pert. It's all like some kind of incredible marionette theater, with the branches doing all this thrusting and maneuvering but all one sees is the fluff at the end. And there is so much of it. The blossoms are enormous! They swell and grow and her mind runs through the analogies. It is like foam on the sea. It is like the dream of the last glacier. It is Marilyn Monroe covered with an oversize feather boa the color of platinum. The flowers fizz and rise and the tree seems to expand, like it is releasing its soul. The strange, spindly branches are transformed into long, slender gestures, like the tree is some kind of embodiment of movement. It seems to be dancing. The upper branches reach up, and the lower branches bend down, and it's like it is impersonating a flock of egrets. The tree seems to be twice the size it was last year, when it refused to bloom, and it is so covered with froth that she forgets about the branches that were trimmed; there are more than enough flowers to make up for whatever was taken.

Morning after morning now it doesn't rain, and the sun comes out and lights the tree so it glows. She sits with Sophie on the patio, both of them wrapped in blankets. It is still cool in the mornings. They drink their coffee, and they stare at Einstein, surrounded by a blanket of tulips and daffodils. The sunlight plays with Einstein's blossoms as it moves between the clouds, and the tree shakes its head, like a colt tossing its mane. "What do you think the tree is trying to tell us?" she asks her daughter.

And Sophie, on the cusp of leaving the age when her imagination comes to her as a reflex, hesitates. "I don't know."

"Think," she tells her daughter. "What do you think it is trying to say?" This would be a question her mother would ask her.

"Spring is here."

"Well, yes." She laughs. "Of course. But what else?"

It's too early for Sophie to be able to tell her. She isn't really asking because she expects Sophie to know. She is asking so Sophie will remember that she asked this question on a cold spring morning in California, an hour before they went inside and decided to make pancakes for the family. The memory will come back to Sophie, maybe in another decade, when she needs the question in her own mind, the way she needed to see her mother's vision board scattered around the house and in the garden.

She doesn't tell her daughter, either, that buried in her mother's possessions was a final clue to the mystery of the vision board. When the nursing home called to ask, politely though somewhat impatiently, that she pick up her mother's belongings so the room could be occupied by a new resident, she made the four-hour round trip to pick up the five boxes of possessions. She had not sorted through everything—most of it still sat in the garage. But she had gone through her mother's wallet in search of ID cards, and there she had found a black-and-white photo of a man, strategically hidden behind a photo of her father. On the back of that photo of the stranger was written the name Carl Joseph.

But she doesn't tell her daughter this. The important story she wants to transmit to her daughter is in the garden, and lies in the fact that the Einstein tree hasn't died. There was a year in which it chose not to blossom, but it had not forgotten how. It is so much older now, and perhaps the year of mistreatment or the drought or whatever it was that happened had made the tree think it could not blossom. But it waited, and then, having gathered itself, it is now charging out with twice as many blossoms as before. As long as the tree is alive, it can do this. It will always have this capacity, perhaps even to exceed itself, and it is really only death that can keep it from blossoming each spring, if it so chooses.

She doesn't tell her daughter this. She just says: "Think about it a bit." And then they go inside.

. . .

Eventually, she can leave her home again. She wears a mask and tests herself often for some new version of the disease. She washes her hands often and takes off her shoes, like her mother taught her. She will never again have the same ease in the world that she had before the sickness arrived, or that she enjoyed with the Tree Doctor. But she adapts to this new world, along with everyone else who has survived.

A few years later she is up late one night, unable to sleep, and she decides not to keep working but instead to check the news, flipping through stories of what is now called the Age of Urgency. She comes across a curious tale that stops her for a moment. The city of San Diego—so far to the south, and so hot now, due to the changing temperatures, that no one would ever think a cherry tree could survive its temperate winters—has recently received a gift of twenty young cherry tree saplings, made from a graft. The cherry trees are said to be particularly resistant to drought. They are the gift of a wealthy and anonymous donor from California, wishing to commemorate the nine million who have passed away during the pandemic. The trees are planted in a small garden, which the public can visit for free. The varietal is also for sale, though production will be limited. It is a strong tree. The branches droop a bit so in the winter—especially in the even briefer winter of San Diego— the tree might seem to be dead. It has branches that look almost like spikes. But it will revive. It doesn't need the cold that a traditional flowering cherry tree needs, and it will make a wonderful addition to the garden of anyone seeking a thing of beauty, as the climate continues to warm, and so many plants and flowers disappear.

She sees the story and for a brief moment she wonders where the tree has come from? But then she feels a vibration in the house. It is the sound of her children walking through from the bedroom to the office, where she is finishing this new book she has been writing, and she realizes that one of them is hungry. She rises to meet them in the kitchen, where the lemon cake she baked earlier in the day has been cooling. And then she forgets about the story of the strange trees that can bloom even without much water, and without the cold of winter.

MARIE MUTSUKI MOCKETT is the author of a previous novel, *Picking Bones from Ash*, and two books of nonfiction, *American Harvest*, which won the Nebraska Book Award and the Northern California Book Award, and *Where the Dead Pause, and the Japanese Say Goodbye*, which was a finalist for the PEN Open Book Award. A graduate of Columbia University in East Asia Studies, she has been awarded NEA-JUSFC and Fulbright Fellowships, both for Japan.

The text of *The Tree Doctor* is set in Rooney Regular.
Book design by Ann Sudmeier.
Composition by Bookmobile Design & Digital
Publisher Services, Minneapolis, Minnesota.
Manufactured by Sheridan Saline on acid-free,
100 percent postconsumer wastepaper.